The Devil's Steps

Bony Novels by Arthur W. Upfield:

1 The Barrakee Mystery / The Lure of the Bush

2 The Sands of Windee

3 Wings Above the Diamantina

4 Mr Jelly's Business/ Murder Down Under

5 Winds of Evil

6 The Bone is Pointed

7 The Mystery of Swordfish Reef

8 Bushranger of the Skies / No Footprints in the Bush

9 Death of a Swagman

10 The Devil's Steps

11 An Author Bites the Dust

12 The Mountains Have a Secret

13 The Widows of Broome

14 The Bachelors of Broken Hill

15 The New Shoe

16 Venom House

17 Murder Must Wait

18 Death of a Lake

19 Cake in the Hat Box / Sinister Stones

20 The Battling Prophet

21 Man of Two Tribes

22 Bony Buys a Woman / The Bushman Who Came Back

23 Bony and the Mouse / Journey to the Hangman

24 Bony and the Black Virgin / The Torn Branch

25 Bony and the Kelly Gang / Valley of Smugglers

26 Bony and the White Savage

27 The Will of the Tribe

28 Madman's Bend /The Body at Madman's Bend

29 The Lake Frome Monster

ARTHUR W.UPFIELD

The Devil's Steps

ETT IMPRINT
Exile Bay

This corrected edition published in 2020 by ETT Imprint, Exile Bay

ETT IMPRINT & www.arthurupfield.com

PO Box R1906,
Royal Exchange
NSW 1225 Australia

First published1946.
First electronic edition published by ETT Imprint 2013.
First corrected edition published by ETT Imprint in 2020.
Reprinted.

ISBN 978-1-925706-69-7 (pbk)
ISBN 978-1-922384-54-6 (ebk)

Chapter One

At Wideview Chalet

The alarm clock beside Bisker's bed called him to his daily life at half-past five. The clock appeared to be armour-clad and completely shock-resisting, for every time the alarm began it was cut short by a callused hand which crashed down upon it with such force that a lesser mechanism would have been smashed flat.

At five-thirty on this first morning in September it was quite dark. Inside Bisker's room it was coal-black, and, until Bisker began the recitation of the first complaint of the day, utterly silent. Bisker's voice was loud with emphasis.

"A man oughter be sunk a million miles below the bottom of the deepest well on earth," he said, in his heart duty wrestling with the desire to strike. "Oh, what a limbless fool I am. Curse the drink! You dirty swine ... it's you that stops me saving enough money to get me outer this frost-bitten, rain-drowned, lousy hole of a joint, get me back to where there's a thousand tons of good, dry wood to the acre, and where a man can lie abed all day if he wants to. Oh, blast! If that old cow sezs two words to me this morning, I'll up and slap 'er down."

Striking a match, he lit the hurricane lamp standing on the wooden kerosene case beside the bed. Then he took up one of two pipes, in the bowl of which had been compressed the dried "dottles" taken during the previous day from the other pipe. Bisker was a connoisseur in the art of nicotine poisoning and he favoured an extra-strong dose before rising in the mornings, to be followed with mere ordinary doses during the day. To avoid wasting time, the special dose was loaded into the pipe overnight. For five minutes he smoked with only his face outside the blankets, even his face being partially protected from the air by a bristling, stained grey moustache.

"Fancy a man coming down to this!" he exclaimed loudly. "An' me an up-an'-at-'em cattle drover most of me life. Just tells you what the booze will do to a bloke. Ah, well!"

Slipping out of bed, he revealed naked, bandy legs below the hem of a cotton shirt over a flannel undervest. He stepped into trousers which appeared to be wide open to accept his legs and small and rotund paunch, pulled on a pair of old socks and then stepped into heavy boots he did not trouble to lace. A thick cloth coat and a battered felt hat completed the ensemble, but to this had to be added the working kit comprising one pipe, a plug of jet-black tobacco, a clasp-knife, a tin containing wax matches and a corkscrew.

Taking up the lamp, he passed outside.

It was not so very cold after all, although his breath did issue in the form of steam mixed with tobacco smoke. By the aid of the light he followed a narrow cinder path to its junction with a wide area of bitumen fronting a row of garages. Across this area he lurched along a path also of bitumen which skirted a large wood-stack and eventually arrived at a small door at the rear of Wideview Chalet. The door he opened with a key which he took from beneath a brick, and on passing into the house he found himself in a scullery in which part of his day was spent.

From the scullery he entered the kitchen, switched on the electric light, blew out his lamp and filled a tin kettle with water to place on a small electric stove. He then proceeded with the least noise possible to clean out the four grates of the cooking range, set in the centre of the kitchen, and to light fires in them.

By the time he had completed this work the kettle was at the boil. Bisker made a pot of tea, and whilst the tea was "drawing" he passed out to the scullery and re-fired the boiler which provided hot water to the bathrooms and to every bedroom. He was pouring milk into two cups when the cook appeared in the kitchen.

"Mornin'!" she said with a kind of lisp, as she was minus her false teeth.

"Day!" snarled Bisker. "Cupper tea?"

"Too right! I don't work till I get it."

Bisker poured tea into two cups. The cook accepted hers without speaking, set it down on the stove and herself on a chair she drew near to the now-roaring fires. Bisker carried his cup in one hand and his pipe in the other to take a position before one of the fires from which he glared down at the cook.

"A man oughter—" he began, waving his pipe on a level with his moustache.

"Aw—shut up!" pleaded the cook. "Give me a light and be a gentleman."

Bisker snorted yet again. He put his cup down on the stove, and from a fire withdrew a billet of kindling wood which he presented to the cook. She snatched it from him and lit the cigarette she had produced from her apron pocket.

Mrs. Parkes was only slightly under forty. She was large, very large. Her brown hair was drawn tightly against her head with masses of curling pins. Her large face was deathly white, and against the background of her face her little red nose appeared not unlike a tiddly-winks counter.

Bisker drank his tea without swallowing.

"'Ave another?" he asked.

"Course. Fill it up. Thirty-seven to cook for, as well as the missus, three maids, a drink steward and you. What a life!"

Bisker took the cups over to the wall bench, filled them and brought them back to the now-warming stove.

"How'd you sleep?" he enquired, now a little more cheerful.

"Better than if I'd had you beside me," replied the cook. "And you be sure to shave early, or the missus will be roaring you up again. You're a disgrace about the place. Thank 'eaven the winter won't last much longer. Must've been another frost by the feel of it."

"She froze 'ard but it isn't so cold outside as I expected," averred Bisker. "Wind musta shifted to the west just before I got up. Well, I s'pose I'd better get on with the blasted boots."

"Yes, and you go quiet about it, too," commanded Mrs. Parkes stubbing out her cigarette. "We don't want the old cat in her tantrums three days running."

Bisker stood before the cook, sliding the palms of his hands together and leering.

"One of these days," he said slowly, "you're gonna hold her while I cut 'er throat—slowly. The old——"

Mrs. Parkes feigned indignation. She snatched up her cup, glared at Bisker, and said a little shrilly:

"You cut out that murder stuff and get along with your work. You'll be havin' me in 'Truth' next, and then what'll me husband say when he comes 'ome!"

"Stick yer teeth in," Bisker replied, and swiftly retreated to the scullery, retreated backwards as though he were withdrawing from the presence of royalty.

From a box on a shelf he obtained a pencil of chalk and, again entering the kitchen, crossed it and passed through a doorway into a passage which led him to the public lounge. Here he switched on lights, passed through the lounge and so gained the passage which led to the bedrooms. Switching on more lights, he collected the footwear of the guests, marking on the soles the number of the room outside of which they awaited him. There were ten pairs of men's boots, sixteen pairs of women's shoes, and three pairs of children's boots. All these he took back to the scullery, and then went on another journey to collect a pair of shoes from outside the door of the room occupied by Miss Eleanor Jade, the proprietress of Wideview Chalet.

Standing at a bench, Bisker began to work on the collected footwear. Every pair was of good quality, and every pair bespoke their utility for walking. This morning Bisker expected to find them dry, for the weather had been fine for the last four days. He was, therefore, easily provoked to profanity when he began work on a pair of men's shoes, size eight and bearing on the sole the figure five.

"Musta been out walkin' late last night, the blinkin' foreign German," he complained. "More work—as though a man 'asn't got enough to do. Musta got 'em as wet as hell."

These shoes took him three times as long to clean as any previous pair. Having done them, he began to whistle, and continued whistling till he came to the last pair. These were a woman's shoes, size six, collected from the bedroom door of Miss Eleanor Jade. Like the shoes from Number Five, they were also damp.

"Ha! Ha!" chortled Bisker. "The old bird! The old cat! The old—old——" Ceasing his chortling he began to brush the shoes collected from the bedroom door behind which slept Miss Eleanor Jade. "Now, lemme see. Number Five goes for a walk late last night. In he comes, has a drink or two—I must ask George about that—then toddles off to 'is room, takes off 'is shoes and plants 'em outside his door for me to clean. Yes, that's how it was. But that same argument can't be applied to the old cat. She wouldn't be out walkin' late last night, and yet 'er shoes are wet same as Number Five's. The old——Ah—yes, she could 'ave. A little bit of love, eh! Ho! Ho! Sherlock 'Olmes me!"

Having completed this task, Bisker placed the footwear on a large wooden tray and went back to the bedrooms. By the time he had replaced them where he had found them it was almost full daylight.

He left the house to return to his room, a hut built in a far corner of the spacious garden. On the way a magnificent panoramic view of valley and distant mountains was presented to his unappreciative eyes. From the wide, stone-balustraded veranda extending the full length of the house-front, a well-kept lawn tilted gently down to the distant wire fence bordering a main highway. The lawn, as well as the small shrubs in beds spaced upon it, was white with frost, a glittering white upon which lay the reflected light of the sun now rising above the far mountains, thirty-odd miles across the valley.

After shaving and washing in ice-cold water, Bisker returned to the kitchen where the aroma of cooking food and simmering coffee caused him to forget momentarily the agony of the first five minutes of his day following the ringing of the alarm clock. Outside, the air was milder. The bushman in Bisker was quick to note the remarkable rise in the temperature after the sun had risen.

A uniformed maid entered the kitchen with an empty tray on which she had taken early-morning tea to Miss Jade's guests. George, the drinks steward and table waiter, was already at breakfast at a side table to which Bisker drifted. Another maid set down before him his breakfast of bacon and eggs, toast and coffee for Miss Jade fed her staff well.

"Mornin', George!"

"Morning, Bisker," replied George, a sleek man of about thirty, pale of face, dark of eyes and hair. "Nice day."

"Yes. Gonna be a warm day after the frost. Wind's gone round to the west. The frost'll thaw off quick. Might get rain tonight. What time you get to bed?"

"About eleven," replied George. "The men were tired and cleared off to bed early."

"You tuck 'em all in nice and comfy?" Bisker enquired with his mouth full.

George smiled in his superior manner.

"All bar the bridegroom," he admitted. "I left him to the bride."

Bisker winked and leered. He glanced furtively over a shoulder observed that one of the maids and the cook were standing close, winked again at George and refrained from making an evil remark. The remark was never made, because George, having finished his breakfast, departed for the dining room.

Presently Bisker rose and shuffled out of the kitchen. He left the building by the scullery door and crossed the yard to the wood-stack where, sitting on a splitting-log in the warm sunshine, he fell to slicing chips from his tobacco plug. The slight problem of the wet shoes had vanished from his mind.

Having smoked for ten minutes, he put away his pipe and took up an axe with which he proceeded to split foot-length logs into billets for the cooking range. In addition to the kitchen and the boiler fires, there were the lounge and dining room fires to be fed, great blazing fires so much preferred to the cheerless gas and electric fires in the homes of the guests.

For half an hour, Bisker split wood and then took a broom and began the daily sweeping of the bitumened areas and the paths. And then, when he had worked round to the long front of the house, he heard Miss Jade's voice.

"Bisker! Have you seen Mr. Grumman this morning?"

Bisker turned and looked upward to see his employer standing at the veranda balustrade, her bejewelled hands sparkling in the golden sunlight.

"No, marm," he replied.

He stood staring at "the old cat," the wonder in his mind, as it was always when he looked at her, that anyone could be so fortunate. Under forty, Miss Jade's hair was as black as night, her eyes were dark and big and even now as she faced the sun her make-up was perfect. Her voice had the faultlessness of tone and accent which must have been acquired only by long practise.

"Very well. Continue your work, Bisker," she commanded.

Bisker obeyed, but his thoughts were not gentlemanly. He was sweeping the path running parallel with the house-front. It crossed midway the wider path leading from the veranda through the lawn to the wicket gate in the bottom fence above the road. He had almost reached the far end of the path when, to his astonishment, he observed a man in working clothes walking up from the wicket gate. Bisker looked involuntarily for Miss Jade, for no person other than a guest was permitted to enter the grounds of Wideview Chalet by that gate.

Miss Jade was no longer on the veranda. Bisker dropped his broom and ambled down the path to meet the social outcast. He knew him.

"Hey, Fred!" he called, when he was twenty feet away from the intruder. "Don't you know that none of the slaves can use that there gate to come in?"

The intruder was tall, thin and bony. His blue eyes watered. The tip of his nose suspended a water drop. He said, with the unruffled calm of the man who will not be hurried:

"Come on down. I've got something to show you."

He turned about and went on down to the gate. Bisker paused, glanced back to see if Miss Jade was watching them, and followed. When hard on Fred's heels, he said, hopefully:

"Got a bottle?"

"Better still," Fred answered without turning about. "Just a bit of a surprise for you. You and me are gonna be famous."

"I don't wanna be famous," asserted Bisker. "If you've brought me all the way down here not to crack a bottle, you ain't no friend of mine any more. A cold mornin' like this, too. And that old cat will be starin' at me with 'er black eyes an' all and will be wantin' to know this and that and who the hell you are, and all the ruddy rest."

On arriving at the wicket gate, it could be seen that a ramp had been cut in the red bank skirting the top side of the highway. Fred and Bisker passed through the gate, down the ramp and so to the macadamised road where they were out of sight of anyone standing on the veranda. Fred stopped, turned and pointed a finger accusingly at Bisker.

"Where were you last night?" he asked.

"In bed. Where d'you think I was?"

"Where was you before you went to bed?"

"Where——I was drinking whisky with you in me 'ut as you well know," indignantly replied Bisker.

"You're lucky," he was informed. "You ever seen a dead man?"

"'Undreds. Why?"

"I've found a dead 'un."

"You have? Where?"

"You're that close to 'im that you're all 'ot."

"You don't say."

"I do say. Come on and I'll show you."

Fred led Bisker along the road bordering the storm-water gutter dug deep against the foot of the bank. He led on down the road from the little bridge at the foot of the ramp which crossed the gutter. The gutter was almost hidden by the briars and winter weeds. When he stopped, he said:

"I only just caught sight of 'im as I was walking along 'ere on my way to a job. Look!"

He pointed into the gutter. Bisker stood quite still and stared downward into the gutter with eyes unusually large. First he saw, beneath lines of vivid green, a patch of scarlet. Then he saw, also beneath lines of vivid green, part of a man's face. He bent his body forward, resting his hands upon his bent knees, and stared still harder.

"That's one of our guests," he said slowly. "A bloke named Grumman. Looks like 'e's dead."

"Too right!" supplemented Fred. "You take a closer bird's-eye view of 'im."

Bisker straightened himself and regarded Fred as though it had been suggested that he step off a cliff a hundred feet high. Then he knelt at the edge of the gutter and lowered himself down into it. With his arms, he parted the tangle of brambles and weeds above the figure of the man dressed in a grey dressing gown and with red leather slippers on his feet. Bisker could tell if a man was dead, having seen dead men. He rearranged the covering of vegetation over the body, and then regained the edge of the road.

Fred regarded Bisker with an expression of sternness in his watery eyes. Bisker looked up and was about to speak when, from above them, a voice said:

"What is going on down there?"

Both men stared guiltily and looked upwards to see a slight and well-dressed man standing on the lip of the road bank. Bisker said:

"Morning Mr. Bonaparte. Better come down an' take a bird's-eye view of a corpse we've found."

"Did you say a corpse?" asked Mr. Bonaparte.

"That's right," affirmed Fred.

"Then I will join you."

In less than ten seconds this guest at Wideview Chalet stood with Bisker and Fred on the edge of the road just above the body.

"Have either of you men been down there in the gutter?" asked Mr. Bonaparte.

"We both 'ave," replied Bisker. "Fred 'ere 'e found 'im and brought me down from me work."

"Ah—pity. You are quite sure he is dead?"

"Too right!"

"Do you know who it is?"

"Mr. Grumman," answered Bisker.

"Mr. Grumman, eh! Oh! Bring me a stick about five feet in length."

Fred found a branch on the lower side of the road and snapped off a stick of the required length. With its point, Mr. Bonaparte moved aside the intervening brambles so that he could see clearly the dead man's face and the clothes he was wearing. Then with the stick he pushed and pulled the vegetation back to hide the body.

Chapter Two

Bisker's Unusual Morning

Miss Jade was taking breakfast in a corner of the dining room. The dining room at Wideview Chalet was Miss Jade's pride, for she had designed it with the purpose of making as much as possible of the magnificent view. Across the entire front were wide panes of glass so that guests whilst eating might admire one of the finest views in all the State of Victoria.

The maid who brought Miss Jade's bacon and eggs said to her:

"Bisker wants to see you, marm."

"Bisker wants to see me?" Miss Jade exclaimed. "Did you say that Bisker wants to see me?"

"Yes, marm," replied the maid, adding pertly: "That is what I said, marm."

"Tell Bisker that I am breakfasting."

The girl departed silently over the thick pile. Miss Jade's finely pencilled brows drew a fraction closer together. There appeared between them two short vertical lines, lines which had caused Miss Jade a good deal of concern, and which she could vanquish only by keeping her brows raised. She heard the maid's voice from beyond the dining room's well-oiled swing doors, and almost choked at the sight of Bisker himself advancing towards her table.

"Bisker!" Miss Jade almost shouted.

Bisker continued to advance, to advance in defiance of Miss Jade's terrible eyes which ordinarily would have petrified him into immobility. He was smiling faintly, a softly sardonic smile, and when he arrived at her table twiddling his old felt hat in his grubby hands, he said:

"You was asking after Mr. Grumman, marm."

"How dare you come here, Bisker!" cried Miss Jade.

"I came to give you a bit of news about Mr. Grumman, marm," Bisker persisted, the sardonic smile lingering in his eyes. "It isn't the sorta news I thought you'd want the guests to know just yet."

Bisker waited. He had news to impart and it was not going to lose anything in the telling. Miss Jade regarded him icily. To her this was a new Bisker.

"Well what have you to say to me about Mr. Grumman?" she asked.

"He's fell asleep, marm, that's what 'e's done."

"Fallen asleep! Why he's not in his room. He's still out."

"Yes, marm—out for keeps—out in the ditch the other side of the front fence. He's dead."

"He's d——" began Miss Jade in a high loud voice. Then she checked herself. Pushing back her chair, she stood up and stared down upon the rotund Bisker. Softly, she asked:

"Did you say Mr. Grumman is dead, Bisker?" Bisker nodded.

Now Miss Jade was a woman of character. She had begun in a small suburban boarding-house, and worked through a succession of larger boarding-houses to small guest houses until she became the proprietress of Wideview Chalet on Mount Chalmers. She was not one to give way to panic. The swinging doors were not so far removed that the maid on the other side could not hear what was being said.

"Come with me to the office, Bisker."

Bisker ambled after her. When within the office, she ordered a young and efficient-looking girl to take her breakfast, and then she waited for ten seconds before closing the door and saying to Bisker:

"Now, Bisker."

Bisker told how he had observed a working man coming up from the wicket gate, how he had "rushed" down to stop him and to turn him out, and how he had been led to observe the body of Mr. Grumman.

"You are quite sure that the man is dead?" questioned Miss Jade.

"In the last war I seen lots of dead men," said Bisker. "Mr. Grumman is dead all right. His body is stiff and as cold as me nose."

"Did he fall over the road bank, do you think?"

"It don't look like it by the way he's lying," replied Bisker, adding cheerfully: "Course he might 'ave. I ain't saying as how he didn't just walk off the bank in his sleep, sort of. Any'ow, he's dead, and we can't just plant him somewheres in the garden."

Miss Jade's brows rose much higher than was necessary to erase those vertical lines between her brows. When she spoke again her voice was cold.

"Don't be foolish, Bisker. Be quiet, I'll ring the police."

"That's what Mr. Bonaparte said, marm," Bisker answered.

"Mr. Bonaparte!"

"Yes, marm. Mr. Bonaparte came to the edge of the bank just as I had examined the body. He's having a look round, sorta. Sent me along to tell you and to ask you to ring for the police and the doctor."

"The doctor! But you said that Mr. Grumman is dead."

Bisker looked patiently at his employer.

"That's so, marm. But the law says that only a doctor can prove that a man's dead."

It gave Bisker satisfaction to observe that Miss Jade was thrown off her balance, that for once she was a prey to her emotions. He stood calmly watching her as with fluttering hands she lifted the telephone and asked the operator to connect her with the Police Station. Whilst waiting she looked up at Bisker, and he was astounded to see in her eyes a look of appeal. The crisis found the man.

"You had better let me do the talkin'," he suggested.

"Please, Bisker."

Miss Jade gladly surrendered the instrument, and sat down in the secretary's chair. Then Bisker spoke.

"This is Wideview Chalet, Mr. Rice," he said. "Bisker talkin'. One of our guests, a gent named Grumman, is lying in the ditch at the bottom of the garden. He's got only his dressing gown and slippers on, and he looks like being dead. Thought you'd like to come down and look him over."

Miss Jade abruptly felt like having hysterics. Bisker proceeded:

"No, we haven't rung for the quack yet, Mr. Rice ... Yes—all right! ... You'll be along directly? ... All right! We'll hang on till you gets here."

Bisker set down the telephone, studied Miss Jade for a fraction of a second and seated himself in her office chair, slumped into it with the same visible relief that she had shown when she sat down. He said plaintively:

"Sorry, Miss Jade, but I'm sort of upset like. Findin' poor Mr. Grumman like that and all. A little drop of brandy—now."

Suspicion leapt into Miss Jade's dark eyes, but the mention of brandy created the want in herself. She pushed a bell button. Bisker rose and lurched to the desk. He again picked up the telephone and asked to be connected with Dr. Markham. He saw George appear at the door, and with exultation he heard Miss Jade order two brandy-and-sodas. Then he heard another feminine voice.

"Is that Dr. Markham's?" he asked, deliberately putting a tremor into his voice. "This is the Chalet. A gent has been taken seriously ill ... What's that? ... The doctor's away? ... That's bad ... Back soon? Oh, all right! Tell him to come along up as soon as he can ... Yes, it's serious."

He had just replaced the telephone instrument when George appeared with the drinks. Miss Jade ordered George to place the glasses on the desk. Bisker waited for George to withdraw, and such was the steward's training that not a muscle of his face betrayed his astonishment. The door having been closed after George, Miss Jade said:

"Take a glass, Bisker."

Miss Jade took three sips at her drink. Bisker held his glass to the light of the window, he sniffed at the contents, then he drank without swallowing and wiped his bristling grey moustache with the full length of a coat-sleeve. He was regretfully putting down the empty glass when Miss Jade said:

"Should it turn out that Mr. Grumman did not meet with an accident, Bisker, that in fact he met his death through violence, everything will be most upset here at the Chalet. I hope, Bisker, that you will remain loyal to me. The guests will doubtless all depart, and the place will have a bad name to live down. Let us hope that Mr. Grumman met with a normal accident."

Bisker's small grey eyes became steady.

"What makes you think that Mr. Grumman might 'ave been murdered?" he asked.

"Don't be stupid, Bisker," snapped Miss Jade. "You tell me the man is dead and that he is lying in a ditch in his dressing gown and slippers. Surely you can recognize the possibility?"

"Oh, yes, marm. I can see that," admitted Bisker.

"Of course you can. How long will it take Constable Rice to get here?"

"About five minutes in his car. Half an hour if he walks. This might be 'im coming now." They listened. Then Bisker said: "No, it's a car coming up the drive from the highway."

The Police Station, staffed by one officer, was at a small hamlet approximately half a mile up along the highway above Wideview Chalet, and, therefore, Constable Rice would take a left-hand turn-off to reach the Chalet at its upper side by the main entrance and the garages. To come in from the city, cars entered through a wide gateway about a hundred yards below the wicket gate and the ramp to the highway. It was thus that Miss Jade and Bisker knew that Constable Rice would be bound to call at the house, and would not see Bonaparte and Fred, who probably were remaining near the body of Mr. Grumman.

The car that came up from the highway could be heard circling on the open space fronting the garages and the entrance to the reception hall. Both thought it was Dr. Markham, and Miss Jade passed from the office to the reception hall, followed by Bisker, who now could hear a car coming down the road from its junction with the highway above the Chalet.

There entered into the reception hall a man dressed in a grey lounge suit of excellent cut and quality. On observing Miss Jade, he removed his hat and advanced. His face was clean-shaven, and his complexion exceptionally pale. In that white face two dark eyes were emphasised. He uttered the formal "Good morning" with a slight foreign accent. Then he said:

"I've called to see my friend, Mr. Grumman."

Miss Jade now had more command of herself.

"Oh, yes! Mr. Grumman is slightly indisposed this morning. In fact, we think he has met with an accident. We are just——Ah!"

Into the reception hall stepped Constable Rice. He was not a large man, but he looked efficient. He was wearing ordinary clothes. The visitor for Mr. Grumman, observed Miss Jade looking beyond him, turned about to face the constable, and Rice looked his astonishment.

"Why!" he said. "I do believe it's our old friend, Marcus! Marcus without his little black moustache, too! No, you don't, Marcus!"

Rice flashed into a crouch and then leapt forward. He was actually off the floor when they heard a distinct "florp" sound. Miss Jade could see the weapon in the visitor's right hand, a weapon having a long and ugly nozzle—a silencer. The velocity of the policeman's body carried it to the place where the visitor had been standing, but he leapt aside, and Rice fell to the floor, an inert and sprawling figure.

He lay quite still. The visitor turned round to face Bisker and Miss Jade. His eyes were twin coals of flame, a dull scarlet behind black. Miss Jade opened her mouth to scream but the sound that issued from it was merely a long-caught sob.

Bisker stood with his hands doubled into his hips, his eyes little points of livid grey. The visitor backed slowly to the main entrance, stood there for what seemed a long time, then vanished beyond the door he slammed shut. Neither Bisker nor Miss Jade made the smallest movement. They heard the sound of a car being driven swiftly down the drive to the highway. Then Miss Jade slumped to the carpeted floor.

To Bisker it seemed that his own voice came to him from at least a hundred feet distant. He was on his knees when he heard it saying:

"Now, now, Mr. Rice! You hurt bad?"

He turned over the body of the constable, and then ceased further movement whilst he gazed down at the small round hole in the centre of the policeman's forehead, and at the thin trickle of blood oozing from it.

"The dirty rat!" he said slowly.

Then he was on his feet and running to the closed front door. He swung it open and dashed outside, ran for a short distance over the bitumened space, then pulled up and said again:

"The dirty rat!"

On returning to the reception hall, he discovered Miss Jade on her hands and knees, and because her hair was all awry he had the impulse to laugh at her. Instead, he bent over and hauled her to her feet, and half dragged her into the office, where he put her in her own most comfortable chair.

"Leave it all to me," he ordered, and was astounded by the timbre of his own voice.

He walked to the office door with the intention of closing and locking the door between the reception hall and the short passage leading to the lounge. Then he had his second brilliant "brain-wave" of that morning. He went back to Miss Jade's desk and pressed the electric button summoning George.

Bisker was standing at the door between hall and passage when George appeared.

"Bring a bottle of whisky and glasses for two and a siphon of soda-water," he ordered.

George was on the point of questioning this order when Bisker partly stood aside to give George a view of the dead policeman.

"Get that whisky quick," Bisker snarled, and George almost ran to obey. When he returned, Bisker let him into the hall and locked the door. He took the tray from George.

"Bolt the front door—go on—quick."

In the office he found Miss Jade still slumped into her chair. She looked up at him, her black eyes wide and unwinking. She opened her mouth to scream, and Bisker said:

"Keep your trap shut, marm."

He poured whisky into a glass, added a splash of soda-water and offered it to Miss Jade, who continued to regard him with a fixed stare.

"Take a holt of yerself, marm. Come on—drink 'er up."

"Bisker!" she cried. "Is Mr. Rice dead?"

"As mutton, marm," replied Bisker.

Miss Jade noted the remarkable metamorphosis in Bisker, Bisker the retiring, apologetic, shuffling Bisker, and she thought it even more strange that she liked him and experienced a feeling of comfort—of all feelings she might be expected not to be expecting. Her arms slid outward over the desk and her head fell forward to rest upon them as she burst into a fit of weeping.

Even as she wept she heard the gurgle of liquid pouring into a glass. She did not observe Bisker fill a glass to the brim and drink it without more than one swallow. She heard the siphon sizzle when Bisker half filled his glass with soda-water for a "chaser." Then she heard him at the telephone calling for Police Headquarters, Melbourne.

Her weeping ceased as abruptly as it had begun. She moved her body upwards. Bisker was sprawling over the desk speaking into the receiver, describing what had happened. She felt inexpressibly tired. Almost mechanically, she picked up the drink Bisker had poured for her and began to take quick sips from the glass. Behind Bisker stood George and she thought how extraordinary it was that George appeared calm and self-possessed.

Presently Bisker replaced the telephone.

"A patrol car in an outer suburb nearest to us will be here in twenty minutes," he told her. "I'm to keep everyone out until they arrive. You had better go and see that the guests don't wake up to what's happened."

"I—I——" began Miss Jade, when Bisker cut her short. It was necessary, in order to execute a little plan he had thought of, to get rid of Miss Jade and George.

"George!" he snapped. "Help me to take Miss Jade outer here."

They had almost to carry Miss Jade from the office and across the reception hall, past the sprawling figure on the floor. At the passage door Bisker glared into George's eyes and snarled:

"Take Miss Jade away to her room, anywhere. And keep your own trap shut, too. Get me?"

George nodded. Bisker unlocked the door, and George assisted his employer out into the short passage. After that Bisker shut and re-locked that door. He ambled back into the office, where he put the siphon behind a lounge chair, the glasses into a desk drawer and the three-parts-full bottle of whisky into his hip pocket. Then he passed out of the office, crossed to the main door, unbolted that, passed outside and re-closed the door, and stood hesitant on the iron foot-grid before the front step of the porch.

Would he have time to take the bottle of whisky to his hut and there conceal it under his mattress? Hardly. There was, too, the chance that someone might see him, and the police might hear of it and want to know why.

Either side of the front door there grew an ornamental shrub in a large tub. Bisker selected the tub on the left side of the door. The earth was friable. He scooped a small and deep hole straight down so that the bottle would not lie longwise with the danger of its precious contents seeping out from the glass-stoppered cork. Down went the bottle into the hole. Bisker covered it in, having to place only three inches of earth above the stopper. That done, he sat on the edge of the tub and produced his tobacco plug, knife, pipe and matches and began to slice wafers from the plug.

The second wafer was cut when round the corner of the building appeared Mr. Napoleon Bonaparte.

"Ah! Bisker! Did you call the local policeman?" Bony enquired.

"I did, Mr. Bonaparte. He's here—inside."

"Indeed! What is keeping him?"

Bonaparte's blue eyes regarded Bisker with a penetrating stare.

"You just didn't happen to see the car what come up the drive and then went down the drive a few minutes ago, did you?" Bisker asked.

"I did. What of it?"

"Didn't note the number, I suppose, Mr. Bonaparte?"

"No, I wasn't near the drive. Why?"

"Well, the bloke in that car came into the reception 'all when me and Miss Jade was waiting for Constable Rice to arrive. The bloke in the car came in and asked for Mr. Grumman, and Miss Jade was putting 'im off, sort of, when Rice came in. Then the bloke saw Rice and Rice recognised 'im, and Rice made a jump for 'im and he shot Rice with a pistol fitted with a silencer."

"Indeed! Is the constable badly hurt?"

"He's quite dead," replied Bisker, and felt disappointment at not observing any alteration in the expression of mild interest on Bonaparte's dark face. Then all that had happened burst from him as the taut nerves began to relax, and when it was told, he sat trembling on the edge of the tub, the brief period of self-appointed authority vanished.

"There is nothing we can do, Bisker," Bony said, "but wait for the police."

Chapter Three

Boots, Male, Size Twelve

When the first police car arrived, Detective-Inspector Napoleon Bonaparte was sitting in a cane chair on the wide front veranda overlooking valley and mountain. Patches of fog scattered over the valley appeared like little woolly clouds spaced on a rumpled carpet of red and green checkers. There was no wind. The air was warm and so clear that he could distinguish the grey of fire-killed trees on the mountain slopes thirty-odd miles distant.

He sat alone at the far end of the veranda, smoking his badly made cigarettes, his ears open to the chatter of other guests who were by now suspecting that something was seriously amiss. Some of them were wanting to take the next bus down to the city and Miss Jade was indisposed and the secretary had vanished. He heard the police car coming several minutes before it turned off the highway and purred up the sharper incline of the tree-lined drive.

Three minutes later, he observed Bisker, accompanied by a large man in plain clothes, on the path skirting the front of the veranda. They came along as far as the steps, and then turned down the path dividing the lawn, which would take them to the wicket gate—and the body of Grumman.

A further period of ten minutes elapsed before Bony heard the sound of more than one car coming up at speed along the highway. These cars also turned in at the driveway and came to a halt beyond the far end of the house. Soon after their arrival, several plain-clothes men followed the path taken by Bisker and the first arrival, and of these two carried cameras and one a substantial leather suitcase. He did not walk with the military alertness of his companions, and Bony guessed him to be the police surgeon.

After they had disappeared through the wicket gate and down the ramp, Bony rolled another cigarette, lit it, and then lounged farther down into his comfortable chair. The cushion behind his head was soft, the contours of the chair fitted his slim body, and the sunshine which poured in radiance over him was warm and delightful.

He wondered what Colonel Blythe would say when he heard that Mr. Grumman was dead. And he wondered what the police would think when they entered Mr. Grumman's room. It was certain that they would be more interested in nailing the murderer of First Constable Rice than in finding the murderer of Mr. Grumman although the killer of Grumman would, of course, be hunted for. Rice was one of them, and it seemed that Marcus was known to them. A point of special interest to Bony was what had Marcus to do with Grumman?

Time passed, and then Bisker was coming up from the wicket gate with three detectives. From where he sat Bony could see them just above the coping of the stone balustrade. The party turned to their right at the top of the path, and took the path leading to the end of the house where the main entrance and the reception hall were situated. The hall and office would certainly be in the temporary possession of the police. Most likely they would use the lounge in which to examine every guest.

Bonaparte experienced a feeling of mental exhilaration. He had reason to feel it. In the first place his case of two days had taken an unexpected and remarkable twist, and, in the second place, he would have to continue to work independently of the police, as he had begun.

This was by no means the first time he had worked for Colonel Blythe. The first occasion had been in April, 1942, when he had been instrumental in locating the leaders of a spy ring acting for Japan.

This Grumman business was a kind of aftermath of the German surrender, and had called him, Bonaparte, from Brisbane to Melbourne, and in Melbourne to a house in the best side of Toorak Road. There Colonel Blythe had offered him a drink and cigarettes and begun to talk.

Had not Colonel Blythe married Colonel Spendor's daughter, it is doubtful whether Bony would have ever seen Mr. Grumman. Blythe was a little over forty, fair-haired and blue-eyed, cultured and charming. He had had something to do with the British War Office for years before being seconded to Australia for special intelligence work, and the only time he seemed put out was when mention was made of the war-time Australian Intelligence Officers at Army Headquarters.

It was but four days before this beautiful morning of September N that Colonel Spendor, Chief Commissioner of Police, Brisbane, had sent for Detective-Inspector Napoleon Bonaparte and gruffly informed him:

"My son-in-law's got a job for you, damn and blast him! I wouldn't let him have you if you were not free for the moment. I've obtained priority for you on a plane leaving at two-fifteen. Before going out to the airfield, call in for some letters I want you to hand over to my daughter, will you? I wouldn't put it past those blasted censors to open anything I posted. And don't forget to give her my love, and tell her husband that he can have you for only seven days."

Then in that quietly furnished room in the house in South Yarra, Bony had presented the letters to Mrs. Blythe, and assured her that Colonel Spendor was very well, as was Mrs. Spendor when he had seen her the previous week. After she had withdrawn, Colonel Blythe got down to work.

"D'you think the civil 'tecs noticed you as you left the plane?" he asked, and Bony had said he thought he had not been especially noted.

"Good! Well, old pal, there's a bird staying at a guest house some thirty miles out in the country who goes by the name of Grumman. If I ask Military Intelligence here to run the rule over this Grumman, they will probably send a lance corporal out to see him and to ask him a set of questions written down on a sheet of paper. They've done it before, the brainless idiots. And they'd like to know what I know, and wouldn't begin to function until I had set out on some silly form all that I did know, which would not be much.

"Listen, we'll go into the details later, but now here is the outline. Mr. Grumman is General Wilhelm Lode, who, it was reported by the Germans three months before they crashed, was killed in action. He was, and still is, a member of the German OKW, an organisation of military experts which lives for ever, in peace and in war, and through defeat. The public name for the OKW is the German General Staff.

"When the German General Staff knew that the game was up, it was announced that General Lode had been killed. Other high officers also were alleged to have been killed. Lode's job, and that of other officers, was to preserve the blueprints and the formulas of the most advanced weapons and scientific results in war-making, including the release of atomic energy, until the time again arrives when the General Staff can begin the blue-printing of another German Army for the third World War.

"How Lode got to Australia, I don't know. I met him in 1932, and I saw him five days ago in Collins Street. You are the only man I can trust, Bony. I want you to rub him over, find what is in his luggage, find his associates, find where he has planted the stuff he certainly brought out of Germany. Those plans and formulas are more precious to us than his carcase."

Well, that had been the introduction of Bony to Mr. Grumman. He had come to Wideview Chalet to stay for a fortnight. He had met Mr. Grumman, who spoke perfect English and not before that morning, when Mr. Grumman was found dead in the ditch, had he been able to take a peep into his room, where he received a great surprise.

Now Grumman was dead, and a friend of his named Marcus had called to see him and had departed hurriedly after having killed the local policeman. On top of all that, there was the surprise given him, and awaiting the investigating detectives, in Mr. Grumman's room. Bonaparte was lost in his thoughts when a pleasant voice close to him said:

"Not Detective-Inspector Napoleon Bonaparte, surely?"

Bony opened his eyes, affected a yawn and looked upwards to see standing just beyond his feet a man dressed in an elegantly cut lounge suit.

"And you?" he asked.

The other smiled.

"I am Sub-Inspector Mason," he replied. "We have never met, I think. But Superintendent Bolt says he knows you quite well, and he's rather anxious to renew the acquaintance. He's in the office here. Care to come along?"

Bony smiled, and rose not ungracefully to his feet.

"Lead me to the Grand Inquisitor," he pleaded. "How's the old temper?"

"Fairish," replied Mason, as they walked along the veranda. "You ever suffered from it?"

"Oh, no. I have observed it only."

On passing through the lounge, Bony observed one of the guests seated at a little table, with two obvious plain-clothes men seated on its opposite side. Several small groups of guests were talking in low tones, some obviously irritated, others merely excited. The body of Constable Rice had been removed from the reception hall. In the office, Superintendent Bolt and two junior officers were seated at Miss Jade's desk.

Bolt was a ponderous man, seventeen stone in weight, with not a great deal of superfluous flesh on his enormous frame. The top of his head was distinctly dome-like, a yellowish rock rising above a fringe of grey hair resting on his ears. Small brown eyes lighted when Bony and Mason entered the office, and he rose from his chair with outstretched hand. He moved with the effortless grace of a cat despite his fifty years.

"So it is actually you!" he said, his voice a purr. "How are you, Bony?"

"Very well, Super," Bony replied, taking the hand offered and careful to avoid having his own crushed in the greeting. "Beautiful place, good cooking, good attention."

"And no work, eh?"

"Nothing to speak of. Glad to see you looking so fit."

"Thanks. Come over and have a chat."

"If—you can spare the time."

"Oh, yes, I can always spare time with you," agreed Bolt, and chuckled. "Meet Dr. Black, our own surgeon. And Inspector Snook.

Gentlemen, meet Inspector Napoleon Bonaparte of Queensland."

Bony shook hands, noting the long cadaverous face of the police surgeon and the square-cut countenance of the Inspector. He accepted a chair and sat with them, Mason making a fifth.

"Been staying here long?" Bolt enquired of him.

"No, only a couple of days," replied Bony, now engaged in the manufacture of a cigarette. "I came up here for a week of quietness and the proper atmosphere for meditation."

"Ah!" breathed the Superintendent. "Meditation."

"Not always is meditation a luxury; sometimes it is a necessity," Bony stated, looking up from his task to survey the others swiftly in turn. "Dr. Black will surely agree with me that physical and mental relaxation are of enormous benefit to men who employ their brain."

"Quite agree," Bolt cut in ahead of the surgeon. "Good yarn for the marines."

"The marines!"

"Yep! Now, my dear old friend, cut out the Justice Darling act of asking what a picture show is, and concentrate. You going to play ball?"

Bony sighed. He lit the cigarette he had made and which was an obvious offence to Dr. Black. The police officers regarded him steadily. Bony said:

"Tell me—who is Marcus?" Bolt leaned forward and glared.

"Bony, tell us first—are you going to play ball?"

"Of course."

"Good!"

"With a proviso," murmured Bony. "I can play ball with you up to a point, and I will explain just how far I can go because you will not want to spend time unnecessarily. I have been, and still am, interested in the man named Grumman found dead in the water-gutter down beside the road. I came down to Melbourne for a special assignment, having been seconded by my Commissioner to the Army people. I am interested in Grumman's past activities and in the person or persons who killed him. You will be interested in the persons who killed him, too, but not for quite the same reason that I am interested. I am interested in the man Marcus because he was connected with Grumman. You will be interested in him because he killed Constable Rice. Our interests, therefore, will not clash, or ought not to, and so I am quite willing to co-operate with you in return for your co-operation with me."

"Good!" Bolt again exclaimed, this time rubbing the palms of his hands together. "Let's begin. You were down by the body soon after it was discovered, weren't you?"

"Yes. I found the man Bisker and a second man standing on the edge of the gutter just after Bisker had been down into it to see the body which the other man first found. I had a look around the place, examined the road-verge up and down, and then along the top of the bank, and finally the ground along both sides of the wire fence and upward from the little gate."

"Did you find anything?" asked the Superintendent, and four pairs of eyes bored into Bony's now-expressionless face.

"Very little," he admitted. "Unfortunately, last night there was a very hard frost which, again unfortunately, was thawed very early this morning by a moist wind coming in from the southwest. I'd like to ask a question here."

"Go ahead," urged Bolt.

"Doctor—I know how difficult it will be to answer this question. How long do you think Grumman had been dead when you examined the body?"

The police surgeon frowned.

"Certainly less than twelve hours and certainly longer than five—going back from 9.54 a.m. when I examined the body."

"Five!" repeated Bony. "That goes back to five o'clock this morning. According to Bisker, who got up this morning at twenty minutes to six, when he left his hut he noticed that the west wind, or rather what was a westerly drift of warm air, had set in. Had set in, remember. Not had just set in when he left his hut.

"We can accept it as a fact that Grumman left his room, or was carried from his room, before five o'clock and before that westerly warm air reached here so rapidly as to bring about a thaw. He was wearing slippers size eight. He weighed, I should think, about eleven stone. I have found no track made by either one of those slippers, either on the ramp leading from the gate down to the road, or along the edge of the road.

"From the face of the bank, I am convinced that he did not fall from its top down into the gutter, and I am certain that his body was not dropped into the gutter from the top of the bank. I am also sure that the body was not dropped into the gutter from the edge of the road. It was taken down into the gutter, and there carefully laid in it and the grass and brambles drawn over it to hide it from any chance passer-by."

"But the man, Fred, was a chance passer-by," interjected Inspector Snook.

"Quite so," Bony agreed. "He saw parts, or a part, of the body, but we should remember that the body was placed there in the dark, by a person or persons not able to be positively sure they had concealed the body, which, from the position of grass stems and brambles, they had endeavoured to do.

"These points may appear to you to be unimportant. My task of tracking was made exceedingly difficult by the frost which made the ground iron-hard at the time Grumman's body was placed in the gutter, and which thawed completely before the body was discovered. However, on the ramp I saw the imprints of a man's boots, size twelve. This man came up the ramp after I did last evening shortly after eight o'clock, for an imprint of his right boot is partly overlaid on one made by mine, and he went down the ramp when the ground was much more frozen than it was when he walked up. The peculiar thing about this is that during the time I have been here, two days and a night, I have not seen any man wearing a boot size twelve, nor have I seen the track of such a boot. No man among the guests has such a foot, and neither Bisker nor the man who found the body has that size. He is, at the moment, a misplaced object and, in consequence, of interest. A man wearing such a boot would be big enough to carry a man of Grumman's weight down to the gutter. How did Grumman die?"

"Poison," answered the surgeon.

"Cyanide?"

"Almost sure. A guess?"

Bony hesitated.

"Yes," he replied. To those assembled, he said: "Find the man who wears a size twelve in boots. He is not a workman. The heels and soles are of rubber, the diamond-shaped trademark is stamped on the soles, and the soles are partly worn, very much so along the inner edge toward the toe, indicating that the wearer is a horseman."

"Thanks, Bony," purred Superintendent Bolt. "Mason, examine Miss Jade and the staff and ascertain who called here last evening after eight o'clock — you know — the man with twelve in boots."

When Mason had left the office, Bolt said to Bony: "Any other point of interest?"

"Yes. A maid was sent to enquire after Grumman when he did not appear punctually at breakfast as was his custom. She first knocked on his door, and receiving no answer, she tried the door and found it unlocked. She opened the door a little way and called Grumman's name. Again receiving no answer, she opened the door wide and looked in. The curtains were drawn before the french windows, but there was sufficient light to enable her to see that he was not in bed and was not in the room. Subsequently, when I went in, I found that all of Mr. Grumman's luggage had been taken away."

"You can't tell us how or by whom it was removed?" asked the Superintendent.

"No. I possess nothing on which to direct suspicion towards anyone. Personally, I find it most annoying," Bony went on, blandly. "I want to go through the late Mr. Grumman's effects."

"You don't want to more than we do," snapped Snook, and Bolt began to chuckle.

Chapter Four

A Pleasant Afternoon

During the remainder of that morning, Bony occupied his cane chair at the distant end of the veranda. Plain-clothes policemen seemed to be everywhere; they walked about the lawn and up and down the paths; in and out of the room lately occupied by Grumman, the french windows of which were immediately behind the reclining Bonaparte; and about the veranda interviewing guests who already had been examined in the lounge as to their identity and occupation and holiday plans. Two of them photographed the house, the lawns, the windows of Grumman's room, and the interior of that room and of the reception hall. The fingerprint-section did their work in Grumman's room, while members of the traffic branch roared their cycle outfits up the drive to report to Superintendent Bolt, and roared down it to slip away again. An ambulance came to collect the bodies. Two men measured the lawns and the bottom road bank, and made a rough plan from which would be made a minutely accurate one.

Lunch was served to the guests at one o'clock. The efficient George waited with the assistance of two maids, his movements smooth and his demeanour courteous. The guests were informed by Inspector Snook that they were released from restriction, and when they drifted from the dining room they found the secretary at their service and the now-composed Miss Jade on duty as hostess.

By three o'clock all but six of the guests had departed, and all but two of the policemen had left. The room occupied by Grumman had been sealed. Three kookaburras in a driveway gum tree decided to chorus their pent-up feelings in sardonic mirth. At half-past three Bony was the only guest occupying the veranda, and to him George brought afternoon tea on a service trolley.

"It's been quite an exciting day, George," observed the little half-caste when helping himself to two of Mrs. Parkes's cakes.

"Yes, sir, it has that," George agreed. "The next stir-up will be from the press, I expect."

"Ah, yes. Those boys will make an appearance at any moment. In fact, they are a little late, but then, I suppose the detectives wouldn't release the news till after they returned to the city. It appears that you will be less busy from now on."

George smiled.

"Oh, the place will soon fill up again. Lots of people will come out of curiosity. Another cup of tea, sir?"

"Thank you. How long have you been employed here?" Again George smiled.

"Three months, one week and four days," he replied. "I had to work it all out for the d.s. Well, I must get along. Thank you, sir."

As he trundled his trolley away Bony glanced at his feet, noted that he was wearing tennis shoes size seven, that he was slightly knock-kneed and walked on his toes.

The sun was westering, and already the house shadow reached far down beyond the highway. The valley lay bathed in colour, and the far mountains had changed their colour from dove-grey to warm brown. Not a cloud broke the blue dome of the sky, not a leaf moved, so still was the air. It was almost as warm as a summer's evening.

George came again to Napoleon Bonaparte.

"Inspector Snook sends his compliments, sir, and will you kindly see him in the office?"

Bony frowned.

"What, again!" he exclaimed. "Hang it, I suppose we'll all be pestered by these detectives for some time."

"They can be very irritating, sir," George said, sympathetically.

"They can be!" echoed Bony. "They are."

He found the office door closed, knocked on it and entered when a loud voice bade him. He re-closed the door and crossed to sit at the table at which Inspector Snook was seated.

"Thought you'd like to hear results to date before we leave," Snook said. "And there are one or two points that want clearing up."

"Go ahead," Bony urged.

"To begin with, our fellows haven't located Marcus," Snook said, his voice containing a trace of anger. "Within ten minutes of Bisker's call this morning all roads leading down from this mountain were blocked, and all cars travelling from here were stopped and examined.

"Careful questioning of Bisker has given us a reasonable estimate of the time which elapsed between the minute Marcus left the house and the minute that Bisker spoke to Headquarters on the telephone as five minutes, so that the roads were blocked fifteen minutes after Marcus left in that car. The nearest road-block was at Manton, nine miles down the highway, Manton being a small township with a railway station.

"It's possible that Marcus got beyond Manton in those fifteen minutes. And it's possible, too, that he took a side road off the highway and two places between here and Manton. Anyway, he hasn't been trapped."

"Tell me about him," Bony requested. Snook leaned back in his chair, placed the tips of his fingers together and pursed his lips before replying. Then he said:

"Marcus is our Number One Gangster. Marcus is our own pet name for Alexander Croft, alias Mick Slater, alias Edward B. Martyn."

"Oh!" breathed Bony. "Ho! Ho! Edward B. Martyn! No wonder the constable didn't have a chance."

"No, Rice had no chance. Rice was a plain-clothes man for six years, and a good man, too. He was shot up pretty badly last year, and when he was able to return to duty he was offered the station up here for a period for health reasons. He knew Marcus—unfortunately for him when he was unarmed."

"I've heard of this Marcus under the name of Martyn," Bony averred. "He never came into my class of investigations. Bad man, eh?"

"The baddest, Bony. He's cold and efficient, and the list of his crimes is as long as your arm."

"What does he specialise in?"

"Dope. He's an international trader in dope. You interested in dope?"

"No." Bony gazed up at the ceiling. "No. It wasn't dope which brought me here. I'll tell you in confidence. My present interest is in secret war weapons and explosives, and such like. Now how does dope fit in with that? In other words, what interest had your bird Marcus in my bird Grumman?"

"Search me," exploded Snook. "I don't get this affair at all—yet. By the way, when you went into Grumman's room, was the door unlocked?"

"Yes—with the key on the outside," answered Bony. "I had with me a key to fit the lock of that door, and I was astonished to find the door key in the lock. Then I learned that the maid had been sent to see what detained Grumman from breakfast, and she had found the key in the lock."

"So that, actually, all Grumman's luggage had been taken away when the maid looked in."

"Oh, yes. I am sure that Grumman's luggage was not taken out of the room after the maid reported to Miss Jade and before I went in."

"What d'you make of it?"

"Nothing so far. I don't understand it."

"Nor me," admitted Snook. "There is this Grumman who gets the drinks steward to bring him a drink at ten thirty-five last night, and then goes off to bed. He gave no intimation of leaving. You say that he didn't fall into the ditch, and wasn't dropped into it. You say that his body was laid in it. Now where was he poisoned? If in his room, then his body must have been carried down to that ditch. Why carry the body to conceal it in the ditch, and why then pinch all his belongings?"

"Perhaps to give his effects a thorough, even a minute, examination, an examination which would require more time than that between the killing of Grumman and daylight."

"Yes, there's that to it," agreed Snook thoughtfully. "But why try to conceal the body, and if to conceal the body why leave it there in the ditch? Why not take the body with them to the place where they took the effects, or at least to a much better place than that ditch? Up here there are millions of places where a body could have been concealed."

"I don't know why. Something may have gone wrong in their planning. If the body had remained concealed, even for twenty-four hours, then during that period the people here would have thought that Grumman had done a moonlight flit to evade paying his account. That might have been the plan, but it just went wrong when the man Fred happened to catch sight of the body in the ditch."

"Probably it was something like that," agreed Snook.

"Did you people get onto the man wearing the number twelves?"

Snook shook his head. Then:

"I'll post a couple of men up here to look around for that gentleman," he said.

Bony lit a cigarette and blew smoke towards the suspended electric-light shade.

"Do me a favour, Snook. Leave the gent with the big feet to me. I shall be staying up here for some time to come."

"You will! Why?"

"Because I like the scenery."

"Nuts!" snapped Snook. He glared at Bony and asked: "Any special reason why you are working for the Army—outside of Queensland?"

Over Bony's brown face flashed that smile which appeared to transfigure him. He had much earlier this day assessed the other's character, and he was aware that Snook's mind was akin to that of the Civil Servant, a mind governed by rules and regulations and precedents and what not. By such is a democracy ruled, and not by such are great criminals brought to the bar of justice. Placidly, he said:

"The Army employs me, I think, because no person in whom the Army might be interested would suspect that an unfortunate half-caste was a policeman. I am staying on here until I am assured that the person wearing the number-twelve boots is not a local resident, and also, until I am sure that the persons responsible for Grumman's death and the theft of his possessions have left the district. That is why I think you can leave this end of the two cases to me."

The Melbourne man rose to his feet.

"All right, Bonaparte. We'll do that. You will keep us *au fait* with any developments up here?"

"Certainly. I may go down to the city tomorrow, and then I'll call in at Headquarters and have a look at your pictures of Marcus."

"Yes, do. We'll help all we can. And don't you take Marcus at all cheaply. He's Satan walking the earth. Now I'll get along. I'll leave the news lads to you and Miss Jade and Bisker. Bit of a character—Bisker. He told the Super that he was entitled to civility as he paid income tax. The old man looked as though Bisker was a talking mosquito."

On leaving the office, Snook left the house and was driven away by a plain-clothes man, while Bony sauntered into the lounge and rang for George. George was away getting a drink for him when Miss Jade appeared.

She was now quite composed and dressed in an afternoon frock. She wore clothes like a Frenchwoman. Bony rose to his feet and gave her a slight bow and his brightest smile.

"I've just asked George to bring me a drink," he said lightly. "Might he bring you one, too?"

"Thank you, Mr. Bonaparte." Miss Jade smiled with her mouth and not with her eyes. George entered with Bony's drink, and she ordered a cocktail.

"I am glad that you are not running away, too, Mr. Bonaparte," she told him.

"Run away! Certainly not! I'd not leave for ten murders," Bony said gaily. "I want a holiday. I like this house, and the air outside and the views. And now that the wretched police have left, I expect to be able to enjoy my holiday in peace."

They touched glasses. She accepted a cigarette from his case, and she looked into his eyes over the flame of the match he struck for her. He was rolling a cigarette for himself when she asked:

"What was your impression of Mr. Grumman?"

"Quite good, Miss Jade. He bothered me a little with his accent. Did you know his nationality?"

"American, I understood. German-American, I think. Plenty of money. My books show a credit for him of some eighteen pounds. He paid well in advance from the day he came."

"He had been here some time?"

"Yes—five weeks last Tuesday." Miss Jade most daintily blew a smoke ring, expertly lanced it and turned again to Bony. "I can't understand how his luggage was carried away without someone hearing it being taken."

"Out through the french windows of his room, across the veranda, down over the lawn and so to the road where, no doubt, a car was waiting."

Miss Jade nodded her superbly coiffured head in silent agreement.

"Do you understand it at all?" she asked.

"I'm afraid I don't understand it a little bit," Bony admitted. "I never could even guess the ending to a mystery thriller. Raising sheep is my long suit. I fear you must have been badly frightened when that man shot the local policeman."

Miss Jade clasped her bejewelled hands together. Her eyes were big when she exclaimed:

"Oh, I was, indeed. It was that man's eyes which frightened me most. They reminded me of the eyes of a jay which Bisker wounded. The birds would come here and take all the berries from my trees, so I got Bisker to shoot some of them. One fell at my feet, and it looked up at me and tried to fly at my legs, and its eyes shone with a red light. That man's eyes were red, shining red, when he backed to the door and pointed his dreadful pistol at us. Red eyes in a paper-white face. I'll never forget them."

Abruptly, Miss Jade became pensive. Bony was about to speak when she motioned with her right hand for him to remain silent. Then she said: "Somehow or other, that man's face reminded me of someone I've met, and you mentioning just now about mystery thrillers brings to mind who that someone is. That man is not unlike a resident here, a writer of mystery stories, a man named Clarence B. Bagshott. Well, now, that's remarkable."

"How so, Miss Jade?"

"Mr. Bagshott's face is very white, and he has dark eyes which at moments when he's talking take on a reddish gleam. He's a mystery, too. I never liked the man. I wonder! I wonder if the man who came here and killed Mr. Rice is a relative of Mr. Bagshott! He might be. But then that's absurd, Mr. Bonaparte, isn't it?"

"Possibly, Miss Jade, but not necessarily."

"Still, as someone once told me, authors of mystery stories are criminally minded. Instead of actually committing crimes, they give vent to their criminal instincts by writing about crime."

Miss Jade gazed straight into Bony's eyes. Then slowly her face, including her eyes, broke into a smile and she laughed.

"How silly of me, Mr. Bonaparte. And I am laying myself wide open to a slander action. Mr. Bagshott is very clever in his way, and, I suppose, like most clever people, is a little neurotic. Now what?"

George entered from the passage connecting the lounge with the reception hall.

"There's a party of reporters come, marm. They are asking for you."

"Bother!" Miss Jade softly exclaimed. Then to Bony: "Do I look all right—if they want to photograph me?"

She had risen, and Bony was standing when he replied in his grand manner:

"Madam," he cried, "you are the loveliest woman I've been privileged to meet for many a long year. A little publicity, I am sure, will not spoil you. Au revoir! I'll take a little walk before dinner."

Chapter Five

Treasure Trove

The giant shadow of Mount Chalmers was extending its thick finger across the wide valley towards the great mountain range, the tree-lined escarpments of which now stood in brilliant relief. Not a leaf moved on the stately mountain-ash gums growing beside the road along which Bony strolled. Early for the season, a whip-bird deep down in a gully gave its warbling note which is followed by a sound like that of a whip being cracked, whilst in the grassy banks of either side of the road the red-capped robins and the blue finches were busy nesting.

To the man of the open spaces of the semi-arid interior, this scene of soft greens and chocolate earth, of silvered tree trunks and trailing vines, gave pure delight. The air was so clear, cool but not cold, and its freshness was like wine in the nostrils.

What a day it had been! The weather had been sublime, the scene one of innocent rustic charm. Yet no previous day had provided Bony with such a crop of questions demanding answers.

He wondered what Colonel Blythe's reactions would be when he heard that Grumman was dead and his luggage removed. At least, the theft suggested that there were others besides Colonel Blythe who suspected the distinguished member of the OKW had brought priceless documents with him from Germany.

He wondered, too, just how Grumman had met his end. Bony himself was to a degree associated with the dead man during the last evening of his life. At half-past six, he had been seated with Grumman at dinner, at the same table with four other guests, two men and their wives. It was a circular table, and Grumman occupied the chair opposite the detective.

The German was raw-boned and lean. He had light blue eyes and a rat-trap of a mouth. His grizzled hair was worn fairly long, obviously, to Bony, as a partial disguise. With his hair cropped close, and with a monocle in his eye, he would have looked just what he was—a Prussian. He spoke like a German who had lived in the U.S.A. for many years, and to Bony's ears the North American accent was emphatic, so much so that had he not been aware of Grumman's origin, he would not have detected the slightest faults due to the acquirement of English as spoken by educated Americans.

Grumman had appeared to be quite free in the company at that table.

He talked interestedly of America and of cities in South America. There was no marked reserve in his demeanour; in fact, he was just one of the well-educated, travelled East-coast Americans who call in at Australia on a round-the-world rest-cruise.

After dinner, the five people who had dined with Bony drifted to the lounge where coffee was served and where smoking was permitted by Miss Jade. When Bony left the lounge at half-past seven to take a stroll, Grumman was talking with two male guests. When he again entered the lounge at about a quarter past eight, the two male guests and Grumman were still occupying the same chairs.

Grumman remained with those two guests until five minutes after ten when he arose, saying in Bony's hearing that he would take a sharp walk before going to bed. He left the lounge by the door opening into the short passage leading to the reception hall and the main entrance. He left without hat or coat for, to have obtained them from his room, he would have left the lounge by another door.

A little before a quarter to eleven, Grumman came back through the same door by which he had left, and the flush on his face indicated a sharp walk in the keen air. An elderly man who had been reading a novel invited him to take a drink, and Grumman ordered whisky. After returning the hospitality, he went off to his room, the time then being a few minutes to eleven.

Grumman's room was the best at Wideview Chalet. It was lighted by a pair of french windows opening on to the front veranda. Bony's room was less expensive, having only an ordinary window facing the top side of the house and the road down which Constable Rice had driven his car.

The door locks were the same, and the key to Bony's door fitted the lock on Grumman's door. He had established that fact just before leaving for his walk the evening before. He was also able to establish at the same time the fact that Grumman did not lock his room when he left it during the day or evening.

Those who had killed him were certainly ruthless. How had they achieved their purpose in poisoning the man? The poison had most certainly not been in the drinks served by George in the lounge. He must have received it in his room, after he had undressed and slipped on a dressing gown over his pyjamas. He had taken two whiskies in the lounge, the first at the other guest's expense, the second at his own. The other guest had suggested a third drink, but Grumman had declined, and therefore, it would be improbable that Grumman would take another drink from a private store after undressing. Had he, before getting into bed, drunk water from the carafe, water containing cyanide? Hardly! For one thing he would not be thirsty, and for another, a whisky drinker would not take water—unless it was to swallow a medicinal tablet.

He wondered whether that "idea" had occurred to Snook or Mason, and whether the contents, if any, of the carafe had been taken for analysis.

He wondered, too, where the man Marcus came into the picture. A dope peddler, even in the international trading scale, would have no business or social connection with such a man as Grumman. He might have discovered Grumman's identity and intended to practise a little blackmail. One thing, however, was certain. Marcus was not responsible for Grumman's death and the theft of Grumman's effects.

He paused in his stroll to look down upon Wideview Chalet lying two hundred feet below the narrow lane he was following. Two hatless men and a woman wearing a scarlet kerchief over her hair were coming leisurely up the path from the wicket gate. There were two cars parked on the open space before the main entrance to the house, and even as Bony watched several men came out to the cars. Another came with Bisker from the direction of Bisker's hut.

All except the handy-man got into the cars which were then driven down the drive to the highway, and Bony smiled a little tight-lipped smile, for they were newspaper men. Had they seen him it was probable that one at least would have known his profession and blazoned it to the world.

He was about to continue down the lane which would take him to the upper road and the Chalet, when he observed Bisker turn from watching the departing cars and cross to one of the ornamental shrubs growing on either side of the front doorway. There he paused, looking first through the open door into the reception hall and then towards the garages. With a swift movement, he thrust forward his right hand, apparently to press down the earth in the tub, and with movement equally quick, he drew back that hand, again gazed furtively all round, and abruptly walked round the corner of the building to enter a rear door opposite the wood-stack.

"Yet another little mystery," murmured Bony, delightedly. "Now what, about that tub, interests Bisker? Either he picked up something on the surface of the earth in the tub, a something I could not see, or he wanted to take something and became too frightened that someone in the reception hall or about the garages might observe him. I must get to know Bisker a little more intimately. Well, here's me for a wash and dinner. I'm hungry. Must be the air."

No one but Bisker knew how dry was Bisker. He dared not "put it on" Miss Jade for a snifter. He dared not ask George to get him a drink for which he would have to pay, in case either George or Miss Jade might recall the full bottle of whisky taken to the office with the alleged purpose of reviving Miss Jade. And it was still too early to "sneak" off to the hotel a mile down the road, for dinner had not started and he had dishes to wash. Anyway, why walk a full mile down to the hotel when there was a bottle three parts filled with whisky right there under his hands? He had been a fool to have attempted to retrieve it in daylight. Someone might have seen him.

Reluctantly, Bisker dragged himself away from the tub and ambled in his distinctive gait round to the scullery door. Deciding he would have to wait until he had "cleaned up" after dinner, he planned how he might reduce the after-dinner chores by doing as much before dinner as was possible. In the scullery he found the beginning of the evening's labours awaiting him, and filling a trough with hot water, he fell to reducing the stack of baking trays and utensils used that late afternoon. When the house gong was struck he was that much forward.

The evening was well advanced when again he left the house, and immediately he was assailed by the temptation to retrieve his bottle of whisky. This was a favourable opportunity. The guests would be going to the dining room, the secretary would be "titivating" herself in her room, and Miss Jade would be hovering about the servers and the kitchen.

Despite the dusk, Bisker chipped at his tobacco plug and loaded his pipe, whilst his eyes searched the neighbourhood for possible enemies. Nothing stirred, not even a cat. He paused casually to strike a match and light his pipe. Still there was no sign of any living thing. Gradually, he worked his way round to the shrub tub, and with a nonchalance he did not feel, he seated himself on the edge of the tub, his body directly above the coveted bottle.

The light suspended from the roof of the entrance porch just failed to reach the tub, but in case someone should come out on the porch and see him, he slid farther round the shrub until it came between him and the door. Then, with his right hand, he began to grope round the shrub to that part of the tub which had become for him an irresistible magnet.

The tips of his fingers had begun to burrow gently into the soft loam when a figure appeared at the corner of the house and slowly approached.

Bisker withdrew his hand as quickly as though it had been bitten by a bull-ant. His body froze into immobility, but he had omitted to put out his pipe from which shreds of burning tobacco were still falling unheeded on his old working clothes.

"Good evening, Bisker!" Bony cheerfully greeted him.

"Ha! Good evenin', Mr. Bonaparte." Bisker's voice betrayed his state of nerves. "Nice night!"

"It certainly is. Has the dinner gong sounded?"

"Five minutes back," Bisker replied.

"Then I must hurry in. Good night!"

Bisker watched Bony enter the area of porch light and pass into the reception hall. He waited—a full minute. Now was the time. It was almost quite dark. A swift delving, a short rush to his hut and——

Again Bisker's hand was withdrawn with the previous swiftness. Bony re-appeared on the porch, and unhurriedly came outside to where Bisker sat on the shrub tub.

"Sorry to disturb you," Bony told him. "I seem to remember having seen you somewhere some time ago, and the thought has stuck in my mind. Are you a native of these parts?"

"What, me!" Bisker exploded. "Me a native of this miserable, fog-cramped, frost-deadened country! Why, I come from west of Cobar where the people are civilized, what there is of 'em, and where there's plenty of wood to keep a man warm. You're a grazier, aren't you, sir?"

"Yes, Bisker. I am interested in Thunder Downs, in Western Queensland. You ever passed through Thunder Downs?"

"That I have," Bisker answered, now cheerful and memory mastering the desire to get at his bottle. "I've come through Thunder Downs with cattle—lemme see, yes, back in 'thirty-seven that was."

"Then what are you doing down here?" Bony asked him, and knew the answer before Bisker spoke it. Bisker didn't hesitate.

"I come down to Melbun on a 'oliday, and I went broke. I 'aven't been anythink else than broke ever since. The booze 'as got me properly."

"Like to go back to the bush, Bisker? Back where it's a real man's life, away back where there isn't any booze for a man excepting perhaps once a year down in Cobar or Broken Hill?"

There was the silence of hesitation. Then Bisker said:

"I can't save enough money to get back to a railway terminus. And I once tramped back through 'undreds of miles of farmin' country and won't do that never no more." Bisker grasped at a straw: "I suppose you wouldn't take me back with you when you went, would you, Mr. Bonaparte?"

"I might," Bony conceded. "I'll think it over."

"Thank you," Bisker said, earnestly. "You see, once I got away from the drink for two or three months, I'd be all right again."

"Of course you would. I'll see what can be done about it, Bisker. Now I must go in to dinner. When do you get yours?"

Bisker slid off the tub and said that he would have to go in for his dinner at once, and thus Bony was satisfied that, whatever it was that interested Bisker in the shrub, it would have now to wait until later.

"Where you been?" demanded Mrs. Parkes of Bisker when he entered the warm kitchen.

"Workin'," Bisker replied in such a tone that the cook stared. Bisker ambled across to the table where the staff ate. In his mind the prospects of returning to his beloved bush almost totally eclipsed the desire for whisky. He ate his dinner hardly aware of what he ate, for he was a member of a small army of bushmen who live hard, work hard, enjoy life to the full, until they smell whisky or hear a cork being drawn. Thereafter, nothing stops them from drawing their money and hurrying to the nearest township or wayside hotel. And like the male spider, they know clearly the danger of courting the siren.

It was not until he was washing the heavy utensils used for preparing the dinner that his mind returned to the bottle buried in the tub, and when he came to the utensil he was looking for, the last, he whistled expectantly through his teeth.

His work done for the day, he walked out without saying even a good night to the cook. He made his way across the open space in front of the garages and so to his hut, where he lighted his hurricane lamp and lit his own fire on the open hearth.

That done, he left his hut and followed the path to the open space at the edge of which he paused to examine the night-shrouded scene. The house porch was aglow with its light. There were lights in rooms to the left. The roof of the big house supported the dark but star-studded sky. Bisker kicked off his boots which all day had remained unlaced.

In his socks, he edged across the bitumened space before the garages. Nothing alive moved within his restricted vision, and he kept the shrub in its tub between himself and the porch. Without sound he reached the tub, and stood there like a darker shadow for a full minute. It was now ...

Bisker dug his hands into the soft loam, and his fingers came into contact with an object both round and smooth, and then a similar object adjacent to it. His fingers went a little more deeply into the loam, and he pulled up what felt like two fountain pens in a leather pocket case. This object he transferred quickly to a pocket, and frantically delved again—to find with an ecstasy of relief the top of the whisky bottle not three inches from the point where he had first touched what appeared to be twin fountain pens.

He hugged the bottle to his chest with his left hand whilst the right smoothed down the earth. That occupied him five seconds, and then he moved silently away across the bitumened space, recovered his boots, and like a black wraith slipped along the narrow path to his hut. With a sigh of relief he closed the door, crossed to the table and there in the light of the lamp examined the bottle gleefully, like a miser counting his gold pieces.

Bisker sat on a case at the table and up-ended the bottle between his lips and drank. The liquid fire coursed down his gullet, ran into and through all his veins and vanquished the depression which had settled on him like an enormous weight. He drank again, a little more slowly and a little less. Then he set down the bottle, loaded his pipe and smoked.

Ha! Life was not so bad after all. That bottle was a win, all right and all. What a win over the old cat, and that blinking George who wouldn't give a dying duck a bit of weed. Bisker's hand brushed his left coat pocket, and touched the first object he had taken from the shrub tub.

He had guessed rightly. In a black leather holder, to which two strong safety pins were attached, there were two large-sized fountain pens. Bisker looked at them. Then he drew an old newspaper towards him, unscrewed the top of one pen and began to write in a terrible scrawl. He tried the other pen with equal success. Both were good pens, gold-mounted. Now how did they work?

Bisker examined them more closely. He raised the gold filler-bar, and then he depressed it. Nothing happened. Yet that was the way a similar pen in the possession of young Frank up at Marlee Cliffs had spurted ink. But what was the little screw at the end of each pen for? Bisker tried to loosen one with a thumbnail and failed. He inserted the point of his clasp-knife into the screw-head and after trouble at last moved it. When he took it out with forefinger and thumb he saw the screw was attached to a tiny cylinder less than one inch in length. The cylinder was covered with a glistening wax-like substance.

"Now wot in 'ell's inside that?" he demanded softly. "Well, we'll cut 'er open and just see."

The end of the cutting edge of his clasp-knife was razor-sharp. With it, he began gently to cut longwise through the wax which was fairly hard. Quite suddenly the material inside the wax burst open, and Bisker sat looking down on a strip of white film less than half an inch in width and about twelve inches in length. On the film was a series of black dots smaller than pin heads.

Then Bisker's blood froze. There was someone behind him. There had not been a sound, but he knew suddenly that someone stood behind him.

"Where did you find those pens, Bisker?"

The blood in Bisker's veins began again to flow. The pens! Poof! He had feared that someone behind him was after the whisky in the bottle. The voice was that of Mr. Bonaparte.

Chapter Six

Bisker's Visitors

"Don't move your hand, Bisker. You might tear that most valuable film."

Into the range of Bisker's eyes Bony slid a long-fingered brown hand which closed firmly on his wrist. Against his shoulder pressed the slim body of the guest who had promised to consider how he could be released from servitude to Miss Jade. The strength in the hand about his wrist astonished Bisker.

Bony's other hand then came into Bisker's view, and the fingers began to disentangle the long strip of what appeared to be a species of celluloid on which the many dots showed clearly. It was not unlike a strip of cine-film.

"I am going to release your wrist. Don't move it until I say so," Bony ordered, and Bisker stared with fascination as the two brown hands slowly and carefully disengaged the strip. He saw that the inner end was attached to an aluminium spindle. "Take this end. Gently now. Take it by the edge and don't let go."

Bony now had the strip straightened between himself and Bisker, and with great care he began to rewind it on the spindle. Without speaking, Bisker watched the brown hands, and then glanced upwards at the brown face in which the blue eyes gleamed like gems, then down once more to the film being slowly re-wound. After what appeared to be a very long time for Bisker, who could observe the whisky bottle beyond Bony's hands, the end he held was drawn against the roll, and now the roll was being pressed into the little waxlike case. Thereupon the cut selvedge's were pressed together as the whole was inserted into the pen. Finally, the containing screw was replaced, and the pen slipped into the leather holder. Not until he saw the filled holder slipped into Bony's inside coat pocket did Bisker speak.

"A bit calm-like, ain't cher? I found them ruddy pens, not you. They might be worth a lot of money in reward."

There was another box against a wall, and this Bony brought to the table and sat upon it to face Bisker.

"Well—wot about——" Bisker began and fell into a strained silence beneath the intense stare of those ice-cold blue eyes in the brown face. He experienced a distinct sense of relief when the blue eyes moved their gaze from him to the making of a cigarette, and the ensuing silence, in which the soft noises of the fire came as though from another world, seemed to Bisker to be interminable. Then, without looking up, Bony spoke:

"Go and draw down the blind. When you've done that, I am going outside to see if anyone is lurking about. You will then come here and sit down again, and you will not touch the whisky. Is that clear?"

"Yes, Mr. Bonaparte, but—what's it all mean?"

"I'll tell you in a minute or two. Now—the blind."

Bisker felt rebellious, but he obeyed, and when he had pulled down the blind on the only window, Bony laid the newly made cigarette across the top of the glass bottle-stopper in fine balance. Then he slipped to the door he had not closed when he entered, opened it wide enough to permit his body to pass outside, and closed it.

The night was dark in spite of the stars. He moved swiftly round the first corner of the hut, then reversed and passed the door to gain the opposite corner. In this way he passed round the entire structure till he came again to the door and was satisfied that no one was playing hide and seek with him. Normal eyes would have failed to see the trunks of the gum trees bordering the driveway, the faint greyish tint of the garages seen from the door of the hut, and the bank of shrubs beyond the window-wall, with tall trees beyond it. Normal ears would not have registered the faint whispering of leaves stirred by an air current, nor have distinguished the foot-falls of a cat crossing a swathe of dead leaves. There were a host of shadows impenetrable even to Bony's half-aboriginal eyes, gulfs and tunnels of black void which might conceal a hundred enemies, but he decided he could be reasonably sure that no one up to that moment had drawn near enough to the window and door to see what Bisker had taken from the shrub tub.

On opening the door of the hut, he found the rotund little man still seated on his case. But he was facing the door, his eyes wide and round and his grey moustache standing straight out from his face. Closing the door, Bony crossed to the table, seated himself on the second case, took the cigarette from the bottle top and lit it.

"You may get a cup or a glass, Bisker, and take a drink. Drinking from the bottle disturbs my appreciation of the niceties."

Bisker blinked, rose and brought to the table a cracked cup. Bony passed him the bottle and watched the cup being half filled. The cup was raised to Bisker's mouth and over it he regarded his visitor. Then he drank moderately and wiped his moustache with his coat-sleeve. He was invited to light his pipe.

"Where did you find those fountain pens?" Bony asked, and warned Bisker to speak softly.

"In the shrub tub to the left of the porch," Bisker replied. "I was getting me bottle of whisky when me 'and felt the tops of the pens, sorta. Of course, I didn't know what they was. The bottle of whisky I——"

"Better not tell me when or how you got the bottle," Bony cut in. "You say that you first felt the tops of the pens. Were they in their case just pushed down into the earth?"

"That was how it was, I think," Bisker agreed.

"How near to your bottle were they buried?"

"Only about two inches away. You see, when I planted the bottle I feared losing some of the grog if I laid her down longwise, so I dug a hole with me 'ands just round enough to take the bottle and just deep enough to take it to allow for a coupler inches of earth over the stopper."

"What time was that?"

"Only a few minutes before you came round the corner of the 'ouse and found me sitting on the tub this morning."

"Humph! Let me think."

Bisker drew hard at his pipe and watched the now-immobile face of his visitor. He wanted to ask questions but was restrained by a feeling of inferiority.

"Between the time I left you sitting on the tub this morning and the time when the police arrived, did you leave the tub?"

"No," answered Bisker. "I kept on sitting there."

"There was a period of a little less than an hour between the departure of the Inspector and the arrival of the reporters, where were you during that time?"

"On the wood-stack most of it."

"Could you see the tub from the wood-stack?" Bisker shook his head.

"Did you see anyone walking about in that direction?"

"No."

"All right. Tell me this. Do you think that you buried the bottle close to the pens, or that the pens were buried close to the bottle, after you had planted it?"

On this call to his intelligence, Bisker visibly brightened.

"I could have planted the bottle within two or three inches of the pens and not know they was there," he said. "You see, Mr. Bonaparte, I took a good guess at the size of the 'ole I'd want to put the bottle in, and when I put 'er in she just naturally slipped down into a good fit."

Steadily regarding Bisker, Bony told him to remain silent for a minute or two. He turned about on his box, to sit with his back to the table edge, and Bisker took up the cup and sipped at its contents.

Bony was decided that the pens in their leather case had been pushed down into the earth in the tub sometime before breakfast that morning, and most probably before daylight. That those pens had been in the possession of General Lode, alias Mr. Grumman, he was morally sure. He felt certain, too, that on the roll of film were photographs in microscopic reduction of the formulas and plans which Colonel Blythe was so anxious to obtain.

Now some person or persons had removed Grumman's personal effects from his room with, apparently, the obvious purpose of examining them at leisure to find the material which Blythe wanted and which came out of Germany before the end of the European war. It could not, therefore, have been that person, or those persons, who had pushed the pens in their case down into the earth of the tub.

Had that person, or those persons, been forestalled by another who had relieved Grumman of the pens before Grumman died and his luggage was removed from his room? Or had Grumman become suspicious that an attempt was to be made to secure the precious films and himself disposed of the pens by pushing them into the place where, by coincidence, Bisker decided to bury the bottle of whisky?

The previous evening, in the lounge after dinner, Grumman had announced his intention of going for a walk. He had left the lounge by the door leading to the reception hall and the porch, beyond which stood the shrubs in their tubs. Had Grumman then buried his fountain pens?

If he had done so, then he must have been anxious about their safety, and must have suspected that an attempt would be made to steal them from him. Or it might have been that Grumman was anticipating arrest. And yet ... When he returned and accepted the drink offered by the guest, and then returned the hospitality, he had not appeared anxious or worried. He was quite calm, and he betrayed no nervousness, even to the watching Bonaparte.

Assuming that it was not Grumman who had buried the pens, then the party who did so must have stolen them from him, buried them, and was waiting to secure them at a favourable opportunity. It was most unlikely that he had had anything to do with the theft of Grumman's luggage. And it might well be quite likely that he had watched the tub from time to time, and had seen Bisker hovering about, and even sitting on its edge. In which case he would be certain that Bisker had taken them, and in order to get them back into his possession might be prepared to go to any lengths, even to murder. For human life would count for nothing in the scales against the importance and value of those secret formula and plans.

Had the man, Marcus, been after them? Had Grumman been

expecting Marcus the night he died? Had he, Grumman, feared Marcus to the extent of, himself, burying the pens where Bisker discovered them? If he had, would he have done so at the time he went for his walk, when the porch light was as dangerous to him as it was to Bisker when he wanted to dig up his bottle?

The longer he surveyed these questions, the more he favoured the thesis that the person who had buried the pens in the tub was independent of the person or persons who had carried Grumman's body down to the ditch and had stolen his luggage.

Why had he buried the pens in the tub? They were easily hidable. If Grumman had not buried them, and it appeared most unlikely, then the other person had done so because he feared they might be found on his person or among his belongings. That would argue that he knew of Grumman's death, and, further, that he was a guest or member of the staff and not someone who had come to the house specifically to steal those pens. And still further, it would argue that the thief was aware when he buried the pens that his effects and his person might be searched before he could leave the premises without suspicion.

The value of the contents of the pens was incalculable, assuming that it was the material indicated by Colonel Blythe.

To obtain it from Grumman desperate methods had been employed, to the extent of murdering Grumman. If it was thought that Bisker held possession of the buried pens, his life would not be worth tenpence.

Now what of Bisker? Had he stolen the pens and buried them in the tub? Had he buried them for the purpose of not being found in possession of them after the theft was discovered? Had he stolen them as fountain pens and not for the remarkable contents in the place of ink? Bony swung himself round to face Bisker.

"Why did you steal those pens, Bisker?" he demanded, staring into Bisker's washed-out eyes.

He saw Bisker's brows rise high, saw the look of indignation flash into his eyes, and knew before the denial was spoken in anger that Bisker had not stolen the pens.

"All right! I believe you," he assured the handy-man.

How much could he take Bisker into his confidence for Bisker's own sake? A man addicted to drink is ever unsafe but Bisker might be wide open to fatal attack if thought to possess those pens. Bony considered further. Bisker was a bushman. He had a certain strength of character, even if alcohol was his downfall. Bony thought he knew his man fairly well, and eventually he decided to take chances with him. He said:

"I am going to tell you a thing or two, for your own good health,

Bisker. I have reason to believe that the man Grumman was murdered for those pens. You saw what was inside one of them. Those series of small black dots are industrial secrets worth untold money. You were messing about that tub, and the man who buried the pens there might have seen you, and when he goes to get the pens he might connect their disappearance with you. Then he might go-get after you. Do you follow me?"

Bisker nodded, and Bony experienced satisfaction when observing no fear in Bisker's face.

"I am going back to my room to bring a couple of blankets," Bony continued. "I'll camp here with you, and tomorrow you and I will go down to Melbourne, and I'll arrange for you to be escorted as far north as Windee Station, where the boss there will give you a job at my request. And you will stay there until you are wanted for the inquests.

"Crummy Mr. Bonaparte!' exclaimed Bisker. "That'll do me."

"Very well then. Not a word to anyone, you understand! I won't be more than a few minutes obtaining a blanket or two. Is there a key to that door?"

Bisker shook his head, and said:

"There's an old axe in that corner. She's light and 'andy."

"Very well. And keep off that bottle."

Bony walked to the door, opened it and passed outside, closing the door behind him. In the darkness, he waited for his eyes to become accustomed to it. Then with the silent tread of a cat, he circled the hut, walked along the narrow path to the open space fronting the garages, and entered the house by the main door. In the reception hall he encountered Miss Jade.

"You did it very nicely, Mr. Bonaparte," she said, smilingly.

"Just what, Miss Jade?"

"Avoiding those reporters," she replied. "They gave me an awful time of it, and kept flashing their camera lights to take my picture. And the questions they asked! They photographed the house and had me standing on the veranda steps. I am to be in all the papers tomorrow. Oh, the publicity, Mr. Bonaparte!"

Bony smiled delightedly.

"You will have your house full of guests by tomorrow night," he predicted, and then added in his suave manner: "I am sure, Miss Jade, that the proprietress of Wideview Chalet will not detract one iota from the picture of the house itself."

Miss Jade was well pleased. She wanted to talk about the coming limelight to be shed upon herself and her house, and it was only with firmness allied with extreme tact that Bony disengaged himself and passed on to his room.

He found that his window had been lowered to three inches and that the blinds were drawn. From his trunk he procured a small-calibre pistol and rapidly checked its loading. He carried the weapon in the right-hand side pocket of his lounge coat. From the bed he took three blankets and rolled them into a bundle he tied with the cord taken from his dressing gown. He occupied himself for three minutes with the pens, then he snapped off the light, and slowly and quietly raised the window. He left the building by that way.

He had to skirt the wood-stack to avoid the pool of light shed by a bulb outside the scullery door, and from the wood-stack he passed to the back of the line of garages and so came to the narrow path leading to Bisker's hut. Like a shadow he "drifted" along the path. The hut came to him out of the void, and he stopped when he noted that the chink of light under the door he had seen when he glanced back on leaving it now was not to be seen.

He stepped off the path and slowly felt with his feet over a vegetable patch to the wall of shrubs beyond the hut. In this way he reached the wall of the hut containing the window. He stood there for a full minute, his ear pressed against the glass. Not the slightest sound came to him from within the hut.

He passed silently round the first corner, waited there for a minute, then passed round the second corner and pressed himself against the wall beside the closed door. Still he heard no sound from within. Slowly, he moved to a position on one side of the door handle, then, with a quick movement, he turned it and flung the door inward. It crashed back against the wall.

"Bisker!" he called.

Bisker did not answer, and again Bony called his name.

The silence within the hut continued. Bony waited for a full minute before he proceeded to edge his face round the door-post. First he could just make out the bed, and presently the red embers of the fire on the open hearth. On the far side, in front of the window, stood the table, the side of which nearest the fire was faintly illumined by the dull red glow. The automatic now held to his front, Bony slid farther still round the door-post until he was able to see the inside of the wall. There was no one there, and he was sure no one could stand behind the door which he had crashed back against the wall.

Nothing moved in the gloom of the interior, and having delayed action for another two minutes, he thrust the blanket roll before him like a shield, and stepped inside. Still nothing moved, but there remained the possibility that someone was under the bed or under the table.

The glow of the fire embers was reflected in the lamp-glass and the bottle of whisky.

"You about, Bisker!" he called again, but softly.

No reply reached him. He put his blanket shield down upon the table and crossed to the door, which he closed. Then he passed back again to the table and lit the lamp. On the floor beside the bed lay Bisker. He was on his back, one arm lying parallel with his head, as though the hand was trying to reach the short-hafted axe.

Chapter Seven

An Insecure Hold

Twenty minutes! He had not been absent from the hut longer than twenty minutes, and in that short period something had happened to Bisker which looked remarkably like violence. Setting the lamp on the floor, Bony fell to his knees and looked the more closely at Bisker's face. His mouth was slightly open and he was breathing quietly. His coat was unbuttoned and beside him was a corkscrew and a savings-bank deposit book. The pockets of his trousers were inside out, and the evidence appeared clear that all the pockets of his clothes had been rifled. When Bony gripped a shoulder with his hand and gently shook him, Bisker made no response.

It was then that Bony saw the blood at the back of his head, a patch as large as a five-shilling piece. It was a wound which could not possibly have resulted from accident.

The rifled pockets indicated that the person who had inflicted the wound had searched for the pens. Beyond Bisker, the blankets of his bed had been pulled away and lay in a heap on the floor. The mattress was turned and tossed as though the searcher had looked under it. Crouched there on the floor, Bony gazed about the hut. On the table stood the bottle with about the same amount of whisky in it that there had been when he left to fetch his blankets. On the shelf above the fireplace an alarm clock stood edgewise to front. Bony remembered that he himself had put the clock there when he brought the box to sit on at the table, but he had not placed it like that. There had been several cheap books at one end of the shelf, and now these lay on the cement slab in front of the hearth. The place had been ransacked. Even the contents of an old and battered suitcase lay strewn on the floor.

One unfamiliar with Bony's facial reaction to taut nerves might have thought he was smiling. The mouth was wide and the lips parted so that his white teeth were distinctly revealed. There was, however, no smile in the eyes, which now and then glistened when the lamp-light met them at a certain angle. Absent now were the deliberate movements of hands and feet. The nostrils were faintly moving like those of a fox scenting.

Bony reached across the unconscious Bisker and drew the blankets under the man's head and shoulders and about his feet and legs. Bisker had not put on his boots, which were under the table. And then seated on the floor beside Bisker, Bony produced tobacco and papers and proceeded to roll a cigarette.

He was aware that the walls of the hut were light-proof, and that the blind was much larger than the window and completely masked it. The only possible vent through which a person on the outside could see would be through the door key-hole. The thin slit between the bottom of the door and the bed-log was too low for a man to get his eyes to its level.

Bony felt he had two responsibilities. One of them was Bisker, and the other was the contents of the twin fountain pens in the leather holder now pinned into a waistcoat pocket. The sooner that material was in Colonel Blythe's hands, the better.

Picking up Bisker's old felt hat, Bony rose to his feet and, silently crossing to the door, hung the hat over the handle and thus blocked the key-hole. As there was little reason why they should freeze, he then went over to the fireplace beside which was a stack of foot-length logs, and there, still facing the door, he bent down and picked up several logs which he threw blindly onto the red embers.

Continuing to watch the door, Bony left the fireplace for the table, from which he took the whisky bottle and the cup.

Then he stepped over Bisker's body, crouching on its far side to enable him to face the closed door whilst he attempted to revive the man. He got Bisker to swallow a little of the liquor but it had no effect upon him, excepting to cause him to breathe a little stertorously. That encouraged Bony to think that Bisker would shortly recover consciousness and be able to relate what had happened during those twenty minutes he had been absent.

By Bony's wrist watch the time was five minutes after nine o'clock.

At ten o'clock, Bisker was still unconscious, and his condition was worrying Bony, who was beginning to think of going to the house to telephone the doctor. He had not done so before, hoping that Bisker's head injury would produce unconsciousness merely for a short time, and thus prevent additional complications to a case already well provided with them. Then again, he felt that if Bisker had regained consciousness to relate what had happened, he could have planned ahead. Now, to call the local doctor would also mean reporting to the police, and although he himself would say nothing to them about the fountain pens, they might well learn of them from Bisker when he recovered. There were such matters as State rights and Departmental regulations under which Superintendent Bolt would claim those fountain pens and their contents.

It was eight minutes past ten when Bony first heard the approaching "drunk."

He was not far from the hut, perhaps at the end of the narrow path with the open space fronting the garages. A low mumbling merged into a burst of profanity. Bony heard a hiccough, then a man's voice complaining:

"Why don't you open the ruddy door, Bisker? Here's me a-wandering around in the flaming darkness, hanging onter a bottle, and there's you lying in bed snoring yer ruddy head orf. Curse it! If I sings out loud the Jade woman will hear. Like she did larst time." A period of silence ended with a hoarse appeal: "Bisker, open the flamin' door so's I can see where I am."

Bony remained seated on the floor beside Bisker.

From beyond the door he could hear the "drunk" talking quietly to himself, the thought of Miss Jade apparently still uppermost in his mind. Presently, when he made another appeal, Bony knew he was much nearer the door.

"A bloke oughter be shot. Trying to take a drink to a pal, and he won't open the door to give a bit of light. Hey, Bisker! If you don't open the door I'll roar the place down and bring Miss Jade along."

There followed more mumbled growling interspersed with oaths, and then a body lurched against the wall of the hut beside the door. The sound of this body sliding to the ground down the wall was illuminating to the listening Bony.

"Well, I'm here," solemnly announced the gentleman without. "This ruddy tree's as good as any other, I s'pose. Silly fool, Bisker! Where's me bottle? Coo ... I thought I 'ad lorst me little darlin'. Wonder 'ow far that 'ut is from 'ere."

A little later, the "drunk" clawed his way to his feet, and Bony heard him say:

"Flamin' 'ut must be the other side this tree. I'll go round 'er and then I might see the 'ut."

Against the corrugated sheets forming the walls, Bony could hear the man's hands and occasionally his feet when they kicked against the iron. He passed round one corner, passed the window and so passed round the next corner, the while complaining:

"Mighty big tree. Biggest tree I ever see. Biggest tree in Gippsland. Biggest tree in Australia." On coming again to the door he said: "Biggest tree in the world." Silence. Then:

"Where the flamin' 'ell am I? Could 'ave swore I was on Bisker's track." Then he began to sing: "'I'm the cock of Glasgee Town.'"

Bony got up from the floor and crossed to the door which he opened and flung back—to look down the ugly snout of a squat black japanned revolver, and above the weapon at the black mask over a man's face.

"Reach high—quick!"

The order was spoken low and menacingly.

Bony raised his arms, and at the same time the heat of anger rose up his neck into his head.

"Back! Back you go!"

Bony backed and as he did so the masked man entered the hut, closing the door behind him with his free hand. He was of medium height and weight. The hand gripping the pistol stock was white; obviously its owner was one who spurned labouring work. The lounge suit of navy blue was well cared for, the trousers expertly pressed, as were the sleeves of the coat.

"Back a bit more mister," came the order, and Bony backed until he came against the table. "A little to your left. That's it. Now sit down on the box. Keep your hands up—I might get nervous." Bony obeyed. The intruder himself began to back away, away towards the body of Bisker and the hurricane lamp. His eyes could be seen beyond the holes in what was a dark blue kerchief, their gleam reflecting the light of the fire. They appeared never to blink. They kept their fixed stare upon Bony even as their owner bent his knees and picked up the lamp and placed it on the table.

"Now then—where's your gun?" he demanded. "Don't back and fill. I'd much prefer to shoot and then take what I want. Where's your gun?"

"In my coat pocket," replied Bony, his voice toneless.

"Stand up."

Bony obeyed, and the business end of the weapon was pressed into the pit of his stomach.

"If you've got any imagination, you'll feel right now what a bullet in the stomach is like. What pocket is your gun in?"

"Right."

The eyes behind the mask bored into Bony's blazing blue ones. The pressure of the gun against his stomach remained dreadfully steady. He felt the hand enter his coat pocket, felt the small automatic being withdrawn. He was furiously angry, not with the masked man but with himself, angry at having been so stupid as to fall into such a simple trap.

"Now we'll have the pens in the little leather holder. Where have you got them?"

"Spit the rubber out of your mouth and talk plain," suggested Bony.

"Smart, eh? Come on. Talk about fountain pens."

Bony hesitated, then decided it was useless to prevaricate. "They are in the top-left waistcoat pocket."

"Good! You just keep your hands up and don't worry about me. I like helping myself."

Bony abruptly found difficulty in maintaining his gaze direct to the masked eyes, and it was greatly to his credit that he maintained the stony expression on his own face, for beyond the masked man he could see Bisker, and Bisker was standing up on his own two feet. Hallucination, surely! If only he, Bony, dared look away from the masked face to make sure that it was Bisker behind the fellow, Bisker standing up, and gently swaying to the right, where lay the axe. A hand unbuttoned Bony's coat, felt behind the cloth for the pens, found them, and began to endeavour to unfasten the pins fastening the leather holder to the cloth.

Bony could not now see Bisker out of the corner of an eye, and he began to wonder whether what he had seen had been a vision conjured by wishful thinking. The hand at his waist-coat pocket was becoming impatient with the pins, and thus the pins became more obstinate. The hand then felt under Bony's right armpit—then flashed across to the left.

"Undo those pins and hand the pens to me," came the order.

"Do it yourself," snarled Bony.

"I'll give you one chance more. Only one. What about it?"

The voice was brittle, hard and merciless. Bony lowered his arms, slowly, for the weapon was aimed at his stomach with a steadiness which was appalling. He was obliged to tilt his face forward to see what he was doing, and then, glancing upward, he again saw Bisker, this time to the right of the masked man. And Bisker had taken up the axe.

"Come on! What are you mucking about for?" demanded the masked man.

"Use your eyes and see," Bony suggested, and hoped greatly that Bisker would do nothing whilst that gun was pressed into his stomach. He freed the holder from the cloth, and drew it out of the pocket and held it forward. It was snatched from him, and the masked man stepped two paces back, two paces nearer the waiting Bisker.

Bony's arms were beginning to tire, but the weapon in the steady hand of the masked man was still aimed directly at the centre of his stomach. Beyond the masked man, he could see Bisker, and Bisker was holding the axe above and behind his own head. Bony could just see its blade. It was rust-stained and remarkably blunt.

It was then that from outside there came a loud and long cry. It sounded not unlike a circular saw jamming in the cut and rapidly being stopped. The masked face confronting Bony tilted upward in an attitude of startled listening. Then upon the roof a heavy object fell with a resounding crash. There followed a slow slithering of some object down the iron roof, and finally a dull thud just beyond the door.

"What's that?" demanded the masked man, and in his voice Bony detected alarm.

"Friend of mine," replied Bony, aware that two opossums had fought on a tree branch immediately above the hut, and that the vanquished had been forced to fall to the roof.

The man's next action placed Bisker at a disadvantage. Knowing that if he struck with the axe the weapon might be fired with fatal results to Bony, Bisker waited in the belief that what had happened to himself was about to happen to Bony. Bony would be ordered to turn about and then the masked man would reverse his weapon and bring the butt down hard on his head. It was Bisker's intention to wait until the moment that the weapon was raised in reverse to deal the blow.

The cry of the opossum and the crash on the roof unnerved the masked man, whose desire now was to escape. Still covering Bony, he half turned and began backing towards the door, when he saw Bisker standing like a very bad imitation of the Javelin Thrower.

"Bit too late," he cried loudly. "Either of you move, and I'll drill him first and the other last."

"Mind the step as you go out," Bony said softly, and so astonished Bisker that the axe above his head wobbled and came to rest on a shoulder.

The masked man had now reached the door against which he stood with his back to it whilst his free hand searched for the handle. Gradually Bony's knees bent, bringing his body in readiness to spring forward, and slowly Bisker's axe moved up from his shoulder and then outward as he prepared to throw the "javelin." The man's hand found the door handle, and he stepped aside to permit the door to be pulled inward. His revolver still did not waver off a line midway between Bisker and the detective.

It was not unlike a slow-motion picture which in a flash was increased to normal speed. The masked man wrenched open the door. For a second he continued to menace Bony and Bisker with his weapon, and then he stepped backward out through the doorway, to emit a yell as he stepped on the body of the opossum which, rolling under his foot, precipitated him on his back on the path.

Bisker's axe was the first to arrive at the doorway. The head got through the opening all right, but the haft caught the left-hand post and the implement fell to the floor. The next to arrive was Bony, and he passed through the doorway without touching the floorboards. The third was Bisker, but he moved over the floor and was slow by comparison. Having emerged from his dwelling, he heard noises indicative of a struggle going on somewhere in the dark, and his primitive mind directed him to return for the lamp and the axe. The lamp in his left hand and the axe in his right, he rushed out once again—to meet Bony staggering towards him and holding a hand to his cheek.

"He got away, unfortunately, Bisker," Bony said, pantingly. "Caught me on the cheek-bone with his gun. Better get inside again and see to the damage. How are you feeling?"

"There 'as been times when I've felt better," replied Bisker. "And I'd be feelin' worse than I do if that bloke 'ad drunk the whisky." Having put the lamp down on the table, he turned to Bony to see blood trickling downward between the fingers of the hand held against his cheek. When Bony removed his hand, he said: "Hum! Bit of a scratch. Better let me pour a drop or two of kero on it."

He brought a beer bottle of kerosene and administered to Bony's superficial wound by drenching a handkerchief with the oil and squeezing the liquid upon the open cut, then giving the handkerchief to Bony to press against the cut to stop the bleeding. Into the palm of his left hand he poured more kerosene and slapped it against the lacerated portion of his own scalp. It was done so casually that Bony could not help laughing.

"Best thing on earth," Bisker said almost cheerfully. "Next best thing to kero is whisky, but what a waste that would 'ave been. What about a taste?"

Bony was liking Bisker more and more perhaps because under nervous strain Bisker was becoming more akin to his natural self. He expressed the thought that the suggestion might be accepted, and a few moments later, when he discovered that the bleeding had stopped, he sat at the table with Bisker and made a cigarette despite the smell of kerosene on his hands.

"What do we do next?" Bisker asked, as though the recent ten minutes were a normal period of life.

"Tell me what happened to you," replied Bony.

"Me? Why, I was stirring up the fire when the door was opened. I thought it was you come 'ome, and I says when me back is to the door: 'You was pretty nippy,' meaning you hadn't taken long to get your blankets. Then I hears a strange voice saying: 'You just stand up straight and turn round.' So I stands up and I turns round to look down the barrel of a revolver. Then I looks up above the gun and sees the bloke with the mask over 'is face.

"'E says: 'Up with 'em!' Well there's nothin' else I can do—like singing a song or doing a bit of a dance. Then 'e says: 'Wot did you dig outer the shrub tub?' and I tells 'im I dug up me bottle of rat death. Then he asks me wot else I dug up, and I tells 'im I don't dig up nothing else. 'E calls me a liar—me, mind you—and I can't seem to do nothing about it. 'E said: 'You dug up a couple of fountain pens in a leather holder when you dug up your bottle. You 'and the pens over to me—quick.' I says: 'I'm telling you I ain't got 'em.' 'E says: 'Then Bonaparte's got 'em. You turn round.'

"So I turns round. Then a comet hit me fair in the eyes. When I wakes up, I finds meself lying comfortable. I 'as a bit of a 'eadache, and I 'ears the bloke talking to you about the pens. Then I turns me 'ead and sees 'im standing with 'is back to me and you standing with your 'ands up. So I gets me axe, and I waits me chance because I can't do nothing while he's got that gun pointed at you. It might have gorn off."

"It certainly might," Bony agreed with feeling, and then related how he had been fooled. "You didn't recognize the fellow by his voice?"

Bisker shook his head whilst he swirled whisky about his teeth.

"Did you notice his hands?"

"Not particularly. I was too interested in 'is gun."

"Think back. Have you seen anyone wearing a hat like that fellow was wearing?"

Bisker pondered, his grey eyes screwed to the size of peas. Then he said: "No, I can't remember anyone special wearing a hat like that. Plenty of blokes wear black felt hats these days with the front of the brim turned well down. 'E's no bushman, that bloke, or he wouldn't 'ave been frightened when them 'possums 'ad a fight and one fell on the roof. That upset 'im sorta."

Bony smiled.

"He was certainly upset when he trod on it outside the door. Tell me, how can I get to Melbourne tonight?"

"Ring up the bus bloke for a hire car. Get a train at Manton."

"Hum! How else—other than ringing for a hire car?"

"Walk, Manton's nine miles. You might pull up a car overtaking you."

"Could you tramp nine miles, d'you think?"

"I could. But why?"

"It might be better for you to pack and come with me," Bony replied. "Then you could leave tomorrow for Windee Station. The owner would take you on. I could send him a telegram about you."

"Mind me askin' wot you're gonna do?"

"No. I am going to Melbourne tonight, and probably will return tomorrow to finish my holiday."

Bisker was staring at Bony, and his gaze shifted to the whisky bottle, remained on that for five seconds, and finally returned to Bony.

"When I was standin' with me axe at the ready," he said softly, as though thinking someone was listening at the key-hole, "I sort of remembered about you. I 'eard about you three years back when I was west of Cunnamulla. You coming back 'ere tomorrow tells me you ain't finished with the lad wot bashed me and stole them pens of'n you. Now wot about you taking me on as your offsider? Blokes don't bash me about and get away with it."

It was Bony's turn now to stare into Bisker's eyes and at Bisker's weather-cum-whisky-stained countenance. Bisker went on:

"I been working for Miss Jade for two years, and I ain't been gettin' round with me ears shut. I 'ad no excitement this last war, and nothing before that after three years in France during the first Great War."

"I'll think about it, Bisker, and let you know when I return," Bony decided. "Remember, a closed trap lets nothing out."

Chapter Eight

Colonel Blythe Receives a Jolt

The house in South Yarra occupied by Colonel and Mrs. Blythe stood back from the street. It was an old house "growing" in about two acres of ground surrounded by a high wall.

Besides the domestic staff, the Colonel was provided with two clerks, a stenographer and a messenger. When this clerical staff, supervised by Blythe's assistant, a Captain Kirby, left at five o'clock the premises were guarded by Peace Officers until nine in the morning. The Peace Officers' quarters were situated at the rear of the house in an outbuilding, and after office hours telephone calls were received by a Peace Officer on duty at the switchboard inside the house. He would connect with Colonel or Mrs. Blythe in the study or the lounge respectively, and, after eleven o'clock, with Colonel Blythe's bedroom.

Bony, having arrived at the front gate at six o'clock in the morning had to make known his business to the Peace Officer on duty there. This man contacted his duty-mate at the switchboard, and following discussion, the telephone beside Colonel Blythe's bed awakened him.

"Bring him in—to the study," ordered the Colonel, and three minutes later he was welcoming his early visitor with keen expectancy. The door having been closed by the Peace Officer, he observed the cut on Bony's cheek-bone.

"Been in a private war?" he asked.

"Er—a slight skirmish," admitted Bony. "Very early to call on you, but I thought you would like to have a report. The Grumman chase has become most interesting."

"Yes, that's so. I heard yesterday afternoon that Grumman had been found dead. Poison, I understand. And a policeman shot. Like a drink?"

"Tea—or coffee—if it's at all possible," assented Bony. "I haven't only just got out of bed."

Colonel Blythe picked up the telephone. He spoke quietly in his customary, unaffected voice and the Peace Officer was only too pleased to leave his switchboard for the kitchen. Then Bony was pressed to accept a cigarette and smoke while his host left him to bring a pot of salve for the cut on his cheek. Anxious though he was over the Grumman affair, Blythe's first thought was for his visitor.

"This stuff will cleanse and heal," he told Bony on his return. "Shove it on. There's plenty more."

"Thanks. The cut was beginning to smart. Done with a gun, by the way. My own fault. Yes, poor old Grumman was found in a ditch yesterday morning. Did the C.I.B. people contact you?"

"No," replied Blythe. "I was informed through other channels."

"Well, the morning papers will have a lot of it," Bony promised. "But I'll run through the details which will include material the papers won't have."

He related how he had found Bisker and another man standing on the edge of the ditch wherein lay the body of Grumman, and how he had subsequently entered Grumman's room to find the dead man's effects vanished. He told of the visit of the man, Marcus, and the shooting of Constable Rice, concluding by asking if the Colonel knew anything of Marcus, otherwise Alexander Croft, alias Mick Slater, alias Edward B. Martyn. Colonel Blythe pursed his lips and nodded.

"Edward B. Martyn is known to me," he said. "Captain Kirby, my assistant, will know much more than I do. Kirby, by the way, is a Scotland Yard man. Er—just a moment. Come in!"

The Peace Officer entered carrying a tray containing coffee and biscuits, and Blythe suggested that both he and his mate on duty at the gate might like coffee—with a little dash of rum in it to keep out the cold. Bony felt that Bisker had made a mistake by not consenting to accompany him that night and morning.

"Well, go on," Blythe urged when the officer had departed with the addition to the coffee in a glass.

"How Grumman was poisoned I expect the C.I.B. people will find out," Bony proceeded. "It's an item which interests me but probably not you. They were anxious to play ball with me and I saw no reason why I should not—up to a point. I could not understand why Grumman should be killed, presumably for his papers, and then his belongings removed. He was found dressed in dressing gown and slippers, and wearing pyjamas, so we may assume that he died before midnight—leaving his killer at least five hours to go through his effects for the papers. It became still more baffling after I observed the handy-man loitering about a tub in which grows an ornamental shrub outside the main entrance."

Colonel Blythe listened with growing intensity of interest as Bony continued the tale of Bisker and his buried whisky, his eyes became wide open and he smiled happily as Bony described the scene in Bisker's hut when he closed his hand over Bisker's wrist to prevent accidental damage to the unwound spool of photographic film.

"Good work, old man!" he exclaimed. "Excellent."

"Yes, it was a tremendous fluke," admitted Bony. "One of those rare coincidences which sometimes favour me. However, the pens were subsequently taken from me."

He related how he had gone back to Bisker's hut and there found Bisker unconscious and his pockets rifled and the hut searched. He related the coming of the "drunk" and how he had been taken in by the ruse, and eventually how he had been held up and the pens in their holder taken from him by the man who escaped.

"What horrible luck!" Blythe burst out at the conclusion of Bony's report. "You'll have to get that chap. We must have those films, you know. They'll be a damn sight more dangerous in the hands of some other Power than in the keeping of the OKW, for the OKW won't be able to do so much with them for several years, and in that time, our own Government will nullify most of their secrets through the discoveries of our own scientists."

"It was unfortunate," Bony said sadly. "They were beautiful pens. I was intending to ask you for them."

"Oh, yes, you could have had the pens, man. It's the contents we want. Hang it! What fearful luck! What do you make of it all?"

"Very little," Bony confessed. "However, I am strongly inclined to the belief that the man who baled me up and took the pens did not come from the city to do it. He was wearing a navy-blue suit which was so well pressed that it was obvious that he hadn't worn it long, and hadn't travelled by car in it. Also, it smelled of strong disinfectant: you know, the stuff that is put with clothes to keep away silverfish. If he had come from a distance, or had been in the open air for even a short time, the smell would not have been so strong.

"Whether he had anything to do with the killing of Grumman and the theft of Grumman's luggage is debatable. I think he's not responsible for Grumman's death and the theft of Grumman's kit, for he put those pens in the shrub tub, or knew they were buried there by some person who had no need to steal Grumman's kit.

"What have we? One party who killed Grumman and stole his kit. Another party who stole the pens and planted them in the shrub tub, and a third party, the man, Marcus, who might well have been after Grumman's papers. This last raises the question of what a dope trafficker had to do with a high German officer in possession of plans and secrets of armaments."

Colonel Blythe audibly sighed.

"Heck of a mix-up. What do you intend to do now?" he asked.

"Find out who killed Grumman. Find out who robbed me of those pens I wanted for keepsakes. Find out who the man is who wears a twelve size in shoes, and one or two other things which have come to interest me."

The Colonel began to pace on the sound-defying carpet. Bony poured himself his third cup of coffee and lit his third cigarette. Neither spoke for five minutes, when Blythe halted before the seated Bony.

"We've got to get those pens," he said. "The blasted Peace Conference may fail to keep Germany in subjection as long as she ought to be, and the German General Staff might well get into the saddle again within a year or two."

Bony, looking upward, noted the anxiety in the other man's face. Blythe went on:

"Hang it, Bony. It's not like you. I don't understand you. You had those pens and then you — —Oh, damn!"

"I'm going to get those pens, never fear," Bony boasted. "I have never failed yet in finalising a case assigned to me. Those pens are going to be mine. They are lovely pens, gold-mounted. I want one to give to my eldest son Charles who has just gained his Medical Degree and the other I want to give to my wife."

"You can have the pens—if ever you get them," Blythe promised. "You must get them. Why, the contents of those pens is without price. I want the contents. And I want the contents right now."

"Oh!" Bony's eyes gleamed. "If it's the contents you are so greedy for, that will be easy."

Colonel Blythe again audibly sighed with impatience. He began again to pace to and fro over the thick carpet. He had been first amazed on seeing General Lode in Collins Street, then his hopes had been raised high when Colonel Spendor had sent Bony down to him, for the little detective's war work for him had been remarkably successful. And then for Bony to have the pens in his possession only to lose them to a gunman!

What was that! Bony was saying:

"I want the pens, and you want the contents, Colonel. Well, I have still to get the pens. The contents you can have now."

Colonel Blythe halted once again before the seated Bony. He stooped down to peer into Bony's upturned hands. His own hands tore through his long and still-fair hair. As a man believing that what he sees is a vision, he took up from Bony's hands two thin cylinders covered with a material like wax, and the covering of one had been slit with a knife and now was bound with a piece of twine. Without speaking, he took the cylinders to a desk and turned on a desk light. With a knife he cut the twine, and out burst the roll of what looked like film. He held it before the light. He looked at portions of it through a glass. He was there a full minute, watched by the smiling Bony. For the third time he went back to stand over the detective.

"You blooming swab, you!" he chortled. "You—you—you not-a-policeman's-bootlace-you, according to old Pop. You tantalising, obstinate, undisciplined shadow of a policeman—again according to Pop Spendor. Oh, joy! Oh, heaven!"

"Better go quiet, or you'll wake the wife," urged Bony, smiling delightedly at the effect of his surprise. "Please remember that I seldom take unnecessary risks. I transferred the contents to another pocket immediately after I left Bisker to go to my room for blankets. I wasn't sure of Bisker, for a start, but I believed him when he said he didn't bury the pens. But—I could not take the risk of staying at the Chalet for the night in case that gunman found that the contents had been taken from the pens he had, and came back with reinforcements. I could not take the chance of ringing for a hire car, or even engaging the local hire-car man to bring me to the station. So I left as soon as I could, and I walked to the station, where I had to stay for five hours to catch a city-bound train. And then, having reached the city, I couldn't take the chance of coming here direct— in case I had been picked up and was being followed."

Colonel Blythe appeared as though he wanted to shake hands.

"Well, you've done a good job, my dear fellow," he said. "Pop Spendor ought to be pleased at having you back with him so soon. All the better! He'll not moan and wince so much the next time I ask him for you!"

"I shall, I think, not be returning immediately," Bony countered.

"Oh! But you've done the job."

"Your job, yes, but I haven't finished my holiday," objected Bony. "When I saw the Chalet on Mount Chalmers, I decided I'd stay for two weeks. When I had lived there twenty-four hours I made it a month. Why the food is super-excellent. The service is good. And I must get those pens."

"But your work is accomplished," persisted Blythe. "You can take a year's holiday at Wideview Chalet as far as I'm concerned. I'm willing to bet that by the post this morning I'll have an air-mailed letter from Pop demanding to know how long I intend keeping you."

Bony rose from his chair.

"You have probably found Colonel Spendor little more difficult as a father-in-law than I have found him as a Chief Commissioner," he said. "He can damn and blast as much as he feels like it. I am going back to

Wideview Chalet to get those pens I have promised to my wife and my son Charles. The Victorian Police can go-get Marcus. The killer of Grumman is my meat. So, too, is the gunman who took those pens from me. Why, if I went back to Brisbane without nailing that gunman, I'd hear his laughter all the rest of my life. So you just tell Colonel Spendor that Bony's still on the job for you. Or else ..."

Colonel Blythe clenched his fists and grinned like a school-boy.

"I'd like to have a bit of you," he threatened. "I would, too, if I didn't admire your guts. Now for a shower and a couple of hours' sleep, eh? Then a late breakfast and a confab with Kirby about friend Marcus. You'd like to get ahead of the Melbourne lads, wouldn't you?"

"Yes, it would be a little comforting," agreed Bony.

Chapter Nine

Calm at Wideview Chalet

As usual, Bisker's alarm clock rang at half-past five on the morning of September O, and, as usual, a callused fist crashed down upon its "stop" button. It was absolutely dark inside the hut. Bisker groaned and got through the first sentence of his morning hate before he remembered the excitement of the previous day.

He lit the lamp, and drew to his mouth the early-morning pipe so carefully loaded with "dottles" and now drawing at this trebly poisonous concoction, he surveyed past events and recalled those last orders given him by Napoleon Bonaparte.

Like all bushmen, he had a profound contempt for the city gunman and thug who made himself temporarily superior to ordinary folk through the possession of firearms, and who exercised his trade by armed force instead of the brain that is necessary in the robbing of a bank. Therefore, it was natural for Bisker, at this early-morning hour, to muse on the indignation he had taken to bed with him following his own ill-usage at the hands of such a man.

Dressing with his customary carelessness, and with his customary care filling his pockets with tobacco and spare pipe, clasp-knife and match tin and corkscrew, Bisker took up the lamp and stepped out into the cold, dank and uninviting morning.

On closing the door, he did not follow the path to the open space fronting the garages. Obeying instructions, he sidled along the wall of the hut to its corner and then proceeded direct to the top fence. This he followed past the rear of the garages to reach the scullery door of the Chalet, and so did not obliterate possible tracks made by the gunman, tracks which would be of undoubted interest to Bony when he returned from the city. He had made the morning tea for himself and the cook when Mrs. Parkes arrived in the kitchen.

"Mornin'!" he snarled.

"Morning!" she snapped back at him. "Tea ready?"

"Too right! Make yerself at 'ome by the fire. I'll do the serving act."

Mrs. Parkes dragged a chair along and sat before one of the fires in the central range, and when she sat there was nothing to spare of the chair seat. Her brown hair was not yet "done," and the absence of her teeth appeared to create an emphatic cleavage between the button of her nose and the line of her wide chin. Brown eyes gazed into the fire, eyes small and now unblinking. Without a word, she took the cup of tea brought to her by Bisker, and not until she had drunk it and handed the cup back to him to be refilled and had taken a cigarette from her apron pocket and lit it, did she begin to articulate.

"Any more murders this morning, I wonder?"

"Dunno. It ain't light enough yet to discover any corpses," Bisker said, faint hope in his voice. "The papers oughter be intrestin' today."

"Yes, they ought," agreed Mrs. Parkes. "You get me all the morning papers when you go down to the store. Thank goodness, I won't be in 'em."

Bisker ambled across to the wall bench and filled his cup. He returned to sit on a part of the stove not yet heated by the fires, and cut chips from his plug for another pipe.

"You never know," he said. "One of them reporters asked me all about the staff 'ere, and I told 'im about George, and you bein' the cook."

"You would. And a mighty lot more about yourself. Any'ow, I'm glad I'm not mixed up in it, for my old man to sling off at me when he comes 'ome. I ain't sure this is a respectable place any longer. One thing about it, there's only six guests to cook for this morning, and the name of the place ought to keep more from coming."

"There'll be only five guests this morning," Bisker said. "Mr. Bonaparte went to town late last-night and won't be back till sometime today."

"Oh! How d'you know?"

"'Cos he told me. Nice bloke that. Talks civilised, sort of. None of the 'Haw! Haw! Bisker! Get me a paper!' about 'im. As for that Grumman bloke, well, I ain't partic'ly sorry he's turned in 'is cheques. 'E wouldn't even say good day to a man."

"I wonder who done him in," Mrs. Parkes said slowly, getting the last "draw" out of her cigarette. "You know, I wouldn't be surprised if it wasn't that Bagshott man. From them books of his he knows all about poisons and how to give them. I did hear that he practises on rabbits and things."

"You don't say!" Bisker exclaimed. "No, I wouldn't put it past 'im neither. I never thought of 'im."

"And you'd better not think of him now," Mrs. Parkes said. "Look at the time. What about the boots?"

Bisker collected the boots—four pairs of men's shoes and the pair he picked up outside Miss Jade's room. During this work he took from a coat pocket a note addressed to Miss Jade by Bony and this he left on the small table set to one side of the office door. Whilst cleaning the shoes he whistled so loudly that Mrs. Parkes came to the scullery door to tell him to "shut up."

He had more time this morning, because of the smaller number of shoes to clean, and he wandered round to the main entrance, the door of which was not yet opened. There he visited the shrub tub to smooth the earth he had so rudely disturbed the previous evening. It was as well, for Miss Jade would certainly have noted the disturbance and asked questions. In the light of day, it appeared as though a rabbit had been burrowing. There was the hole from which he had taken the whisky bottle, much larger than when he had made it, and there beside the hole were the impressions of four fingers and a thumb of a man's outspread hand.

Whilst filling in the bottle hole, Bisker's mind worked with, what was for it, abnormal speed. He went over his own actions during the time he had sat on the edge of the tub, and during the last time when he had dragged from the soil the two fountain pens and the bottle and he could not recall that he had pressed either of his hands flat out like that on the soft earth.

Had the impression been made by the hand of the gunman? Bisker worried at this question. There were, of course, no fingerprints, but the shape of the hand was clear, a left hand, and the impression had certainly not been there when he had sat on the edge of the tub the previous evening as dusk was falling. The man whose left hand had made the impression had stood at the tub and used his right to delve into the earth, and the only man beside himself who had had an interest in the tub was the gunman.

"Whay!" murmured Bisker. There was yet another man—the bloke who had buried the pens. The impression might have been made by his left hand.

Now what to do? If he left the impression, the gunman, or the man who had buried the pens might come along and see it, and then press it out. And Mr. Bonaparte might like to see it. He might want to measure it, measure the span and so get to the size of the hand. Yes, what to do?

It was almost full daylight. The sun was due to rise. All was still quiet inside the house, and it was yet ten or fifteen minutes before one of the maids would open the front door and sweep the porch. The idea of placing a strip of tin over the impression occurred to Bisker, and then he saw that this would attract attention to it. So better leave it alone.

He crossed back to the wood-stack and from there passed along the rear of the garages. In this way he came to his hut at its rear, sidled along the wall to reach the door, and at the same time regarded with interest the narrow cinder path he had avoided on going to the house.

Bisker was thoroughly enjoying himself this morning. He shaved with cold water, taking unusual care. He washed in cold water, and instead of leaving his hair to dry in conformity with the cast made by his hat, he combed it, and then, on impulse, hunted for and found among his effects a pair of scissors, with which he trimmed his unruly moustache, taking years off his age and eighty per cent off his appearance of dissipation.

Now ready for breakfast, he buttoned up his old coat, stooped and laced his heavy boots, stood up and regarded his bed upon which the blankets lay in disarray. He lifted the top end of the mattress and took therefrom the bottle which had brought him such adventure. It was still a quarter full, and for several seconds he regarded it with desire writ plainly on his weather-beaten face. Then he put the bottle back beneath the mattress, and left the hut to go to the house the same way he had previously gone to it. In the kitchen he sat down to breakfast with George.

"Goin' to be a nice day," began the drinks steward.

"Yes," Bisker agreed. "Won't last, though. 'Ow's the old bitch this mornin'?"

"Haven't seen her yet." George poised bacon on his fork and stared at Bisker. He had heard a new Bisker the previous morning when summoned by Miss Jade's bell, and now he was seeing a new Bisker. He added: "What have you been doing to yourself?"

"Doin' to meself?" Bisker echoed. "Wot d'you mean?"

George regarded Bisker with his dark eyes narrowed.

"You've been combing your hair and training your mo'," he said, accusingly, to which Bisker belligerently demanded:

"Wot the 'ell's wrong with that? I don't comb me 'air into a quiff like you."

"All right, don't get shirty. Get me a paper when you go down to the store, will you?"

"I might! If you pass me a snifter about ten o'clock."

"That reminds me," said George, and Bisker cursed himself for reminding George. "That reminds me. You said that Miss Jade ordered a full bottle of whisky yesterday morning, and I haven't checked up on what became of the bottle."

Bisker snorted and regarded George with open contempt.

"Now what would any ordinary bloke think would become of a bottle of whisky left in an office full of detectives? I asks you, George, to tell me that one."

George offered no further comment, which pleased Bisker, who said, presently:

"You kept up late last night?"

"Fairish. They was all talking about the murders and it kind of made 'em thirsty. They were arguing about who was likely to have killed Grumman, and when."

"You reckon the 'tecs will be out again today?"

"Almost sure," replied George. "When that feller shot Rice, did you think he was going to plug you, too?"

"No not whiles I stayed still, George, and you can bet I stayed as still as a statue. So did the old cat. He 'ad a nasty, mean, pasty-looking dial, George, and I didn't like the look in 'is eye. I knows when a bloke means business."

"How tall was he—how big?" pressed George, who looked up over Bisker's shoulder. Bisker was about to reply when a maid spoke:

"Bisker! Miss Jade wants you in the office directly after you've had breakfast."

"Righto, Alice." Then to George, Bisker said: "'Ow tall was that murdering bloke, did you ask? Lemme see. About like you. Might be an inch higher. Say five feet eleven, and weighin' around nine stone six. He 'ad wavy black 'air, and a dark smudge on his top lip like as 'ow he 'ad only just shaved orf a moustache."

"Hum! That's interesting. You tell the police that?"

"Expect so. Can't remember all I told 'em."

"Did you notice anything else about him—about his hands, his shoes? What kind of a suit was he wearing?"

"He was wearing a grey suit, a double-breaster, with a bluish sort of tie. His shoes I didn't take stock of, but I did notice the 'ands. They was narrer with long fingers—like yours. A foreigner of some kind—a cold snake of a man I'd like to jump on with me boots. Well, here's me for the old dragon. See you later, George."

On entering the office, Bisker found Miss Jade at the telephone, and while standing waiting for her, he was able to hear that she was answering an enquiry for accommodation. She spoke quietly but well, and this morning she looked to Bisker as she always had done, a woman who knew how to dress, a being who lived in a different world. The black skirt revealed admirable lines, and the dark brown cardigan moulded her bust to suggest that she might be a woman of about twenty-five. Her hair might have been done by a maid born for just that artistic work, whilst her make-up was perfectly suited to her colouring and the morning.

"Ah! There you are, Bisker!" she exclaimed on putting down the telephone. "On the table outside I found a note from Mr. Bonaparte. Do you know anything about it?"

"Yes, marm." Bisker could see that Miss Jade noticed his clipped moustache. "I met Mr. Bonaparte when I was going for a walk last night down at the store. He was talkin' with some people in a car, and he asked me to deliver a note he wrote on a mudguard."

"What time was that?"

"About half-past nine, marm."

"Then why didn't you deliver it last night?"

"I forgot it, marm."

"Forgot it!" echoed Miss Jade, her brows carefully raised.

"Yes, marm," Bisker confessed. "I'm sorry if it's important."

"Not precisely important, Bisker. But don't dare to forget the next time. Er—there are some people coming by the midday bus. A gentleman and his wife, and two single gentlemen. Don't forget to be down at the road when the bus arrives."

"All right, marm." Bisker looked doubtful, adding, dubiously: "But what 'appens if I'm being baled up by the detectives when the bus is due?"

"Detectives, Bisker? What do you mean?"

"Well, marm, it's likely that there'll be more detectives out today. They'll want to ask all the same questions they asked yestiddy. It's a nice day, and it'll be a nice motor drive for 'em. Then there'll be more reporters and more photographers. Still I'll do me best, marm."

Miss Jade regarded Bisker as though she were seeing visions. Her brows were no longer raised. They were depressed and the two dreadful vertical lines showed plainly between them. Then she said:

"Yes, I suppose they will, Bisker. It is all going to be a great nuisance. Well, do your best to meet the bus. That'll be all. But wait! Don't dawdle coming back with the papers."

"Very well, marm."

It is possible that had Bisker not been rotund he might have bowed to Miss Jade. He withdrew as he invariably withdrew from the presence of Mrs. Parkes, back first to the door and beyond, due to habit, for Mrs. Parkes had been known to throw things.

The first bus from the railway town of Manton arrived at the Mount Chalmers store at ten o'clock, and Bisker was there to receive the Chalet papers, with the extras ordered by George and Mrs. Parkes. The place was crowded with residents and visitors, all as anxious as Bisker. His next call was at the Post Office, and when it came his turn to collect the letters he saw the back of a stranger seated at the telephone switchboard, and without smiling, he slowly closed one eye at the postmaster.

Bisker did not "dawdle" on the walk back, uphill and about half a mile, but when he reached the Chalet driveway, he had read most of the front-page reports on the double murders at Mount Chalmers.

As Fred, the casual man, had predicted, Bisker was famous.

Several cars had passed him, and three were parked outside the main entrance. A group of men were standing in the porch. Two others were taking photographs from positions on the lawn. A little self-conscious, Bisker walked through the group on the porch and so entered the office with the mail and newspapers. There he found Miss Jade talking to Inspector Snook.

Silently, he placed letters and all but two of the papers on the secretary's desk, and withdrew as he had previously done and this time regarded suspiciously by the detective, who was not to know of Mrs. Parkes's addiction to throwing things.

When the midday bus arrived, Bisker was down to meet it. A large modern vehicle, it disgorged half a dozen people and the driver, who removed several suitcases and a hat box from the luggage grid at the rear.

"Mr. and Mrs. Watkins!" called Bisker. "Mr. Downes and Mr. Lee. Make sure, please that all your luggage is put down."

The people named sorted themselves from the rest, and Bisker noted them for their tipping value, he having already become adept in this summing-up. Watkins was heavy and well dressed in sports clothes. His wife was overloaded with furs and jewellery. Mr. Downes was a man about forty, grizzled and short-moustached, and Mr. Lee wore clothes in the manner of a countryman on holiday. The party followed the loaded Bisker, who staggered up the driveway, chatting about the scenery. Bisker decided that Mr. Lee was the best tipping prospect.

Chapter Ten

Bony Resumes His Holiday

Towards three o'clock, a car deposited Bony at the driveway to the Chalet, and then proceeded on up the mountain road. The sun was no longer shining, for the sky was almost filled with cloud moving slowly from the west. The continued clarity of the atmosphere, together with the wind-direction, indicated rain before the following morning.

As he had left the Chalet, so he returned. He wore no hat, and the wind ruffled his fine black hair. His clothes had been brushed and pressed by Colonel Blythe's valet, so that he might have been returning from a stroll, after lunch in Miss Jade's beautiful dining room. The cut on his cheek-bone although noticeable, was no longer angry in appearance.

Instead of passing up the driveway, Bony followed the road to the ramp leading to the wicket gate. On the bank above the place where the body of Grumman had been found were standing four men, and these Bony assessed as pressmen. At the wicket gate he met Inspector Snook.

"Ah—good afternoon, Inspector!" he said in greeting. "Beautiful scenery—wonderful view."

"Damn the view!" remarked Inspector Snook. "You just arrived?"

"Only just," admitted Bony, smiling provocatively. "Know anything?"

"Only what I learned during a visit to your palatial Headquarters. The Super wasn't in a healthful frame of mind."

Snooks regarded Bony with a stony stare.

"Healthful!" he repeated.

"Yes, that is what I said, my dear fellow. Temper is dangerous to one of Bolt's physique. Upsets the stomach and brings about ulcers, and ulcers bring about——Well, you know what ulcers bring about. The cause of his annoyance was the clear getaway of friend Marcus. He appears to have the idea that Marcus got away to Melbourne, or Timbuctoo, or some such place, and when I suggested that Marcus might have retired to a house somewhere on this mountain, his annoyance increased."

"Did you read up Marcus's history?" enquired Snook.

"Yes. Quite a broth of a boy. Four known murders and about a dozen suspected killings between here and New York and London. Goes in for disguises and what not, and is by no means a poor linguist."

"And you think he might be still hanging around here?" Snook said, a hint of contempt in his voice. "What makes you think that?"

"Intuition," Bony blandly replied. "Ah! I observe George serving tea to guests on the veranda. You will have to excuse me."

Inspector Snook scowled at Bony's back. Intuition! Well, what could you expect from a half-caste promoted to the rank of Detective-Inspector? Must have influential friends to get him up to that rank and send him on such joy-rides for the blinking Army. As for Marcus's getaway, well, that wasn't his fault. With five minutes to spare in a mile-a-minute car on ninety-miles-an-hour roads, there were five gateways to freedom for Marcus, and Marcus had got those five minutes.

Having reached the veranda, Bony caught the eye of George and drifted to a quiet corner where he sat in a wickedly sensuous lounge chair and was waited on by the smiling steward.

"Looks like rain, George," Bony remarked. "Do I observe some new guests?"

"Yes, sir. Several new guests arrived today. Just back from the city?"

"Just back, George. My friends brought me as far as the drive. Plenty of policemen still meandering about."

"They are apt to do that, sir, after the crime."

"Naturally," Bony agreed.

"Another cup of tea, sir?"

"Thank you."

"I see that you've cut your cheek, sir. Rather badly, too," George said solicitously. "Miss Jade keeps a surgical box, and she could dress the wound, if you wish."

Bony smiled. He regarded the dark eyes gazing down upon him.

"I might accept your suggestion after dinner," he said. "I bashed my cheek against a projection in the friend's car as I was getting out. They put some plaster and stuff on it, but I washed it all off before I left to return home. It looked worse than the cut. I see a guest waiting to catch your attention."

"Thank you, sir," George murmured, and wheeled away his serving trolley.

The wind contained a cold finger, so Bony did not long remain on the veranda. He had seen Inspector Snook walk up from the wicket gate, and he had observed the roof of the bus which had stopped below the gates to pick up the pressmen who had gone down to meet it. And now, slowly and pensively, he left the veranda and strolled along the path which would take him to the driveway and the end of the house where the main entrance and garages were situated. He was in time to see Snook and three other plain-clothes men get into a car and leave.

He began to admire Miss Jade's shrubs, many of which were

flowering. Her selection of rhododendrons was excellent. Having crossed the drive to admire these, he came presently to the path leading to Bisker's hut.

The path was composed of cinders. It was hard and level, but not sufficiently hard to prevent boot tracks being registered on its surface for such as he to see. There were many marks made by Bisker's hob-nailed boots number eight. There were the tracks made by another eight boot, worn by a man who had gone towards the hut and then had returned. And there were the impressions of a twelve-sized shoe or boot made previously to the visit of the man wearing the eight size, for his boot-mark frequently overlaid the impressions of the twelve size.

On either side of the path there was a border of painted-wooden boards, and upon the outside of these boards the ground was cultivated and grew varieties of early-spring flowers planted somewhat widely apart. One of these, a heath, was a miniature hillock of heliotrope.

It grew within a few yards of Bisker's hut, and near to it the ground bore evidence of recent disturbance.

On either side of the path the ground had been roughly dug, and since the operation had been completed it had rained much and this had tended to level the soil, a dark loam of fine texture. Where Bony had struggled with the gunman, there were patches of ground pressed into a greater degree of levelness and he saw the impressions of toe and heel marks, and several impressions of the abnormal shoe or boot size twelve. They had been made by the same man on the path and down on the ramp leading to the highway.

Here, a little off the path, the impressions made by the large boot or shoe could not be considered as an impression which the wearer would normally make when walking, but the impressions on the path were normally made.

Bony proceeded towards Bisker's hut, slowly and with the interest of the guest captivated by the sylvan scene of garden and trees and the smoke-blue view beyond. He came to the hut, and, with his hands clasped behind him, often stopped to admire this and that. He circled the building to see his own tracks and those made by the large-size boot or shoe of the gunman, who had pretended to be drunk and who had also pretended that the hut was an abnormal tree trunk.

Having made a complete circle of the hut, Bony wandered towards the back fence of the property, then came back, passing along the front of the trees growing at the rear of the hut near the window. He observed that anyone standing under the trees could easily see into the hut when the blind was up and a lamp was lit inside, and there he found again the tracks of the man who wore twelves in footwear.

A man of the height and weight of that gunman must be deformed in both feet to have to wear so large a boot, and his feet were the only extremities Bony had not noted during the encounter the previous evening.

Had there been two men acting in alliance—the man wearing the large boots and the gunman? There were the impressions on the path made by boots or shoes size eight, and those might have been on the feet of the gunman. It might not have been the gunman with whom Bony had grappled on one side of the path.

This matter was occupying him when Bisker approached direct from the rear of the garages.

"Well, Bisker! How's the head?" Bony asked the fat little man with the bushy eyebrows and the now-clipped grey moustache. Bisker smiled with his mouth only.

"I'd forgotten all about it, sir," he replied, and stared at Bony's cheek wound. "Looks like you copped it worse than I did. I'm glad to see you back. I've found a clue."

"Ah!" murmured Bony, theatrically. Bisker glanced furtively all about them as though he had swiftly caught the melodrama in Bony's voice.

"Yes, a clue. That gunman, when he was looking for 'is pens in the shrub tub, leaned with his left 'and pressing on the earth, and 'e left the marks of every finger and his thumb and the curve of 'is palm, so's we can estimate the size and shape of 'is 'and. It's still there, or was when I took me last bird's-eye view of it."

"And that was—at what time?"

"'Bout two hours back."

"Might be useful, Bisker, but we cannot very well examine the impression now. Too many people wandering about. Do you know where we could obtain some plaster of paris?"

"Too right, I do. There's some in the tool shed."

"Excellent. Later on, after dinner, I'll make a cast, although it will be difficult in the dark. You might do it with greater success because you know the exact position of the impression. When you've finished for the day, bring the plaster to your hut in readiness. How's your day gone?"

"Not so bad," Bisker said, adding after a distinct pause: "One of the detectives grabbed me and made me bring 'im 'ere to the hut. He made me show him all I possessed and then he went through the place looking for something. I asked 'im what he was 'oping to find and he said he just wanted to look around, sorta."

"You don't really know what he was after?"

Bisker shook his head.

"Did you bring him along the path?"

Bisker grinned.

"I did not," he replied, now smiling with both his face and his eyes. "Him and me first went to the tool shed, where he done a lot of fossicking about, and when we left there, remembering what you 'ad tole me about that path, I sort of edged 'im away from it so that we came down along the back fence. After 'e had done 'ere, we sorta made a round trip of the garden, going down as far as the front fence and slewing right to the drive and so back."

"To your knowledge, no one has walked on that path since last night?"

"No one, s'far as I know."

"Good!"

Bony gazed about him like a countryman in a city. Then he pointed at a shrub a little way back along the path and told Bisker to follow him and to pretend to be talking about it, in case someone was observing them. When they were standing before the shrub he asked:

"Did you by any chance observe the gunman's feet?"

"Not partic'ly," answered Bisker. "After I come to and before I got up I did see that 'e was wearing shoes."

"What kind of shoes?"

"Kind!" Bisker echoed. "Why, just ordinary shoes, I suppose. Lemme think. Yes, they were ordinary shoes—looked a bit big for a bloke of 'is size—that's all."

"Looked big, eh?" persisted Bony. "Try to think back. I estimated that he weighed about ten stone and that he was about five feet ten or eleven in height. Something like my own weight. I wear a size seven in shoes."

Bisker stared hard at the ground and frowned, but he found himself unable to state definitely that the gunman's shoes were abnormally large, just a "bit big for a bloke of 'is size."

"You have no idea what the detective was after?" Bony continued.

"Not a glimmer."

"At any time yesterday or today, were you asked where you came from before you obtained employment here?"

"Yes, I was. I told 'em the truth, that I was down from the bush on a bender when I went broke and 'ad to take the job 'ere. Why?"

Smiling, Bony explained what he thought was the reason for the search. He asked when Bisker's history was gone into, and Bisker said it had been the day before. That morning he had been interrogated about the stations on which he had worked. Grumman had been poisoned with cyanide, and bushmen may with ease purchase both cyanide and strychnine with their groceries, and use it for poisoning foxes and rabbits for the pelts.

Bisker began to chuckle and to say repeatedly, "Wot d'you know about that?"

"Why the happiness?" mildly asked Bony.

"Well, that's funny, that is," chortled Bisker. "If that d. was lookin' for poison, all 'e 'ad to do was to ask me if I 'ad any and if I'd bin in a good mood, which I wasn't, I could 'ave produced nearly a full bottle of strych wot I 'ad in me swag when I come to Melbun, and wot's now in a tin stowed on a roof beam of the 'ut. I put it up there with me reserve of tobacco and a drop of warmin' fluid for use when things were very, very dry, sort of. That d. never looked up at the roof."

"How much is there?"

"Pretty near a full ounce bottle I put into the tin."

Bony sighed, knowing the extraordinary carelessness of bushmen with poisons. He said:

"Just as well, Bisker, for you that your hoard does not contain a quantity of cyanide and that cyanide wasn't found in your possession."

Bisker wanted to know why, and when Bony told him that Grumman had died from cyanide poisoning, he whistled softly, looked grim for a moment, and then regained his present good humour.

A raindrop fell upon Bony's bare head. Already the afternoon was waning into early dusk.

"I took your blankets back to your room," Bisker said. "And I laid 'em out under the quilt like you told me. Nearly got nabbed, too, after I got outer the winder. It was that dark that I nearly collisioned with Miss Jade, who was making for the scullery door from the top-road gate. And that was after midnight, too."

Chapter Eleven

Meditation

Bony decided to be particularly charming to Miss Jade. That would not make demands on any reserve of courage or natural shyness, for Miss Jade was far from being repellent and Bony had more to him than a mere brain.

This decision Bony made immediately on leaving Bisker, when he sauntered through the gentle rain, down along the narrow cinder path to the open space in front of the Chalet; for there was a little more behind the word "intuition" he had uttered to cold Inspector Snook when intimating that he thought the killer of Grumman and the man Marcus were still in the vicinity.

Standing with the closed door at his back, Bony studied his room. It was fairly large for a bedroom in such an establishment, measuring about twelve by fourteen feet and lighted by double windows in the one frame. The failing daylight increased the shadow by the three-quarter bed and at the foot of the wardrobe, but the plated-backed hairbrush, the buckle of the leather box containing his shaving kit, the pot of hair grease and an ivory stud box all on the dressing table gleamed like old silver.

A maid had been at work in this room since he left it the previous night. There was nothing out of place. There was not a speck of dust to be seen even if the sunlight had streamed through the windows, now open as they had been all day. On the little bedside table a vase held pink amarias, and on the walls hung framed photographic enlargements of local views of mountain and valley. A sleeping place far removed from the interior of a stockman's hut, a tent beneath a mulga tree, and that cabin on the lugger in which he had been imprisoned for three weeks by gentlemen in the pay of Japan. It was a bedroom even superior to that occupied by his wife and himself—sometimes—in their own home at Banyo. But who cared about the cost when the money came from somewhere through Colonel Blythe?

Bisker had explained that a Mr. and Mrs. Watkins now occupied the room on one side of him and that Mr. Sleeman occupied that on the other. He had met Mr. Sleeman, who had been staying at the Chalet for some time. The Watkins couple had arrived only that day.

Coming back to this room Bony found very pleasant. To one who had spent by far the greater proportion of his professional life in the interior of

Australia, such a luxury as this room presented, with its thick floor carpets and electric radiator, was not quickly to be abandoned. Neither was to be abandoned this case of two murders, although Bony's actual work for Colonel Blythe was completed.

The electric clock set into the wall, where the visitor could see the time when lying in bed, indicated that it was eighteen minutes to five. The call to dinner would be made at half-past six. The rain was falling ever a little heavier faintly thrumming on the roof. Bony switched on the radiator, drew a lounge chair to sit before it, with the essentials of cigarette manufacture on the wide arms of the chair, he settled down to review the events of the past two days.

Considering that frankness was the best policy, Bony had confided in Superintendent Bolt by explaining where each of them stood, and in return Bolt made available to the Queenslander copies of statements so far obtained, copies of reports made by the fingerprint-section and also he opened the door to complete co-operation.

That the murder of Grumman had been "an inside job" Bony's intuition made him sure, and Bolt was inclined to agree. The poison had been put into his bedroom water carafe, and the one careless omission made by the murderer was to leave the remainder of the poisoned water in the carafe instead of emptying it out, cleaning the vessel and re-filling it. To strengthen Bony's "intuition" was the fact that the gunman's clothes had recently been taken from a box or case and worn for the especial occasion of holding up Bisker and himself. This indicated that he had not come an appreciable distance, but rather was living close to Wideview Chalet, if not in the hostel itself.

From the staff at the Chalet it was known that Grumman's effects comprised two heavy steamer trunks, three large suit-cases, a set of golf clubs in their leather bag, and a smaller leather grip.

Bony was inclined to accept one of two suppositions. The first was that the murderer had found what he wanted in the two fountain pens, and then decided to remove the body and the baggage to create the thought that Grumman had "skipped it" to avoid paying his dues. He had, however, failed somewhere in his planning, and after Rice was shot, believing he would come under suspicion, had hidden the pens in the shrub tub. The second was that, for a reason unknown, Grumman himself had pushed the pens into the earth of the shrub tub. In doing this he had been observed by the man who later held up both Bony and Bisker, a man who knew what the pens contained, and who, therefore, could be absolved from the murder of Grumman. It would seem that on that night there were two men after Grumman's secrets brought out from Germany.

That the man Marcus was associated with Grumman's murder, or with the man who had held up Bony and Bisker, appeared unlikely. Knowing Grumman to be dead, Marcus would hardly arrive at the Chalet the next morning asking for him, and come openly without disguising himself other than by removing his moustache. He had not even taken into his reckoning the long chance of meeting a policeman, and that he was confronted by one who had recognised him was as unfortunate for him as it had been for Constable Rice.

Marcus was no fool. He had been an actor. He had earned big money as a mimic. For every occasion he had been obliged to shoot his way out of a corner, there had been a dozen occasions when he had slipped through the fingers of the cleverest officers by his gifts of mimicry and disguise.

Bony argued that if Marcus had come to see Grumman from Melbourne, he would have adopted a better disguise than merely shaving off his moustache, otherwise he would have run grave danger of recognition by a smart policeman on beat duty or by a smart traffic patrolman, for Melbourne is fifteen to twenty miles across in any direction. It appeared more than likely that Marcus had spent the night Grumman was murdered in a house not so far from Mount Chalmers, and that he foresaw no danger of recognition by any chance-met policeman after leaving his lodging to visit Grumman.

With all this, Superintendent Bolt agreed, and until all likely areas where Marcus could lie up had been combed, the road patrols out of the wider Mount Chalmers district were to be maintained.

Bony smiled and felt exhilarated. It was just a lovely case for him. A glorious mix-up of a case, and in sweet addition, he was to have competition from the Victorian C.I.B. team under the renowned Superintendent Bolt. He would be given all assistance—up to a point. He, Bony, would collaborate—up to a point. To add zest, there was a distinct spice of danger, a taste of which he had already experienced. What had astonished Bolt and Snook was that Marcus, on being named by Rice before Miss Jade and Bisker, had not shot them both dead. Had he done so it would not have been known that he was in Victoria.

It was almost dark when he rose and drew down the window blinds before snapping on the light. It was half-past five. He would set out his evening clothes, obtain a clean shirt and collar and under-clothes from his case, and then after he had dressed he would seek Miss Jade's assistance in attending to his cheek wound.

The dinner clothes were in the wardrobe. The coat hung from a wooden hanger, as did the trousers. He took the garments one at a time to examine them directly beneath the light, a slight frown puckering his eyes. Within the coat was a silver cigarette case containing cigarettes of good quality which were kept to smoke when "in polite company." Within the case were ten cigarettes. The coat was not on the hanger as he had placed it the night Grumman was killed. The cigarettes within the case had been moved and not put back exactly as he had left them.

Bony unstrapped his suitcase, and raised the lid. Every article he removed after having noted its position, and as he took the shirt, collar and under-wear to lay on the bed, he was convinced that all his effects had been moved, examined, and then carefully replaced—but not exactly as they had been found.

He was quite sure of it, because he had himself taken care to memorise the position of every article he possessed during those twenty minutes he had been away from Bisker's hut. Nothing had been taken, not even one of the thirty-eight pound notes stuffed into a pocket of the suitcase.

There were no documents of any kind for the scrutineer to examine. Bony had deposited all his papers with Colonel Blythe before first coming to Wideview Chalet.

Chapter Twelve

Interest in Grumman's Luggage

"Oh, good afternoon, Mr. Bonaparte!"

Miss Jade was wearing a dinner frock of black chiffon trimmed with white satin. Her black hair gleamed beneath the electric light of the reception hall, and her make-up was perfection itself.

"Good afternoon, Miss Jade," he murmured, bowing in his inimitable manner. In a dinner suit, he appeared more like the conventional Indian Rajah than the bushman he more generally appeared. His hair, as black as Miss Jade's, also gleamed in the light. His dark face emphasised the whiteness of his collar, but there was nothing sinister in the face lightened and animated by the smiling blue eyes. The white teeth almost matched the collar.

"What have you been doing to your cheek?"

Bony made the explanation he had offered to George, and then quoted the steward as an authority for believing that Miss Jade possessed a surgical box.

"Why, of course, Mr. Bonaparte," Miss Jade said warmly. "You go along to the office, and I'll bring the outfit. It is a nasty gash! Have you done anything for it at all?"

"Well, yes, my friend provided me with a salve," replied Bony. "He said shove it on. It cleanses as well as heals. The word 'shove' is his, by the way."

Miss Jade stepped close and with the tips of her fingers gently examined the cut. Watching, he noted her eyes narrow just a fraction, and he appreciated that, for it indicated that Miss Jade was not as cold as her demeanour might suggest.

"It's quite clean that's certain. I won't be a minute," she told him, before flowing out of the reception hall on her errand of mercy.

Within the office he encountered the secretary, a fair-haired girl about twenty-two, not too good-looking, an excellent foil for Miss Jade's personality—an item, no doubt, which Miss Jade had had in mind when she engaged Miss Philps. She looked up from her work when Bony entered, in her eyes the shadow of recent events.

"I have been instructed by Miss Jade to wait here for her," Bony announced, smiling in his friendly manner. "You won't mind?"

Miss Philps was about to say that it was not her office, but the smiling eyes brushed that assertion from her mind. It had been a difficult afternoon for her, an aftermath of murder crowded with grim-faced, tight-lipped policemen, and hence her nerves were not restful and her mind was unsettled. She said:

"Won't you sit down? Miss Jade will not be long, I'm sure."

"Thank you. I hope I am not disturbing you."

"No of course not." Miss Philps smiled for the first time. "You see, I am used to being interrupted in my work. How do you like Mount Chalmers?"

"Very much. It's the most beautiful place in Australia, and I have yet to walk down into the fern gullies which, I am told, have a beauty all of their own. So different, you know, from my own part of the country. There, it is all open and flat and sun-glary and hot."

Bony was beginning to describe Western Queensland when Miss Jade came in with a bowl of warm water and a large cardboard box bearing a red cross on the cover.

"I'd just love to go out into the real outback," she said, brightly. "I've never been farther out than Mildura. You must love it, Mr. Bonaparte."

"Yes, I suppose I do," admitted Bony. "There's plenty of space to move about in, and one hasn't to wear dinner clothes and a starched collar and be extra polite, and all that kind of thing."

"Don't you like being polite?" asked Miss Jade, pouring a few drops of antiseptic into the bowl.

"Perhaps the word was not quite the one for me to use," he countered. "Formal would have been better. You see, Miss Jade, were we outback—er—after an acquaintance of four days you would be calling me Bony and I would be addressing you by your Christian name."

Miss Jade advanced to him with cotton wool saturated with the antiseptic. She laughed softly:

"If anyone on Mount Chalmers were to hear me calling you Bony, and you calling me Eleanor, it would immediately go around that we were lovers," she said, half seriously. "One has to be so careful, you know, in a place like this. Now, this might sting just a tiny bit."

"Pleasure is often born of pain," murmured Bony. "No pain, no expert administration by you, Miss Jade. When my man friend gave me the box of salve, he said, 'Here, shove it on.'"

"It's what a man would say." The antiseptic did not sting, neither did the ointment which Miss Jade applied with the tip of a little finger. The ointment at once soothed a wound which was beginning to ache, and then with gauze and a narrow strip of plaster Miss Jade completed the operation and requested Bony to look at it in a wall mirror, saying:

84

"It won't make you unsightly at dinner, Mr. Bonaparte, and it will keep the air from the cut and heal it more quickly."

He turned to see her withdraw her fingertips from the bowl of antiseptic, and begin to dry them on a towel.

"I thank you," he said gravely. "I look, and feel, quite presentable. Next week, should I go off in a friend's car, I'll arrange to gash the opposite cheek. A cigarette?"

Miss Jade glanced at the office clock, and then accepted. It barely reached her lips before the lighter was held by a brown hand in service, and above the tiny flame she gazed into the blue eyes whimsically regarding her. During that flash of time she decided she would like to call him Bony.

No proprietor of a guest house is dull in psychology. Miss Jade was aware that the least travelled people were the most difficult with whom to deal, and that the loud-voiced people were those acutely suffering from an inferiority complex. All her guests at Wideview Chalet were in comfortable circumstances, and her high tariff secured a high degree of selectivity.

The soft and clear enunciation of this outback man both charmed and mystified her, mystified her because she had thought that people who lived far beyond the railways were hoarse and coarse. She sensed the mental power behind the wide, low forehead, the power which in a rare flash became visible, and after her cigarette was alight, she turned to say something to Miss Philps that Bonaparte might not read her mind.

"I hope that you are quite happy in your dining companions, Mr. Bonaparte. I am asking Mr. Sleeman to sit at your table, and also two guests who arrived today, a Mr. Downes and a Mr. Lee." Swiftly Miss Jade smiled. "There will be no ladies at your table. Mr. and Mrs. Watkins especially requested to be given a table to themselves."

"I shall find that arrangement entirely satisfactory," Bony agreed, adding in his grand manner: "Madam, there is but one lady in this house who interests me."

To which Miss Jade countered, really charmed:

"I am glad there is only one gentleman from Queensland here at the same time."

"I find that extremely gratifying, Miss Jade. And thank you for attending to my slight injury. Au revoir!"

Miss Jade herself arranged the seating at Bony's table and introduced the new guests to Bony and Mr. Sleeman and another man who had been staying at the Chalet for several weeks, a Mr. Raymond Leslie.

Leslie was an artist who knew every inch of Mount Chalmers and much of the mountains beyond the valley. He appeared to find pleasure in occupying the chair so recently occupied by Mr. Grumman, and he lost little time in announcing that fact to the two new guests at this table, Mr. Lee and Mr. Downes, eulogizing Grumman's brusque manner of speech and his forceful descriptive power. He appeared to think little of the reticent Bonaparte, and still less of the even more reticent Mr. Sleeman. Bony covertly watched the two new guests, of whom Lee appeared the more transparent. When this large and weather-beaten man stated that he owned "a small place in the Riverina," it was evident that he spoke the truth. He was unmistakably a pastoralist.

Downes was slight with hair turning grey, although he did not appear to be beyond forty. It was difficult to guess his profession and he showed no inclination to announce it. His moustache was short and smooth and dark, there were tiny pockets under his dark eyes, and his hands were long-fingered and white. Seated on Bony's left, he was content to listen to Raymond Leslie talking about Mr. Grumman, and complaining of the treatment he had received from the detectives, who suspected everyone.

On Bony's right sat Mr. Sleeman who, Bony had been informed, was the representative of an English firm of engineers. He was quiet-spoken, interesting, and possessed of a little weakness during the evenings, a weakness in which George took a most prominent part.

"Seem to be settling down again, don't we?" he murmured to Bony beneath the rapid-fire of Raymond Leslie's talk. "Did you clear out last night to get away from the atmosphere?"

"Hardly that," replied Bony. "I was down the road and by chance saw some friends of mine in a car. Hadn't seen them for a couple of years. They took me to their home near the city for the evening."

"Was that where the war was?" Sleeman asked, his eyes glinting.

"Oh, no! It was quite peaceful down there. I was getting out of the confounded car. My friend who was driving had switched off the dash lights and my cheek came in violent contact with a projection from the windscreen. Only five guests here last night?"

"That's all. Elder left this morning. The place is better to live in now, more peaceful now those chattering, screaming women have gone."

The girl, Alice, waited at table. Bony observed her thoroughly for the first time. She was tall, vivacious and efficient. Too young, he thought, to have had any direct part in the murder of Grumman, but not too young to have gone through his own kit whilst he was away. In her statement to the police, she had said that she was a native of Barnsdale, single, and had been employed by Miss Jade for four months. Her duties had included the cleaning of Grumman's room, and she had every morning emptied the water carafe, washed it and re-filled it. In the mornings she had noticed that Grumman had used about half the water contents. Grumman had kept a bottle of tablets on his dressing table, but just what they were she did not know.

The artist was saying:

"Yes, the police thoroughly examined poor Grumman's room. Took all his luggage off, too. At least it was all gone when I passed along the passage to my room this afternoon and was able to look in through the open door."

"I didn't see 'em carting it away," interjected Sleeman.

"Oh, they must have taken it," objected Leslie. "What else would they do with it? Becomes State property until the next of kin is established."

"Well, you may be right, but I saw the police cars depart both yesterday and today, and I did not see Grumman's luggage taken away."

"They probably got Miss Jade to store it," volunteered Downes.

"Maybe! But that doesn't seem to accord with their usual procedure," Leslie argued, for the first time this evening experiencing opposition, and obviously not liking it. A brown-bearded man who apparently believed that people engaged in art should ever appear arty, he was naturally endowed with a temperament.

"Well, we'll ask Miss Jade about it," Downes said mildly, and went on eating.

The matter was put to Miss Jade later on in the lounge, the subject being raised by Leslie. It was then about nine o'clock. The Watkins couple had gone out for a walk despite the rain, Mrs. Watkins having announced to everyone that her husband suffered "frightfully" from indigestion. Leslie and the squatter from the Riverina were talking in one corner of the spacious room. Sleeman was writing letters, Downes was reading, as was Lee. Bony was lying full length in a chair.

"Mr. Grumman's luggage!" Miss Jade echoed. "I don't know what the police did with it."

"There you are, Sleeman!" cried the artist. "What did I say?"

Bony raised himself a fraction that he might observe the others. Miss Jade was standing near the artist and Lee. Downes had lowered his book to his knees and was regarding Sleeman with obvious interest. Sleeman said, with strong conviction:

"I stick to my guns. I am sure that Grumman's gear wasn't taken away by the police. As I said at dinner, I saw all the police cars depart, yesterday and today."

"Well, then, where the devil is it?" demanded Leslie. "It isn't in his room now."

"No, the room is vacant," Miss Jade said in support. "It was unsealed this afternoon by Inspector Snook just before he left. One of the maids has cleaned it since then."

"The police said nothing to you about Grumman's luggage?" pressed Leslie, with what seemed unwarranted heat. Miss Jade shook her dark head.

"Give in, Sleeman," ordered Leslie.

"I can't change my conviction," Sleeman said, firmly.

"All that I know," contributed Miss Jade, "is that yesterday morning I was told that the room had been sealed and would not be made available to me again until the police had completed their investigation of it. And, as I have told you, Inspector Snook said I could enter the room just before he left this afternoon."

"Very strange," remarked Downes from his chair. "Perhaps one of the staff saw the luggage being removed. Ah—here's the steward."

"George!" called Miss Jade. "Did you see what became of Mr. Grumman's luggage?"

George was crossing the room, carrying a tray on which were a bottle and a glass and water for Mr. Sleeman. His mind must have been wandering, for, on being addressed, he tripped slightly, and then came to stand in the centre of the lounge and faced his employer. The water in the glass jug, Bony noted, almost spilt out onto the tray. In his soft and precise voice, George answered:

"No, marm."

"Perhaps Bisker carried the luggage out for the police, or saw them take it away. Would you run out and ask Bisker?"

"Very well, marm."

George presented his tray to Mr. Sleeman, and Sleeman helped himself to a liberal nobbier of whisky, added water, and settled himself further into his chair. George carried his tray back to his pantry.

"You know, that's mighty strange," Leslie burst out. "I'm not disbelieving you, Sleeman, when you say that you saw all the police cars, but, you know, they must have taken the stuff. What did Grumman have, Miss Jade?"

"Oh, there were two large steamer trunks, and several suitcases," replied Miss Jade. "I remember seeing Bisker and George carry them from the car which brought Mr. Grumman. They carried them past the office off the hall, and I was standing at the open door of the office. I remember— —"

Miss Jade's voice was slowly cut off as the scream rose in pitch and volume. It was a scream from the throat of a badly horrified woman. It began on a high note, and rose to a note still higher, the last note drawn out to an unbelievable length. Abruptly it was shut off. Miss Jade became a Junoesque statue. Bony rose to his feet, but Mr. Downes got to his with remarkable alacrity. He was near the door leading to the reception hall and the office. Bony was near that door through which George had appeared and had departed. Then the scream began again. It began on a high note, rose and fell into a pulsating gurgle, then burst once again into a long-drawn ear-torturing shriek.

The sound of it came through the door by which George had gone and which had been left open. Bony leaped from the standing position beside his chair. Leslie and Lee remained just where they were. Downes was even quicker in his actions than was Bony, but Bony was first through that door. He heard Leslie roaring behind him. He heard Miss Jade cry out.

The door led to a passage midway along which were the double doors giving entry to the dining room. At the far end of the passage another door stood wide open, and through that Bony could see the kitchen range. The scream had stopped, and now was beginning again. The terrified woman was undoubtedly in the kitchen.

Chapter Thirteen

The Kitchen Party

With the scream ringing in his ears Bony raced into the kitchen of Wideview Chalet, closely followed by the dour Mr. Downes, Sleeman, Lee, Miss Jade and the artist.

Beyond the large cooking range, Bony saw the rear vision of Mrs. Parkes. Her large body was clothed in black, neatly halved by the white bands of an apron. The sleeves of her blouse were rolled above the bends of her arms where, in normal persons, elbow joints would be visible. One arm was raised and in the hand of that arm was gripped a flat-iron.

Upon the table where the staff ate, the girl Alice was kneeling. Her hands were resting upon her bended knees, and her head was tilted back. Her eyes were closed and her mouth was open, and from that mouth issued another long-drawn-out shriek. In the instant that she paused for breath, Mrs. Parkes snapped:

"Shut your trap, Alice! Leave him to me!"

A moment, two, three of paralysing inactivity held everyone in the kitchen. Then Mrs. Parkes said, conversationally:

"He's coming out!"

"Oh! Oh! Oh!" cried Alice in an ascending octave, and began all over again her scream of horror.

Slowly, reminding Bony of a show figure revolving in a shop window, Mrs. Parkes began to turn in the direction of Alice on the table. As she turned so did the girl's shriek rise up the scale. Then, like a classical javelin thrower, Mrs. Parkes threw the flat-iron. The missile thudded upon something on the floor, skidded and crashed into the wall.

"Got him!" cried Mrs. Parkes. "Now then, Alice, come down from that table and stop behaving like a young gal wanting to be kissed."

The cook moved forward, and Bony, with the company behind him, also moved forward after Mrs. Parkes, who came to a halt, glaring triumphantly down upon the mangled body of an enormous rat.

Miss Jade assumed command.

"Mrs. Parkes," she exclaimed, "what *are* you doing?"

Mrs. Parkes turned, and the motion of her body was not unlike that of a crane swinging a load from ship to wharf.

"I'm not doin' nothing, marm—at the moment," she said. "I have just killed a rat what must have come in through the scullery door what must have been left open by George when he went out a minute ago."

Running feet sounded on the floorboards of the scullery, and George rushed into the kitchen, followed by Bisker. The steward's face was dead white and his eyes were big. Bisker's moustache and eyebrows appeared to be standing straight out. Mrs. Parkes crossed to the girl on the table whose eyes were still shut and whose mouth was still open and about to utter another shriek. Bony, who had turned slightly, was able to observe the reactions of all the others.

The brown moustache and beard of Raymond Leslie seemed to lie flat beneath his bulging eyes. The squatter was the least affected. Sleeman's eyes were winking rapidly, and Downes was standing utterly still, and upon his face was no expression. His eyes were fixed in a wide stare, and his arms were bent, with the fingers of both hands extended like the legs of crabs. When Miss Jade again spoke, animation was resumed. She was the first to regain composure.

"Alice, stop that noise!" she commanded.

The girl, however, appeared to be wound up. Mrs. Parkes rolled over the three yards of tiled floor to the girl. She smacked her face—hard. Then she picked the girl off the table as though she were a vase and enfolded her within her arms against her prominent bust, saying:

"Now, now, dearie, hold your tongue. Here's Miss Jade wanting to know what all the fuss is about. It's all right! I killed the animile. There, there, now "

"George, did you leave the scullery door open?" demanded Miss Jade.

George began to breathe. His eyes blinked.

"No, marm," he replied. "The door was open when I went out to ask Bisker about the luggage belonging to Mr. Grumman."

"Bisker, did you leave the scullery door open?" demanded Miss Jade.

Bisker's moustache twitched. Then his eyebrows twitched, and Bony wanted to laugh, for he wondered what the effect would have been had eyebrows and moustache twitched at the same moment. Like the others, he was experiencing reaction following those terrible screams.

Bisker said that he did not recall having left open the outer scullery door, and he stood like a wilted toadstool beneath Miss Jade's withering condemnation of him, condemnation which Bony considered unjustified, as others in addition to Bisker doubtless passed in and out through that particular door. It was Mr. Sleeman who offered a suggestion which gained Bony's approval.

"Well, all's well that end's well," he broke in, the several drinks already presented to him on George's tray that evening having mellowed him. "Miss Jade! I seek your favour. Will you be so kind as to permit me to call upon George to bring us all a dose of nerve-steadier? Our nerves have been subjected to great strain, and a little bracing fluid would restore them to normal." Miss Jade's anger was melting. "In view of the circumstances," went on Mr. Sleeman, "I'd like to suggest that George wait upon all of us here that we might do honour to Mrs. Parkes. It was the most beautiful shot with a flat-iron I have ever witnessed."

Miss Jade bent her head towards Mr. Sleeman, and George walked forward. He accepted the orders without the aid of a memo pad and departed.

"Dashed good idea of yours, Sleeman," said Raymond Leslie. "I thought there had been another murder."

"Oh! Oh! Oh!" began the girl in the mighty arms of the cook.

"Stop it, Alice, or I'll belt you one," Mrs. Parkes said, kindly. "Now, now, a little drop of brandy will settle you. Be quiet and sit down here with me."

Mr. Sleeman began to relate an anecdote about his wife and a pet mouse released by his son. Mr. Downes patiently listened. Miss Jade began ordering Bisker to fumigate the wood-stack the following morning, for that was where the rat must have come from. Bisker stoutly denied the presence of rats in his wood-stack, but he was talked down. Bony crossed to look at the dead animal which, he saw, was a bush rat large even for that species. Then George came with the drinks, and Mr. Sleeman called for three cheers for Mrs. Parkes. One tiny cheer was given, as it became obvious that this frivolity did not have Miss Jade's approval. After that, the kitchen party broke up.

In an atmosphere of anticlimax, Bony went back to the lounge for a quarter of an hour, after which he slipped away to the hall and out through the main entrance, ostensibly to take a walk, as the rain had ceased. Bisker was loading his early-morning pipe with "dottles" salvaged from the day's smoking, when Bony entered his hut.

"The rain will have ruined the impression made by the man's hand on the earth in the shrub tub," he told Bisker. "To make a plaster cast now would be useless. Anyway, I have memorised the impression. Want to go to bed?"

"No, not for an hour," Bisker replied.

"Any whisky left in the bottle?"

"A little drop I've been saving for a night-cap."

"All right! I won't keep you up long. Er—tell me, when you leave here in the mornings, how do you get into the house?"

Bisker proceeded to load the early-morning pipe with great care, and without looking up from that important task, he answered:

"Before George turns in, he locks the scullery door from the outside and he puts the key under a brick what lies 'andy. Then 'e goes round the house to the front door what he locks for the night. Of a morning, I gets the key from under the brick and goes in by that scullery door to begin the chores."

"Did you see Miss Jade enter the house by the scullery door last night?"

"Yes, I did."

"Did she use the key left under the brick, d'you know?"

"No, she didn't. She musta had a key of 'er own. I 'eard 'er unlock the door, and I 'eard 'er lock it again when she was inside. Me, I was sorta froze against the wood-stack. I could've swore she saw me, but she couldn't 'ave."

"Just what time was that?"

"Well, by me clock 'ere it was two minutes to 'alf-past twelve."

"Was the house locked up at that time?"

"Oh, yes. There wasn't a light anywhere. I made sure everyone was abunk before I got through your winder with the blankets."

Bony regarded Bisker's fingers and noted with an inward shudder how the mass of "dottles" was being pressed into the pipe bowl to be smoked first thing in the morning.

"You clean all the boots and shoes, don't you?" he asked.

"Yes," replied Bisker.

"Dig into your mind and tell me if you have ever cleaned a pair of boots or shoes size twelve."

"Size twelve!" repeated Bisker, looking up into Bony's eyes. "That's a mighty big boot. I take an eight boot, and you take a seven. Crummy! Size twelve! A bloke with that size in feet must be a very big man or a policeman. I remember cleaning a pair of gent's shoes size ten—but size twelve! Why Fred, 'e takes a nine, and that's bigger than the average."

"Who is Fred?"

"'E was the bloke what first found Grumman in the ditch. You know, 'e was with me when you came to stand on the bank yestiddy morning."

"What does he do?"

"Just works about, here and there, cutting wood, digging in gardens. 'E comes 'ere every week to cut the lawn." Bisker laid aside the early-morning pipe and proceeded to cut chips from his plug for the pipe which had been dangling from his mouth. "Not a bad bloke, Fred. Been a shearer in 'is time. Me and 'im is sorta cobbers. When either of us 'as a win, we shares a bottle."

"A win?"

"Yes. A win on an 'orse. Fred's pretty good at pickin' 'em. And then sometimes I 'as a win from a guest. Sometimes 'alf a quid. On two times I've been 'anded a full quid tip."

"Oh!" Bony rolled and lit a cigarette. Then: "Did George ask you about Grumman's luggage?"

Bisker brightened. "Yes," he replied, "I told 'im I never seen any of it shifted by the police. Course it could 'ave been done without me seeing. I wasn't outside the main entrance all the time. What's the strength of that?"

"Nothing very much, Bisker. The subject came up at dinner. One of the guests said that he happened to see into the room occupied by Grumman and saw that all his luggage had gone, and another guest said the police couldn't have taken it because he saw all the cars leave. Then Miss Jade said she knew nothing about it. Just a little argument, that was all. When you took Grumman's cleaned shoes to his bedroom door yesterday morning, about what time was that?"

"About quarter to seven."

"You saw no light beneath his door?"

"No."

"There was nothing unusual about Grumman's bedroom door?"

"Didn't notice, Mr. Bonaparte."

"Nothing unusual about his shoes that morning?"

"They was a bit wet, I remember." Bisker's weathered face expanded into a grin. "Yes, I remember that," he continued, chuckling. "They was the only wet pair that morning for me to clean, the only pair bar one other pair."

"Indeed!" Bony said encouragingly, as Bisker halted before further explanation.

"Yes, that other pair belonged to the old cat," Bisker proceeded. "I says to meself, Hoh! Hoh! The blinkin' foreign German was out walking in the grass last night, and the old cat musta been out walkin' in the wet grass, too. A bit of love, I says. Looks like it, didn't it?"

Bony smiled. "I'm assuming," he said, "that you are referring to Miss Jade. The evening before last was dry and frosty. I was out for a walk after dinner, but I kept to road and paths. My shoes were not wet."

"That's right. Your shoes weren't wet at all. No one else's was either, bar them two."

"Have you ever noticed Miss Jade returning to the house very late at night before last night?"

Bisker shook his head.

"H'm!" murmured Bony. "Interesting. Take particular note of Miss

Jade's shoes tomorrow morning. Note if they are the same shoes that you cleaned this morning."

"All right. D'you think Miss Jade was in at Grumman's murder?"

"Bisker, don't be a fool," Bony said, sharply. "If you are to continue to be an offsider to me, you'll never ask such a stupid question again, or ask any questions. You'll just stay silent about everything, and do just what I ask you to do, and when I ask it. Clear?"

Bisker nodded.

"Good!" Bony said briskly. "Now I want you to do a job for me. I suppose you know every room and cupboard in the house?"

"That's so, Mr. Bonaparte."

"Well, d'you think you could draw a plan of the inside of the house, showing every room and cupboard and store-room?"

"Yes, I reckon I could."

"Excellent. I've brought paper and pencils with me. You do it now. Take your time, and if you make a bloomer, begin again. There is plenty of paper."

Bisker fell to work, his pipe forgotten, the end of the pencils being chewed to splinters one after the other. Bony sat silently watching him. It was raining again, pattering on the iron roof low above their heads.

Chapter Fourteen

An Item of Gossip

Four days passed and Bony gained precisely nothing other than a pound or two in weight. It seemed that neither did the police gain anything during those four days, for on the fifth day when Bony visited Superintendent Bolt at Headquarters he was told that nothing was known of the whereabouts of Marcus, and that Grumman's luggage had not been traced.

"Our loved friend will have got out of the State by this time," growled Bolt. "Probably travelled quite openly by air or rail, looking like anything but Alexander Croft, alias this and that."

"Mind if I have another glance through his record?" asked Bony.

"Of course not. Want to look for anything special?"

"Yes. I'd like to examine your pictures of him. Kirby, you know, Colonel Blythe's assistant, suggested that Scotland Yard might have photographs of Croft, and the Colonel cabled to find out. The London crowd replied that they had photos of Marcus, and were air-mailing copies."

Bony fell to tapping his teeth with the pencil he had used to write a memo. Then:

"When I was last here I saw three pictures of Marcus. They were taken eleven years ago, I understand, when Marcus was imprisoned for manslaughter. What Scotland Yard pinned to him, I don't know, and that is of small importance to us compared with the fact that they also have photographs of him. Now, with their photographs added to those we have here, do you think your experts could build with reasonable accuracy a mould from which a cast could be produced of the head of Marcus?"

"They could do that all right, but with what degree of accuracy, I don't know," replied Bolt. "Why do you suggest it?"

"Well, you see a man *can* disguise his features so effectively as to pass unrecognised by his own wife, or the cleverest policemen, but even friend Marcus would not think to disguise the shape of his head. Profile pictures do give the shape of the head, and I remember that you have one of the rear of Marcus's head, but a near-exact of his head in plaster of paris would enable us to memorise his head-shape, and from that someone might get under the very best disguise."

"H'm!" Bolt regarded Bony with his piercing small brown eyes. "Might be worth doing. Wish I had your confidence that Marcus is still in the State. We don't think so now. In the first place, there was sufficient time for him to get past the road-blocks before they were fixed, and in the second place, his mastery of disguise has proved such a winner not only in Australia but in Europe and in America."

Bolt, watching Bony roll a cigarette, decided that he had never seen a man manufacture worse. He had many crowded hours ahead, but notwithstanding, he patiently waited for his visitor and colleague to finish making the cigarette and light it. Aware of Bony's impatience of regulations and legalities, an impatience with which he was securely sympathetic, he was able to appreciate Bony's peculiar gifts and to value them as an addition to the orthodox and modern methods of crime detection. The huge Superintendent was, as he had always been, anxious to learn.

"There is something else which a man forgets to disguise," Bony said, softly blowing smoke in a spear over the conical top of Bolt's cranium. "The something else is his feet and the way he walks. No two men walk alike, and because I am able to read man-tracks as easily as you read a report, I could teach others to read. In the long ago, I put a suggestion to my Chief that in addition to recording a man's fingerprints, a record should be made of his footprints. I suggested that all convicted persons, and, in some cases, suspected persons, should be made to walk in boots or shoes over a new cement block, and then made to walk over that block in their bare feet. The cement should bear the imprints of at least six steps, and the impressions would then be photographed for the record. The graduate from my school of tracking would be able not only to follow tracks unobserved by the ordinary detective, but also he would be able to recognise the tracks made by any person whose tracks had been recorded. If I had ever observed the tracks of friend Marcus, I would recognise them now and anywhere, so that disguise would be ineffective to me."

"Good idea, I think," Bolt said, slowly.

"Sound sense," Bony stated, and then smiled: "But you know what any Government Department is like."

"Ya," growled Bolt. "And I know particularly well what Australian Government Departmental heads are like. The only way you could get that school of yours started was to have gone abroad and called yourself Spiffoski, and then the Police Department of every State would have adopted the scheme saying what a great thing it would be in crime detection."

Bony's eyes opened wide and then half closed in laughter.

"Spiffoski!" he repeated, throatily. "Bony Spiffoski! I'll have to get the Russian for Bony. Ah—Boniski Spiffoski! When I go back to Brisbane, I'll ring through to the Chiefs secretary and say: 'Morning, Lowther. Tell the Colonel that Inspector Boniski Spiffoski has reported for duty this morning.' It'll sound good. And I'll be in the clerks' room directly below the old boy's office, and I'll be able to hear him bouncing about in his chair and demanding Lowther to tell him who the hell this and that. But then, it wouldn't work. Lowther wouldn't have the courage. Well, I'll get along to your records room, Super." He rose, still smiling. "And give consideration to the idea of making a bust of Marcus's head. I'll ask Colonel Blythe to send along the photos from Scotland Yard."

Also on his feet, Bolt said they "would give it a go." He accompanied Bony to the door, smiled broadly and shook hands, then passed back to his desk to give orders to the Records Branch to serve Inspector Bonaparte. When Inspector Snook entered a few minutes later, Superintendent Bolt did not mention Bony's scheme for the recording of footprints.

It was a Friday, and it was half-past five when Bony emerged from Police Headquarters in Russell Street, coming out through a small door into a back street. There he paused to light one of his cigarettes and to take stock of all persons in view. There were fewer than a dozen, and there had been fewer still when he had entered the great building through that same innocuous doorway. Before he reached Swanston Street via Spring and Flinders streets, he was reasonably confident that he had not been followed either going to or coming from Headquarters.

He spent half an hour in a tea-shop, and then became a unit of the river of humanity flowing towards the one railway station. The speed of the stream was that of a fast walk, and the few people who battled against it in the opposite direction were buffeted and jostled. Bony was halted at the Flinders Street intersection, a unit of the river temporarily dammed, a dam which appeared about to burst all restraint when the traffic lights showed green and the traffic policemen beckoned.

To Bony, the experience held exhilaration. He was swept across the street, up the steps of the station entrance, across the great hall and through the barriers, a unit of a river which flowed in flood for more than an hour. Whilst waiting on the platform for his train to Manton, he watched the river pouring down the ramp and flowing up the sub-ways to be halted for a space thick against the edges of platforms. Trains came in and the river flowed into them. They whirred out filled to capacity, taking the "edging" with them, and immediately the human stream would once more grow thick along the platform edge, waiting to be poured into the next train. Brisbane had nothing to show like this.

It took his train just short of an hour to reach Manton. When he arrived at the waiting bus it was almost full and he got a seat at the front end just in time to avoid having to stand. The seating was arranged along the sides and at the back, and he had for neighbours a man on his left hand and an office girl on his right.

At the foot of Mount Chalmers, a little more than halfway to Wideview Chalet, the bus was barely half filled, and the girl on Bony's right who had been talking to another girl mentioned softly the name of Clarence B. Bagshott. That name brought Bony from a bout of meditation, and he came presently to understand that the author of mystery novels was also travelling in the bus.

A little further along the road, his neighbour's friend alighted, and after a little period, he said in a whisper:

"Am I right in thinking that Bagshott, the author, is in this bus?"

The girl nodded, and regarded him sharply. Bony smiled.

"Please forgive me for speaking to you," he pleaded. "You see, I have read several of Bagshott's books, and I am curious to see what he is like."

When she spoke again, her lips barely moved.

"That's him in the far corner," she said.

The interior lighting was good—for a bus—and with interest he studied this man who had been reported to him via Bisker, via Mrs. Parkes, as addicted to experimenting on rabbits with poison, that the data obtained might be put into his crime books.

Bony felt disappointed. Never before had he consciously seen an author in the flesh, and he had somehow built up in his mind that authors were a particular species of the race, a species not quite like poets and not quite like artists. He had thought to see in Bagshott a man with massive brow, large and staring eyes, a loud and penetrating voice, and distinctive clothes.

Clarence B. Bagshott's appearance was disappointingly ordinary. He was wearing a raincoat over a navy-blue suit. His hat was lying on his knees, so that Bony was able to study his face. His brow was low and narrow, but the back of his head was exceptionally wide. His eyes were constantly alert, and when he smiled he seemed human enough. Even whilst Bony was unostentatiously observing him, he lifted his hat and crossed his legs, and it was then that Bony noticed his shoes. They were exceptionally large—the only oddity in all his make-up.

Unfortunately his feet were in the shadow cast by the legs of a man seated at the side, and Bony was undecided about their correct size. They were certainly higher than tens. The girl said:

"What d'you think of him?"

As a man, Bony thought him to be quite ordinary. He had looked up his name in the Who's Who, with the result that he was aware of this author's record in the writing world. He thought the girl's question was put to him to elicit his impressions of an author, and, in consequence, he replied:

"Not much."

Already becoming familiar with her travelling companion, the girl said:

"He ain't much, neither."

"Indeed!" Bony murmured, encouragingly.

"No," she said out of the corner of her mouth whilst she gazed straight ahead. "You see the girl he's talkin' to?"

Bony admitted that he did.

"Well, she's single."

Bony waited to be enlightened further, for he could distinguish nothing out of place that Bagshott should be talking with a single or a married woman in a public conveyance. Then his travelling companion supplied further information in the form of another question. She said, still out of the corner of her mouth:

"You see the child sitting at the girl's side? That's hers. And some say that it's his, too."

"Dear me!" murmured the "shocked" Bonaparte. "Is that really so?"

His deepening interest warmed his travelling companion.

"They say it is," she told him, and he asked:

"Who are 'they'?"

"Oh, everyone about the Mount," she replied airily. "He's married, you know. Lives in that place opposite the top garage. Big hedge around it. You never see his wife. He don't let her come out. I know what I'd do if I was the policeman."

"What?" asked Bony, thrillingly.

"I'd walk in once every week just to see if Mrs. Bagshott was still alive. I wouldn't put it past him to kill her one night and bury her in the garden, so's he could marry that girl with the kid. Nasty bit of work, I says."

The harsh nasal voice, deliberately kept low, ceased, and Bony once more tried to estimate the size of Bagshott's shoes. The shadows, however, persisted and he gave it up. There would be time and opportunity to look over Clarence B. Bagshott, and to determine just what size shoes he did wear, and just how he wore them and the impressions they made. The vehicle was travelling slowly in second gear and was passing round a bend a thousand feet above the valley. Down in the gulf gleamed clusters of stars, the lights of hamlets, and away in the distance millions of fallen stars lay upon the black velvet—the lights of Melbourne.

"Has Mr. Bagshott been living up here long?" he enquired of his companion, in a whisper.

"'Bout ten years, I think," was her reply. "Thinks himself somebody, too."

Bony regarded Bagshott again in the light of this latest information concerning him. Just then he was talking and laughing and his travelling companion and the child were both laughing with him. What he said could not be heard, but he did not have the appearance of a man either conceited or overbearing in personality.

Still, his feet were of very great interest. If he had made the impressions on the ramp that night Grumman had been murdered, and also the following night on Bisker's path and about Bisker's hut, then his feet would become even more interesting.

Bony was sorry he had to alight before Bagshott. Had the author alighted first he would have been able to see his shoes in clear light as he walked past him to the entrance to the bus.

Chapter Fifteen

Clarence B. Bagshott

Lounging on the Chalet veranda, Bony gazed at the panorama of mountain and valley spread in colourful glory before him. On the wide arms of his chair were a cup of tea and a plate of Mrs. Parkes's short-bread biscuits.

At this moment, he was absolutely satisfied with life.

He was meeting new people and this was always refreshing. They were, of course, vastly different from the people of the interior, but he was coming to understand these southern people, and the growth of understanding added to his interest.

There was the Watkins pair. They had arranged to have a table in the dining room to themselves. Watkins was heavy-jowled; his wife was big and overloaded with powder and lipstick and jewellery. Why had they insisted upon having a table to themselves when always they spoke loudly enough for everyone to hear? The subject of their conversation was invariably travel—their own travels to New Zealand, Tasmania, and to Sydney. Strange how the sense of inferiority does become manifest. Bisker, and the man then mowing the lawn, had both travelled fifty times more than the Watkins couple, but one never heard either of them mount his travel experiences upon the stand of conversation.

George never mentioned that he had been a liner steward for six years. He never spoke loudly, assertively. He seemed to be a well-oiled machine running smoothly and gliding silently along the rails of life. There was more in George than in the Watkins couple combined; for underneath his suaveness lay character of a kind, a character felt rather than seen by the sensitive Bonaparte. Bolt had expressed satisfaction with George's history, a deal of which had been learned from sources other than George himself.

To compare Miss Jade with the Watkins woman made the latter appear superficial. Although Miss Jade appealed to Bony's romantic nature, he had to confess that he did not understand her. She possessed character—of that there was no doubt. She could command herself and, therefore, could command others. Never once had Bony seen her a fraction careless in dress or appearance, or in speech. Success in her business was due to that application of self-discipline nicely tempered with the warm feminine traits of sympathy and understanding.

Of the guests, only Sleeman and Downes were men of character, but whether good or bad Bony was undecided. Raymond Leslie, the artist, was a wind-bag, and Lee, the squatter, appeared to find himself at a loss in a community uninterested in livestock and fodders. That Wideview Chalet was almost empty of guests appeared to please everyone, including Miss Jade.

Presently, Bony decided to exert himself by taking a walk and, possibly, both seeing and learning something more of the man Clarence B. Bagshott.

Not troubling about his hat, he left the veranda and proceeded down the path towards the wicket gate. Fred was pushing the mower across the incline of the lawn to the left of the path, and of that section he had already cut about half. The grass, as Bony had observed, was fine of quality and luscious of growth, but not over-long, although to his own knowledge it had not been cut during the past eight days.

"The grass doesn't grow very fast, does it?" he said when Fred had brought the mower to the edge of the path. The man was tall and rangey and about fifty years old. He turned his watery blue eyes upon Bony, who noted the abnormally red nose and the weak mouth.

"It never grows much this time of the year." Fred's drawling voice placed him at once as an inlander. "Just startin' to grow now. Another fortnight, you'll see how she can grow. Don't grow longer than a dog's hair all through winter, but once spring comes there's no stoppin' her. Everything then busts wide open, all of a sudden like."

"Well, spring cannot be far off by the feel of the air today," remarked Bony. "How far up along the highway is the next garage?"

"Oh—about a mile." A smile flitted across the man's weathered face. "I never mind going up the 'ill for a start. If you goes down'ill for a start you gotta start walkin' up the 'ill to get home."

"That's true," Bony agreed. "Whereabouts do you live?"

"Me? Oh—down at the bottom of the road turning off the main road at the fruit shop. I built me own shack down there some ten years back. The road peters out at my shack, and you can go on from there by a track what takes you to The Way of a Thousand Steps."

"Way of a Thousand Steps!" repeated the detective. "That sounds romantic."

"Yes." Fred's eyes regarded the veranda, probably to locate Miss Jade. "Bagshott, the author, give it that name. It's a gully and there's a path following the gully from top to bottom and the Reserves Committee at odd times uses the trunks of fern-trees to make steps so's that anyone going up or down won't slip and slide for yards in the mud. The Way of a

Thousand Steps begins at the highway where she turns over a stream and it ends 'way down on the edge of the valley forest."

"I might take a walk down The Way of a Thousand Steps one of these days. Bagshott's house—it's beyond the garage, isn't it?"

"Yes, hundred yards or so. You can't mistake it. Big cyprus hedge round most of the place. You'll see a coupler wireless masts in his garden. I was told that the Secret Service was up here during the war about them masts. Looks like that Bagshott was sending wireless messages to Japan or somewhere. Funny sorta bloke, although I think 'e's all right, him having been a lot outback where people is sort of civilized. You come from outback, don't you?"

"Yes," Bony admitted. "So do you. How d'you like being in these parts?"

"Oh, it's all right in a way. But the people! I can't make 'em out."

Bony's brows rose a fraction and he looked interested. Fred searched the veranda and garden for sight of Miss Jade.

"Well, it's like this," Fred explained. "If you don't wear no collar and tie you're a bit of dirt. If you has a drink, you're just an outcast. If you tries to be friendly, they spits at you. And if you tell 'em to go to hell, they screeches at you and goes around telling all the lies about you they can think up. If it wasn't for Bisker, I wouldn't be 'ere. He's the only civilized one in the district. Cripes! I must be doin' a bit."

Miss Jade had emerged from one of the french windows opening on to the veranda, and Fred waited no longer. Bony waved a hand, and Miss Jade gaily waved back to him.

Having passed through the wicket gate and down the ramp, Bony strolled up along the highway. Before long he crossed the road on the lower side of which had been erected white-painted guide posts. Here a gravelled path had been put down, the surface of which was smooth and soft and able to take the impressions of many boots and shoes.

The first impressions that he recognised were those made by Mr. Watkins and his wife. They were at times overlaying those made by Fred when on his way to work at the Chalet that morning. Much farther on, he found the shoe-prints left by Leslie, the artist, and these several tracks were included among very many others which he had never seen before.

The highway turned and twisted around the shoulders of the mountain, and on the top side he could see here and there a house, and here and there a grass paddock widely separated by areas of tall bracken from which towered the smooth and slim trunks of the mast-like mountain ash. Now the road was curving about the slopes of a wide gully and down there grew masses of tree-ferns, the new growth of fronds vividly green against the dark green of the older growth.

He saw the fruit shop long before he reached it, and when he did so, he accosted a man standing at the door beside a stall loaded with apples and oranges, soft drinks and lollies.

"Is Mr. Bagshott's house much farther on?"

"Aw, no! A couple of chains and a bit. Place with a tall hedge 'round it. Can't miss it."

"Thank you."

Through the shop door Bony could see several small tables flanked by chairs.

"Have you got any real dry ginger ale?" he enquired.

"Too right! The real mackie."

The man led the way inside and Bony sat at one of the tables.

"There aren't many people on the road today," he ventured.

"Never is much during the week. This afternoon and tomorrow there'll be cars enough—hundreds of 'em." The shopman set down a bottle of ginger ale and a glass, and at his customer's invitation, he brought another glass and bottle and sat down opposite the detective.

"You intend to visit at Bagshott's?" he enquired.

"No. I am not acquainted with him," Bony replied. "Read his books, and then, hearing that he lived up here, I became curious to see his place. I would like to live here myself."

The shopman settled down.

"Some of his books arse pretty good, and some ain't so good," was his verdict. "He can write all right, but he's a bit wonky in the conk, if you know what I mean. Don't associate with no one. Told me once that he's got everyone at bay and intends keeping 'em there. Don't blame him much for that, any'ow. They're a funny lot hereabouts, and it's me saying it what has lived here for forty-odd years."

"What's the matter with them?" Bony mildly enquired, and the shopman rose to walk to the door to spit. When he returned, he said:

"Well, you see it's like this. The mob up here are atwix' and between. They're neither country nor city. There's two sorts too. There's the kind what's come up here to live till death doth claim 'em, and there's the kind what's lived here most all their lives—like me. Bagshott don't care two hoots for either kind, so he told me. All heated up about it, too, when he was telling me. Course, he was mixed up in a murder over in W.A. some years back. I never rightly got to hear the strength of it, but I've been told that he sooled a bloke on to do a murder or two."

"Indeed!" Bony said, politely. "Mixed up in a murder—or two! Did he go to gaol?"

"I don't rightly know about that. Mind you, he's just the kind to commit a murder so's he could put it in a book."

"H'm! Strange man. He doesn't appear to have a very good character."

"You're telling me."

"I have heard," Bony said, lowering his voice. "I have heard that Bagshott has a wireless and that the Secret Service was out during the war trying to trap him sending messages to the Japs. Is that right, do you think?"

"I think so. I wasn't up here during the war. Down making munitions. But there was talk of it."

"And I heard, too, that he's friendly with a single woman who has a child by him."

The shopman pursed his lips and looked wise. Then he winked both his eyes one after the other. He said:

"Well, personally speaking, I don't see nothing wrong with that. Still, that's what has gone around up here."

"And even that he catches rabbits and poisons them to watch them die so that he can use the information in his books," persisted Bony.

"Oh, that's a fact," claimed the man. "I told him about that once, and he said that in between rabbits he grabs a local dog and tries out some special stuff on them."

"And that he never allows his wife to leave the place."

"That's so, but I don't believe it. I don't believe in painting a man blacker than he is. He's black enough, from all that's said."

"Very black," Bony added with emphasis. "Well, I'll be getting along. See you another day, perhaps."

Continuing his stroll along the path outside the white posts, Bony admitted to himself that Clarence B. Bagshott must have a picturesque personality. It could not be all smoke without some fire, and if he had really been mixed up in one murder—nay, was it not two or more?—he might well be mixed up in the murder of Grumman.

He passed a house, over the front gate of which was a sign announcing that it was a Police Station, and saw nothing of Sub-Inspector Mason. Then he passed a service garage with its petrol pumps, and finally came in sight of a house, only the roof of which could be seen above the tall cyprus hedge. There was a side road flanking this hedge. One gate opened on to the side road, and there was another gate fronting the main highway. The latter was open, and as he approached it, a car backed out. From the car alighted the man who had been pointed out to him on the bus as Clarence B. Bagshott.

Bagshott was middle-aged, tall and thin. He was wearing khaki drill trousers, a pair of old boots, a drill shirt and no hat, and by the time he had closed the gate, Bony was standing beside the car. Keen hazel eyes examined him. The breeze lifted dark brown hair growing low to the man's forehead. And then Bony saw that the hazel eyes recognised him for what he was—a half-caste. He said:

"You are most fortunate in being able to live up here."

Bagshott smiled, saying:

"Bit of a change from carrying a swag west of the Paroo. What part do you come from?"

"West of a line from the Paroo River north to Longreach," replied Bony.

"Is that so!" Bagshott's face beamed. "I haven't been out west since 'thirty-two. How's the country looking?"

"Very bad just now. Wants rain badly. The stock is poor."

"Bad condition to start the summer in, eh? Well, I must be going." Bagshott went round to get into the car, and then he halted and looked across the bonnet. "I've been promising myself a month's holiday up at Wanaaring. Know it?"

Bony nodded, his eyes alight, the smell of the place in his nostrils.

"I've promised myself a full month on the beer at Wanaaring," Bagshott continued. "For the first week I'll be going around on my hands and knees. After that I'll be feeling very good. I've been a long time away from civilised people. Cheerio!"

Bony laughed, delightedly. The car was backed out to the centre of the road, and turned to travel down the highway. Bagshott smiled at him as he passed, and Bony continued to walk on. He walked on for perhaps a hundred yards, regarding the painted wireless masts. Then he turned, strolling casually back until he came to Bagshott's gate, where he paused for two seconds. The marks of the motor tyres were plain on the softened gravel between gate and roadway. So, too, were the impressions of Bagshott's shoes. They were size twelve. They were soled with rubber, still bearing a well-known trademark. They were the shoes, or the twin of the shoes, that had left impressions on the Chalet ramp and about Bisker's hut.

Chapter Sixteen

Satan Takes a Walk

It was on Saturday morning that Bony met and spoke to Clarence B. Bagshott outside the latter's front gate, and he arrived back at the Chalet to hear the luncheon gong as he was walking up from the highway. It was then one o'clock and Fred was returning from his lunch to his grass-cutting job. He had completed the section of lawn on the left of the path to the wicket gate, and now he prepared to cut the right-hand section. When Bony entered the famous dining room, the other guests were all seated.

"Been out on the tramp?" asked Raymond Leslie.

"Yes," Bony replied. "A great morning for a walk. There's no doubt about this mountain air making a man hungry. I think I've never seen air so clear as it is today. By the way, you've been up here some time. Ever met Clarence B. Bagshott?"

"I have not. The man's an utter bounder."

"Have you read any of his books?" persisted Bony.

Raymond Leslie sat bolt upright and the tip of his brown beard moved outward from his narrow chest in what he fondly thought was the Captain Kettle angle. To increase the effect, he set down his knife and fork, before saying:

"My dear Bonaparte, when I read literature, I read literature, not trash."

He spoke so loudly and emphatically that the Watkins couple stopped their high-pitched chatter about trout fishing somewhere in Tasmania, and Bony observed Miss Jade intently listening. The artist had gained the attention of everyone in the room, and he desired to retain it.

"Educated people don't read Bagshott's stuff," he went on. "No one knows him outside the readers of newspaper serials. Our glorious Australian literature has had too many obstacles to surmount in order to become established without having Bagshott's tripe added to them. They call his books Australian, and people unfortunately read them and judge Australian literature by them."

Leslie glared at Bony, who said, meekly:

"I asked merely if you had read his books. I haven't because I have not happened to come across one. I asked, too, if you had met Bagshott, as you have been staying up here for some time."

"I would not want to meet him, Bonaparte," Leslie said rudely.

Then came the quiet voice of Mr. Downes:

"As a matter of fact, I've read several of his books. I like them. You would not insinuate, Mr. Leslie, that I am not educated?"

Everyone at Bony's table looked at Mr. Downes, whose face was now utterly devoid of expression. Leslie was about to say something when he looked into Mr. Downes's eyes. For three long seconds he stared at Downes, into those dark eyes. He felt a chill down his neck, and he actually stuttered.

"Er—no—Downes, I wouldn't say that of you," he dribbled. "I was only speaking generally."

"I am glad to hear that, Leslie," Downes said, employing his knife and fork. "Naturally, I can quite understand your enthusiasm for the real Australian literature," and Bony wanted to chuckle at the plain emphasis on the second personal pronoun.

"I met him this morning," Bony said casually, and the strain vanished, leaving Leslie like a stranded fish. Out of the tail of his eye, Bony flashed a glance at Miss Jade, to see her hands still and her head bent in an attitude of concentrated effort to hear what was being said. "Happened to be passing his place when he backed his car out of the gate. I made some remark or other about the locality, and he appeared quite friendly and breezy. Said he had promised himself a month on a diet of beer up at Wanaaring."

"Why go to Wanaaring—wherever that is?" asked the now more than interested Sleeman.

"Well, you see, Wanaaring had three pubs and about fifteen houses when I was last there," Bony informed them all. "The inhabitants are very friendly and they can really drink beer, in some cases perhaps not too politely, but certainly with grand efficiency. The climate is either very hot or very dusty, and more often than not both at the same time. There are other advantages, too."

When Bony paused, Sleeman prompted him.

"Well, you see, up in Wanaaring, which is a few hundred miles west of Bourke in New South Wales, one feels free of restrictions. For instance, a chap doesn't bother about what his neighbours might think if he chooses to go without a collar. Then the police are both friendly and diplomatic. Should you be found crawling about on hands and knees, they order your friends to put you to bed or to carry you into the local lock-up to lie for a few hours till consciousness returns."

"How do you get to Wan—that place you said?" Sleeman asked.

"Better stay put," suggested Downes, and for the first time Bony witnessed a smile on the normally cold face.

"And Clarence B. Bagshott is thinking of going to Wan—that place?" persisted Sleeman. "Hang it! I'd like to go with him."

Again Downes spoke, and again he smiled.

"I still say you'd better stay put, Sleeman. The police mightn't be so tolerant if they saw two fellows going around on their hands and knees at the same time."

"Meaning?"

"Bagshott and you," replied Downes, disarmingly.

The idea, however, remained attractive to Mr. Sleeman, and he became avid for information concerning Wanaaring and the easiest way of getting there. Raymond Leslie maintained the silence which Downes had evidently imposed with his eyes. The meal which had been threatened by unpleasant boorishness eventually proved to be highly successful, and Bony retired to his chair at the far end of the veranda, feeling very well satisfied with himself.

He was thankful that he did not have to push a lawn mower this quiet and restful afternoon, thankful that he was able to sit and smoke in the acme of comfort and watch the colours pouring against the slopes of the distant mountains as the sun began its descent from the zenith.

The noise of motor cars was more persistent this Saturday afternoon as they came humming up the highway bringing week-enders. Bony recalled the previous Sunday, when the Chalet seemed filled to capacity with guests, and when the road traffic was astonishing. The fruit-stall man had predicted a fine day on the morrow, and that the traffic would then be extra-heavy.

Bony dozed for a little while, but he could not properly sleep because Leslie's enraged face would protrude into his consciousness, followed by the icy voice of Mr. Downes and his piercing eyes which had caused the artist to shut up like a man in a bar when his wife breaks in. Bony awakened long enough to change position in his chair, when he observed Fred still cutting the lawn, and was faintly irritated by the wireless in the lounge, a race description being given.

With eyes closed, he tried again to settle his mind, but this time it was Bagshott who persisted in intruding. He wondered how much of those stories about him were true, and decided he would confer with Miss Jade, who appeared to have a degree of nervousness of local gossip. Notwithstanding, there was the fact that Bagshott wore shoes size twelve, and that the imprints of a similar shoe were left on the ramp on the night Grumman was murdered, and all about Bisker's hut on the following night.

Today, Bagshott had not been wearing the same shoes as those which had made the impressions for the position of the trademarks on the rubber soles was not identical. Still, Bagshott would have to be examined.

It appeared to the lethargic Bonaparte that he had been a long time staying at Wideview Chalet. He had not visited Colonel Blythe now for five days, and the Colonel was bound to have at least one letter from Colonel Spendor demanding in hectic language what he, Bony, was supposed to be doing all this time.

Regarding that query, Bony was not worrying. A man had been murdered with cyanide poison in this very house. His personal effects contained in heavy steamer trunks and suit-cases had vanished. A local lad had "pinched" Grumman's priceless secrets, and only by the favour of Dame Fortune had those secrets come into Bony's possession. Well, after the excitement, there had followed this period of calm. It was strange how there were always periods of calm in an investigation, and how a period of calm inevitably gave place to another period of excitement and action. Crime is a most peculiar manifestation of human psychology. It never lies down for very long, especially the crime of homicide.

"I really cannot allow you to sleep any longer Mr. Bonaparte."

Bony opened first one eye, then the other. Then he was on his feet and smiling into Miss Jade's dark eyes.

"Madame, forgive me!" he said, mentally alert the instant he awoke. "That I should sleep in your presence is a crime. Has the roof fallen in?"

"No, but George has just fallen out—with the afternoon tea, and I thought I would have afternoon tea with you. May I?"

Bony gave the slightest bow, and his pleasure was expressed in his dancing blue eyes.

"There is nothing which would give me greater pleasure, Miss Jade," he told her with conviction in both eyes and voice.

George was waiting with his trolley just behind Miss Jade, and before she could direct him, he brought the twin of the chair Bony had been occupying, arranged the cushion with expert hands, and then hurried to bring a small table which he placed before them.

About the centre of the veranda, just back from the steps leading down to the path which bisected the lawn to the wicket gate, a group already at tea comprised the Watkins couple, Lee, Sleeman and Downes.

"You know, Miss Jade," Bony murmured. "Earlier this afternoon I found myself glad that the number of your guests is very small. Selfish of me. But I am doubly glad now. Had the number been large you would not have found the opportunity to honour me like this."

Miss Jade smiled, and when she smiled Bony liked her the more. Such a speech from another man might have sounded cynical and she would have been quick to detect it. From Bony it came easily and was natural and genuine.

"I could have had more guests, Mr. Bonaparte, but after what happened here, I felt it would be unfair to the staff to have a crowd. Just the few of us provide the staff with something to do, and the organisation is kept running. Next week we shall again be full up. I didn't wish to be surrounded by a lot of—er—rubber-necks, you understand."

"Quite. Rubber-necks with money are as objectionable as those without." Bony waved his disengaged hand to indicate the scene presented to them—Fred and his lawn mower in the foreground against the backdrop of valley and mountains now so coloured that better artists than Raymond Leslie had failed to reproduce them. "What a place to dwell in! You know, Miss Jade, you are a remarkably fortunate woman."

"Yes, I am," she admitted. "A few years ago, when I stood here amid trees and bracken and gazed through tree trunks across the valley to those mountains, I said: 'This is where I shall build my dream house.' Lo—it is built. I'm not old enough yet, however, to forget the days and the nights when my feet ached, and my back felt broken, when I first set up in a guest house. I had only one woman to help me, and I was cook, waitress and manageress all together."

"And the secret of success is—personality," stated Bony.

"The secret of success is—organisation," countered Miss Jade. "The study of details so that unnecessary labour is eliminated. Success is not dependent on the appearance of the hostess—it might be in a saloon bar."

Bony chuckled. "I stand reproved—or rather I sit reproved. How do you get along with the local people?"

Miss Jade's dark eyes opened a fraction.

"You have been talking to people—to local people?"

"I have been gossiping," he admitted. "I think I understand now the remark you made when I was imaginative enough to see us on a far-back station, when you called me Bony and I called you by your Christian name. I regret that I was the unwitting cause of the little unpleasantness at lunch, but I have read many of Bagshott's articles and really was interested to learn that he lived up here. It would appear that, in the minds of the persons I spoke to about him—as about any public person—that he's a thoroughly bad character. I wonder how much of it is gossip."

"What did they tell you?" Miss Jade asked, her eyes abruptly hard.

"Let me tabulate. One, that he was carrying on with a single girl for many years, for a child of eight or nine is said to be their son. Two, that Military Intelligence investigated him on suspicion that he was sending messages to Japan. Three, that he keeps his wife a prisoner and is likely at any moment to kill her and bury her in the garden. Four, that he was mixed up in a murder, or it might have been two or even three murders. And five, well, I can't remember number five. It couldn't have been so lurid as one to four inclusive or I would have remembered it."

"Are you being serious?" asked Miss Jade.

Bony nodded, saying: "Perfectly."

Miss Jade lay back in her chair and laughed. Her laughter caused the party above the steps to glance across at her. It reached Fred, who looked towards the veranda. He had completed the cutting of three quarters of the left-hand section of the lawn, and was working near the bottom fence. In that instant Bony heard someone give a shrill whistle at the far end of the house and beyond his vision and Fred stopped his work and raised both hands in vigorous acknowledgement. Then he went on with his work, and Miss Jade, who had apparently not heard the whistle or seen Fred's answering signal, said, with laughter still in her voice:

"For goodness sake, Mr. Bonaparte, don't go round asking people about me."

"Oh, indeed!" Bony exclaimed gravely. "Is your character worse than Mr. Bagshott's?"

"Probably at least as bad. One has to be more circumspect than when living in a suburb, you know. You needn't believe all that about Mr. Bagshott. Why, it's just silly. He's been living here for several years now. I've never heard such things from the nice people living about here. What is the matter?"

"I've just remembered the fifth item about Bagshott. It is said that he catches rabbits and domestic dogs and poisons them to watch them die so that he can put the effects of poisons into his books."

"Rubbish!" snapped Miss Jade, and for the first time Bony saw anger in her dark eyes. "I was once at a meeting when Mr. Bagshott spoke, and he gave me the impression that he doesn't mince his words, and is careless of the impression he makes. Temperamental! Well, so am I sometimes."

"I am always temperamental. Tell me, is Bagshott a sociable man?"

Miss Jade regarded Bony with eyes which were steady.

"I don't really know. He doesn't visit the people I know here."

"Have you ever seen him?"

"Only at that meeting I mentioned I attended."

"Forgive me. I forgot that reference." Bony turned from her to gaze out over the top of the stone balustrade and across the lawn. Fred was standing with his hands on his hips and staring up the slope of the lawn towards the house. "Yes," he went on, "as in all near-country districts, the gossips are really professionals. The bush people are so different, you know. They seem to have so many more important matters to think about, besides which they are so scattered and therefore warmly human. I wonder what that man is looking at so intently."

"He's wasting the time I'm paying him for," Miss Jade said, once again the controller of an efficiently run organisation. She rose and Bony rose with her. As they advanced to the balustrade, George started to leave the far corner of the veranda with his service trolley. Then Miss Jade exclaimed:

"Why, it looks like footprints on the grass!"

"It certainly does," agreed the interested Bony. "They begin here near the steps and they proceed parallel with the path right down to the gate, or where Fred has stopped with the mower. It's rather extraordinary."

Hearing George with the trolley collecting the tea things from their table, Bony turned and called softly to him, and the man, politely interested, came to stand a little behind Miss Jade.

"What do you make of those marks, George?" Bony asked.

"I—I don't know, sir," replied George. "They look—they look——"

"To me they look like a man's boot-marks," reiterated Bony. "See the way they are spaced here at this end. Are you ill, George?"

"No, sir. A slight headache, that's all."

The others gathered about them and George withdrew to collect the tea things from the table at which Miss Jade and Bony had been seated. Miss Jade pointed out the strange marks on her beautiful lawn. Everyone agreed that they looked just like a man's tracks.

"The grass appears to have been burned straw-white, as though someone had poured acid on it," remarked Downes.

"As though someone had walked down there in red-hot metal shoes," supplemented Sleeman. "Never seen anything like it before."

"Must be the Devil walking about," Downes said. "Now I wonder just how that happened."

Miss Jade spoke, and there was anger in her voice.

"Then why didn't he walk along the path, which is only three or four feet to the left? Perhaps that casual man knows something about it."

She was the first to leave the veranda, going down the steps to the path running parallel with the veranda, and then along the path going down to the wicket gate. The large Mrs. Watkins followed with her husband. After them went Sleeman and Lee. Downes sped a swift glance at George, and Bony looked that way, too, to observe the steward standing by the table, both hands holding the tea utensils, and looking outward over the lawn. Then Downes went down the steps and Bony followed him.

114

Chapter Seventeen

Bagshott in the News

"Fred, how do those marks come to be there?" asked Miss Jade, her eyes wide and blazing at the unfortunate man. Fred removed his ancient felt hat, sniffed, and regarded the marks with an expression on his face of profound misery. Then he looked again into the dark eyes still concentrated upon him.

"I don't know, marm," he said. "I've only just noticed 'em."

"Only just noticed them!" echoed Miss Jade. "Why, you have been cutting this section of the lawn all the afternoon. What d'you mean—you've only just noticed them?"

It was a difficult question to answer and Fred made no attempt. He gazed sadly down the slope at the marks laid upon the velvety green in almost a straight line. Then, as though relieved of great responsibility, he walked on down behind Bony, who was slowly moving away, his hands behind him, his head bent forward.

The marks of the boots or shoes were as distinct as though they had been made on soft sand. The size of the footwear which had made the marks was number twelve.

Each stamp of the boot or shoe was almost perfect, almost, but lacking in several important essentials. Such a mark made on sand would have revealed to Bony peculiarities such as areas of greatest pressure and the exact manner in which the person who had made the marks lifted his feet off the ground. Those peculiarities were the vital tell-tales. The grass was not able to reveal the vital peculiarities—it could only register the flat impression of the soles of the boots or shoes.

Arriving at the edge of the still-uncut portion of the lawn, Bony saw how he had come to miss seeing the marks when walking up the path before lunch. The uncut grass was approximately two inches in length and was lying at various angles from the perpendicular. The "burned" patches could be seen among this uncut grass, but not so clearly as when the grass was cut. Bony could see that the man whose feet had made the marks had gone on down the lawn to the bottom, and then had turned abruptly to reach the path just above the wicket gate.

Along the inside of the wire fence running above the top of the road bank there was left a strip of some four feet which had never been cut by a mower, and the grass along this strip was high, about nine or ten inches, and very rank and coarse.

Bony stood on the inside of the wicket gate and regarded the surface of the ramp leading down to the road. It was fairly soft. He saw his own foot-marks made this day. Those left when on his way from the house were overlaid by others, but those made on his return were undamaged right down to the road, indicating that he had been the last to come up the ramp to the gate. He saw the foot-tracks left by Mr. and Mrs. Watkins, by Fred, by Lee and Sleeman, and by people he did not know, and later he learned that the strangers to him had been four people who had called to visit the Watkins couple.

Miss Jade and her several guests were still standing in a group at the top side of the lawn. Fred was standing aimlessly beside his lawn mower. Downes was mid-way between Fred and himself, walking slowly beside the line of tracks. And slowly Bony began to walk to meet him.

"Mighty strange," observed Downes a moment later, when they both returned to the edge of the uncut portion of the lawn.

"Very," Bony agreed. "I don't understand it. Do you?"

Downes shook his head.

Bony sank to his knees to bring his eyes nearer one of the tracks. The grass was not burned, it was merely dead—quite dead, dead right down to the soil. All over the lawn the grass was growing thickly. Bony took a pen-knife from a pocket of his coat and with its point began to loosen the earth at the roots of the dead grass. Then, with his fingers, he teased upwards several roots, to find that near the surface they were also dead. Only down at a depth of an inch and a half did he discover living roots.

He rose to his feet and walked down to the uncut portion of lawn, and again went to his knees beside one of the tracks. Here he moved aside the slightly overhanging living grass, laying bare the dead herbage. A blade of this he picked, finding it exceedingly brittle but not to the degree that he could powder it between the palms of his hands. It had certainly not been burned with heat or with acid. It had merely died like ripe wheat stalks.

Plucking a handful of the dead grass, he rose to his feet and presented the grass for Downes's inspection. Downes took some of it, held it closer to his eyes and felt it with his fingertips.

"It doesn't look as though it had been burned by anything, does it?" he said in his cold and precise voice.

"No," Bony agreed. "It appears to have died quite naturally. Yet it cannot be a natural phenomenon for it to have died in areas like those which obviously are shaped like a man's boot soles. It lies outside my experience."

"And mine, too," Downes said, and dropping the grass he had taken from Bony's hand, he turned to walk up towards Miss Jade and those with her. Bony ostensibly tossed away the grass he had plucked, but he concealed a quantity which he thrust into a pocket.

Fred proceeded with the cutting. Several of the group at the same time asked for the answer to this riddle, and neither Bony nor Downes could supply it.

"It's the most remarkable thing I've ever seen," Sleeman burst out. "Must have been the Devil who rose straight up from Hell to take a walk on your lawn, Miss Jade. And what large feet, too!"

When he placed one of his own shoes over a mark there was a wide edging left all round it.

"What size do you take?" asked Downes.

"Seven," Sleeman replied. "Oh, I didn't make those marks. You can all see that."

"It's a *man's* foot-marks, isn't it?" shrilled Mrs. Watkins, and her husband assured her that it was.

"Wonder when it was done?" asked Lee, the squatter. "I've never seen the like of it. Why, a man having that size feet must be bigger than I am."

"Or a man smaller than you but having deformed feet or diseased feet," added Downes. He noticed George standing at the top of the veranda steps. "Just a moment, George!" he called.

The steward came down the steps to them. His face was as politely placid as always.

"Know anyone with feet as big as those?" Downes asked, pointing to the marks.

"No, sir, I don't," replied George, looking steadily at the questioner. He placed one of his shoes over a mark, and to Downes said: "I take a size seven."

"I'm curious to know when it was done, too," Downes said. "You being a countryman, Lee, ought to be able to tell us that."

"Yes, Mr. Lee, you should be able to give an estimate," Miss Jade added.

Lee looked a little uncomfortable.

"When was the lawn mowed last?" he asked.

"Let me think," pleaded Miss Jade. Then: "Yes, I remember. The last time it was cut was last Saturday week."

"Well, then, the marks weren't made before last Saturday week," Lee grinned. "Helpful, aren't I? What about you, Bonaparte? Can you give an opinion?"

"Lawns are outside my general knowledge," Bony said. "That at my place is of buffalo grass, and a steam roller would not injure it. I think that those marks have something to do with frost."

That brought further questions, but Bony evaded giving a plain answer to any of them. He had evolved a theory which might explain how those footprints came to be so ineradicably imprinted on Miss Jade's lawn, and he was strongly inclined to the belief that they were made on the night that Grumman was murdered.

Of momentary interest was the reaction displayed by Dowries, Miss Jade and the steward. Subtract the natural annoyance in anyone owning a well-kept lawn, and still Miss Jade's anger appeared to be unnecessary. Bony thought that perhaps her anger was assumed to hide another emotion, or it might be to conceal an expression of knowledge, say the knowledge that the marks had been made by the feet of Clarence B. Bagshott. It would certainly be a remarkable coincidence if there were two men living on Mount Chalmers who wore boots or shoes size twelve.

The interest displayed by Dowries might well be based on the type of mind called scientific. He wondered what Downes was, where he came from, and he determined to ask Bolt to establish all that could be established about him.

As for George, well, George had become somewhat of a mystery. On first seeing the marks, the man had suddenly stuttered and looked ill. He had explained that he had a slight headache, but he had not shown any indisposition when he arranged the chair for Miss Jade and the table.

And now, dash it! further to complicate the matter, Fred was actually almost running to and fro across the lawn with his mower and was whistling: "The Campbells Are Coming." And that followed the scolding he had had from his employer.

After dinner, Bony announced to those in the lounge that he was going for a walk, and he passed out from the lounge through the reception hall and the front entrance, and then walked down the drive, humming a tune. Arrived at the open gates, he returned up the drive, keeping off the gravelled surface and under the bordering trees. Before coming to the open space at the front entrance, he veered towards Bisker's hut, passing that at its rear, and noting that the interior was in darkness. In this way he came to the rear of the garages and eventually to the open gateway leading to the top road.

To avoid sound, he walked along the edge of this road down to its junction with the highway. Then he continued up along the highway past the junction of that road at the bottom of which Fred lived and opposite which was the fruit shop where he had called earlier in the day.

Presently he came to the service garage and the Police Station. Here there was an electric road-light, but there was no way of avoiding anyone seeing him enter the Police Station. In the office, he found Sub-Inspector Mason, and Mason jumped to his feet and welcomed him with a smile.

"How's the world treating you?" asked Mason.

"Fairly easy. And you?"

"Fairly hard," replied Mason, "Chair?"

"Thank you. Kindly shut the door and lock it. Any of your men about? ... Good! Ask him to lounge about the front gate while I'm with you."

On returning, Mason found Bony occupied in making several of his cigarettes.

"Now, what's the latest?" Bony asked.

"Nothing of much importance, I'm sorry to say. I was wondering how to contact you, though, because I have a letter for you from Headquarters. Here it is."

Bony ripped open the envelope, to find enclosed a note from Superintendent Bolt, saying that a plaster head had been made from the photographs of Marcus in the possession of the Victorian Police. They had been assisted in this work by a Professor of anthropology who had stated that the result, whilst not completely accurate in measurements, was sufficient to give a picture of the head of the photographed man which could be added to other data confirming identification. When the photos arrived from London, they would be checked with the bust and alterations, if necessary, made.

Bony passed Bolt's letter across the desk to Mason, and smoked whilst the Sub-Inspector read it.

"How has the search gone up here?" he asked. Mason pursed his lips.

"We've made a thorough job of it, I think," he replied. "We have gone into everyone living up here permanently, and have examined all the persons renting furnished houses. We found a sly-grog joint, four gambling joints, and a man wanted for theft, but not a trace of friend Marcus."

"H'm! Disappointing! You have a neighbour named Bagshott. Know anything of him?"

"Plenty," Mason answered, smiling broadly. "Read all his books, know all about him from a cousin over in W.A. in the C.I.B. in Perth. Called on him three days ago to get him to sign a paper. He's a Justice. When I mentioned the cousin whom he knows very well, he called for afternoon tea. I was in a hurry, and he said if I didn't stay and meet his wife he'd read the Riot Act."

"Notice his feet?" Bony asked.

"Not particularly. Why?"

"You should always notice people's feet—particularly, Mason. They tell more about the character of a man than does his face. Then, again, people cannot get around without their feet. Some people's feet even scorch a perfectly green and virile grass lawn."

"How so?"

"Take pen and paper and write a few notes whilst I describe what has happened on the lawn at Wideview Chalet." When he had described the foot-marks, and Mason had jotted down memoranda, Bony went on: "I have a theory about those marks, but as it is merely a theory please keep it to yourself. Your notes on the marks I want you to present to one of the City Park curators and obtain his opinion of their cause. It might be necessary to obtain the opinion of two such men. You remember that the body of Grumman was dressed in pyjamas under a dressing gown, and that it was evident that the body had been laid in that ditch and an attempt made to conceal it. It is my theory that the marks on the lawn were made by the feet of the man who carried Grumman's dead body from his room down to the ditch, and that the double weight on grass made excessively brittle by the severe frost that night, followed by a very rapid thaw just at sunrise, so crushed the grass stems and the surface roots that life became extinct. If that is so, then those boot-marks were made by Grumman's murderer. And I am beginning to think Grumman's murderer is Clarence B. Bagshott."

"Eh!" exclaimed Mason.

"Bagshott wears a size-twelve shoe," stated Bony. "And the size of the shoe which burned its outline on Miss Jade's lawn is number twelve. You will admit that so large a foot is rare. Remember, however, that I said I am beginning to think, not that I do think, that Grumman's murderer is Clarence B. Bagshott. I have to check up on Bagshott's tracks against others I have observed in the grounds of the Chalet. So you see the importance of obtaining expert opinion how those marks came to be made on the lawn."

Mason leaned back in his chair and regarded Bony with raised brows.

"Well, that's strange. We live and learn, don't we?" he said slowly.

"We are always learning, Mason, those of us who are intelligent. There is something else I want done. I am not quite satisfied with what Bolt has concerning Miss Jade and the steward, George. Without doubt the information about themselves given to you people will have been checked over, but I suggest a re-check. Then there are two guests who interest me. One is an artist fellow named Leslie. He's been living up here for some time, and he knows the district in and out. Get me all you are able about him, in addition to that obtained from him the day Grumman's body was found. The day following Grumman's murder four new guests arrived at the Chalet. Note their names, please." Mason did so at Bony's dictation. "Of these four, Downes appears to be the least frank about himself. Lee may be more clever than he appears. The Watkins couple talk ever-lastingly about their travels, but that weakness may be assumed. Oh, by the way! Give me an envelope."

From his pocket Bony took the quantity of dead grass taken from Miss Jade's lawn and placed it in the envelope provided by Mason.

"The curator might like to examine this grass, as it was taken from one of the boot-marks," he explained. "Tell the Super I'd like him to send the bust of Marcus's head up here for me to see. Also tell him that I am thoroughly enjoying the restful holiday and do not wish to be disturbed. Can I use your telephone?"

"Certainly."

Bony called for Windsor 0101. He had to wait three minutes before contacting Colonel Blythe. Then Mason heard him say:

"Evening, Colonel! This is Mr. Boniski Spiffoski speaking... . Yes, the Russian-iski investigatoriski. Didn't you know? ... I beg your pardon! ... Oh! Colonel Spendor is annoyed about something—especially about me. Yes. You tell him I'll be back one day soon. I am having a wonderful holiday. I thought you'd like to know that and to hear my sweet voice. Now please don't worry about Colonel Spendor... . Yes, I know You apply to your wife. She knows how to calm down the old boy... . A plane! ... But I am not returning to Brisbane by plane. No, I am going back via Wanaaring. Yes, by car. I'm going to have a month on the beer with a friend of mine—I hope. Good night!"

Chapter Eighteen

Fungi and Swordfish

The following day, being Sunday, the traffic on the highway was heavy all the morning, and particularly so after two o'clock in the afternoon. It was a day which was to be remembered by Bony for a long time.

Firstly, a frost fell and whitened all the open places. Miss Jade's lawn was whitened but not the shrubs growing here and there on it and this latter fact recalled to Bony's mind that Bisker had said that the shrubs were covered with frost on the early morning when Grumman's body had been found. Since that morning there had been no frosts.

The valley was hidden beneath a thick, still fog, a fog declared later by the weather man as being at least a thousand feet in depth. When Bony stepped out upon the veranda of Wideview Chalet, the sun was well above the range of distant mountains, and the scene held him spell-bound.

Over the valley floor the fog-clouds were massed into an unbroken pseudo ice-pack. Above the ice, far to the north-west, was an island, the top of Mount Macedon, Eastward of it, jutting in to the ice-pack, lay a giant's finger joined to a long arm of Mount St. Leonard. From Mount St. Leonard, the range swept in a great arc round to the Baw-Baws, a blue coast beneath a low-angled sun which had painted out all its minor features with a broad brush of indigo. The ice field appeared to come within a stone-toss of Miss Jade's front fence. Its surface was varied in shape but uniform in its brilliant white. Far away to the south there sailed as though upon its surface huge icebergs which accepted the light of the sun in a glory of shimmering daffodil-yellow. Over upon the far coast the ice-pack was curled like curling white waves about to break upon the rock-armoured land. A square mile of it lay as flat as damask cloth. Yet another square mile of it was rumpled like the train of a bridal dress.

Where Bony stood the sunlight was warm. No current of air disturbed one leaf of the nearby trees. As though from the sky above, not from beneath the ice-flow, the hoot of a train cried its pitiful blindness.

Two hours later, the southern bergs were melting as though they floated in a sea of warm milk, and the waves curling upon the coast of the distant mountains had become gigantic. Seeming vast upheavals were tossing the ice-flow into hillocks and miniature mountains, and the flow itself was sliding past the Chalet, sliding away over the City of Melbourne and into the Bay. There came a wind which lifted stupendous masses of ice into towering ramparts, and which dug enormous and dreadful chasms into an ink-black darkness.

Eventually the valley, fields and paddocks and the forest areas came up out of the chasms to meet the sun and lie spread before Bony's enchanted eyes.

The only jarring note was the voice of Mrs. Watkins constantly repeating the phrase: "Oh, how lovely!"

The second event which made this a memorable day for Bonaparte occurred in the afternoon when, having decided he would take a walk up the highway, he arrived outside the rear portion of the garden belonging to Clarence B. Bagshott. This rear portion was not bounded by a hedge, and just over the fence the mystery-story writer himself was trenching a plot of ground.

Bony leaned against an iron fence post and rested his arms along the topmost barbed wire. A little to the left was the gateway to Bagshott's garage. Before him, and beyond Bagshott, were the two wireless masts, the subject of the conjecture that the owner had been in touch with Japan. Then Bagshott plunged his spade into the firm earth and stooped to poke at something with a stick, and this action so aroused the curiosity of the watching Bonaparte that he called out:

"What have you found?" Bagshott turned towards Bony.

"Hop over the fence and come and see," he shouted.

It was not an easy fence to "hop over," but Bony managed it without damage to his clothes and joined Bagshott, to see him turning over with the stick what appeared to be an undersized soft-shelled egg.

"Ever seen one of these before?" the author asked without looking up.

"No. What is it?"

"The naturalist gentry call it the *Clathrus Gracilis,* but ordinary people name it the net fungus. When this thing, looking like a small egg, 'hatches' or ruptures there is expelled a net which unravels large enough to cover a tennis ball and at the same time disperses its spores. I've never seen one 'hatching,' but I'm hoping. I found a net a few minutes ago. Let's try and find it. Over here."

Bagshott strode across his land, followed by the smaller man whose interest in life included all things. Bony noted in a detached manner how Bagshott lifted his feet in the over-large shoes he was wearing. They were old shoes from which the gloss had long since been removed by the rough usage they had undergone. However, the subjects of tracks and homicide were now being swiftly swept into a mental cupboard to give room for this new interest which was claiming both their minds.

"Ah—here it is!"

Bagshott halted and stooped and Bony stooped with him. He saw a delicate net-like object which would cover a tennis ball. It was springy and stained with dull browns and a dull green. No strand of the net was broken.

"I understand that there are considerably over fifty thousand species of fungi," remarked Bony, taking up the specimen in his hands. "I've never seen this kind before. Rather wonderful, isn't it?"

"Yes." Bagshott was regarding the fungus lying in Bony's hands. "Don't know much about 'em myself," he went on.

"There are some fine specimens of 'Shelf' or 'Saddle' fungi to be found growing on the underside of fallen trees down in the gullies about here. Got one or two in the house. They keep well. But this basket one beats the band. You wouldn't think that all that network could have come from so small a container, would you? I understand that when it springs out from the shell it sheds its spores and then swells through its power to absorb moisture."

"There must be many wonderful things up on this mountain," Bony said, and found Bagshott's hazel eyes regarding him. "It is a charming place. I looked at the fog lying in the valley this morning for almost two hours. Never thought there was such a place in Australia. You know, you're very lucky to be able to live here. Interested in natural history and that kind of thing?"

"Yes—superficially. There are many strange things even in this garden. Sometimes I dig up a yabbie. You wouldn't think to find them so far above the nearest gully stream, and they are almost white. You want to take a walk well off the road at night and listen to the earth-worms. They make a sucking noise, like water going down a bath outlet. They're yards in length, too. Come on in. I'll show you that Shelf fungi."

Bony was taken out of this part of Bagshott's garden which was devoted to the cultivation of vegetables and raspberries, conducted through an arch in the dividing hedge and into the garden surrounding the house, where ornamental trees and flowering shrubs inhabited a secluded world. His eyes were busy with the surface of the paths, too. Everywhere he saw the imprints of Bagshott's shoes, and not only of those shoes the man was then wearing. All these imprints had the same peculiarities, revealing the maker of them to be mentally energetic, slightly neurotic, and longer in the right leg than the left.

Having wandered through city botanical gardens and having seen many gardens laid out with unnatural orderliness, this garden was a new experience to Bonaparte. Here and there he saw foreshortened vistas in which things appeared to grow just as Nature placed them, and he thought that the sacrifice of the view was worth it. Bagshott was saying in reply to a remark Bony had made:

"Yes, beautiful district. But like everything else, the human animal comes to appreciate beauty less as he becomes more familiar with it. There are days when I pine for an inland gibber plain, and want to have to strain my eyes to see the distant horizon. I'd give all this for the outback. A man can become too respectable." He chuckled and glanced back at Bony. "Sometimes I find respectability very wearing. One of these days I am going to break out."

"You lived for many years, didn't you, outback?"

"About twenty," replied Bagshott. "Got around a bit too."

"And are you really determined to have a month at Wanaaring?"

"Too right I am," replied Bagshott forcibly. "Been out of the bush for ten years now. Haven't had a holiday since before the war, and I'm becoming dyspeptic, mentally unbalanced and affected by advanced senile decay. So would you be, too, if you lived in a place like this for long. Come on in."

Bony was taken into a small room furnished with a writing desk, a lounge, stiff-backed chairs and book-cases crowded with volumes. On the walls hung framed original drawings of illustrations of the man's stories. There hung also the skin of what appeared to be an enormous snake.

"What d'you think of that?" Bagshott asked on observing Bony regarding it. "Nice specimen, eh? Shot it myself. See the shot-mark? Measured twenty-three feet in length."

It was beautifully marked with green lines branching outward from a central grey ribbon, all on a ground of dull brown, and Bony was wholly taken in.

"That," said Bagshott, "that is a piece of bark from a mountain-ash gum. Remarkable likeness to a snake's skin, isn't it?"

Bony had to finger the bark before he could accept the reality.

"Well, now, sit down and behave yourself," Bagshott commanded, and waved his visitor into a chair.

Bony was startled, being unaware that he was misbehaving, and then his eyes gleamed with humour, for his host meant nothing more than to put him at ease. He was shown the specimen of the Shelf fungi, which had been lightly varnished and was as hard as stone and appeared to be indestructible. He was holding it in his hands when his host vanished.

Left alone without explanation, Bony gazed round the room in which mystery stories were concocted. It was very masculine, and comfortable though small, and it looked out upon ornamental trees backed by the tall hedge that banished the highway to the far end of the world. Quite by accident, he espied on the mantel above the great open fireplace an exceptionally large fish-hook.

He was fingering this hook when Bagshott came in. His mind was hundreds of miles away. He was seated in the stern of a launch, with his electrified hands poised above the great reel attached to the rod, through the guides of which hundreds of feet of stout cord were being swept away into the dancing sea by the great fish which had taken his bait. And then when his mind clicked back to the present he looked up to see Bagshott regarding him with a strange expression.

"If you ever want to be really and properly alive," he said, "go and angle for swordfish."

"I have been really and properly alive," averred Bony.

"You have! Where?"

"Off Bermagui. Have you been there?"

"Too blinking right!" Bagshott almost shouted, his eyes alight and in them strange fires. "Come here."

Bony was practically hauled from his chair and dragged out of the room into another, where mounted on a plaque was the head of a marlin. Bony stood in the centre of the room, looking upward at the gleaming sea-green-and-blue specimen of the greatest fighting fish in all the oceans. Bagshott was talking game fish, but what he said did not register in Bony's mind, for Bony's brain had become a torch set on fire by the head and sword of the fish and by the huge hook he still carried in his hands. He could smell the sea. He could feel the tautness of every nerve whilst waiting for the moment to strike. A million pictures passed before the eyes of his inner mind, and he lived again through the greatest moments of his life.

Then he and Bagshott were asking questions of each other and not waiting for the answers. Mrs. Bagshott came in and her husband did not give him time to acknowledge the conventional introduction. She had accompanied her husband on his fishing expeditions, and she knew the background equally with him and this stranger to her house.

For five minutes all talked at the same time, Bony being shown photographs of fish and sea-scenes, and views of the coast which he readily recognised and which brought out of the store of memory incidents of his own experiences. Then he was being rushed by the volcanic Bagshott back into his study, where on the desk Mrs. Bagshott had set a tray of tea and cakes. His hostess was valiantly trying to ascertain if he took sugar or not, milk or not, and he being badgered by questions by his host concerning big game angling, so that he began to lose the sense of knowing whether he were on his head or toes.

Yet he thoroughly enjoyed it, and Mrs. Bagshott did not appear at all fearful of being buried in the garden, although it is wonderful what mountains are removed by faith—and/or arsenic. He left them standing at their garage gate, and began his walk back to the Chalet, his mind a little chaotic with the admixture of Net and Shelf fungi, swordfish, snake-skin cum tree bark, and the impressions left on earth by a pair of large shoes.

He was halfway clown the road to the guest house when Mason met him, Mason returning from the city in his car. Without getting out, the Sub-Inspector told him that he had the bust of Marcus, and Bony wanted to take and kick the bust of Marcus to pieces. Mason had other information, and Bony agreed to call back at the Police Station later that evening. Bony told him he had been calling on Bagshott, and Mason asked if he was considering the fellow's arrest.

"Arrest!" echoed Bony. "Arrest—nothing! Why, I'm going swordfishing with Bagshott and his wife." And he left Mason looking after him from the car door, on his face an expression of blank bewilderment.

Chapter Nineteen

Bony Entertains

The barometer hanging on the wall of the reception hall at Wideview Chalet began to fall at about four o'clock, and when Bony arrived back from his visit to the Bagshotts' the sky was festooned with white streamers heralding wind and rain.

He found Sleeman and the artist in the lounge and was invited to join them in a drink, and thereupon he stipulated one round only, knowing that he had work to do at the Police Station before he retired to bed that night.

To his surprise, Alice, the maid, brought the order, and when she was questioned about the absence of George she explained that George had received a telephone call from the city. He had obtained leave of absence for the rest of the day and would not be back until the coming of the first bus from Manton the following morning. As she presented the serving tray to Sleeman, he placed the tip of a finger on the back of her hand and said:

"You see to it that the scullery door is kept closed tonight, Alice. We don't want any more nerve shocks like that one you gave us the other night. All that fuss over a rat."

The girl flushed.

"I hate rats," she said. "They make me shiver all over. I don't mind snakes. I've killed several upon my dad's place, but rats I abominate, sir. Thank you, sir."

Having received back the chit-book signed by Sleeman, Alice tripped away through the service door, and Raymond Leslie began a story which did not greatly interest Bonaparte, who was glad to get away after forcing a smile at the tale's climax. At dinner, he found Downes absent and, remarking on this, he was informed that Downes had had visitors that afternoon and had gone off with them. Bony was also informed that the Watkins couple had left. Thereupon, observing Miss Jade seating herself at her solitary table, he arose and crossed the almost forlorn dining room and bowed to her.

"Madam, I seek your favour," he said softly.

Miss Jade gazed upward into the beaming eyes and decided that he was not being cynical or trying to be funny. With his left hand, he indicated the table at which sat only three men.

"If you would take dinner at our table, Miss Jade," he said, "we would be honoured, and I feel sure that we would at least attempt to talk interestingly."

Miss Jade rose to her feet.

"It is most kind of you, Mr. Bonaparte," she said in the tone of voice she always used with her guests. "I would be delighted. Tomorrow we have quite an influx of guests, and the place will no longer seem deserted."

"That is bad news," Bony said gravely. "A houseful of guests will distract your mind from us fortunate men here this evening." They crossed to the one guest table in use and Bony said, grandly: "Gentlemen, Miss Jade had done us the great honour of consenting to dine with us. I have promised that we will talk intelligently."

"We'll do our best in that respect," Lee, the squatter, boomed, placing the chair for Miss Jade.

That dinner, with Miss Jade as a member of his table, was the third item of that day which Bony was to remember for many a year. Miss Jade's presence was a stimulant to them all, and they were a stimulant to her. She was vivid, and a good foil to the artist and to Bonaparte.

A few minutes after half-past eight Bony entered the Mount Chalmers Police Station, and there to his surprise he found Superintendent Bolt with Mason. At his entry into the office, Mason slipped outside to close the front door. Bolt, observing Bony's dinner clothes, said:

"There's no doubt that some fellers strike lucky patches in life. Lolling around all day, and eating and swilling at the taxpayers' expense when ordinary men like me and Mason have to work for a crust."

"It's a crying shame, Super," Bony lamented. "But tell me the reason for your tour this evening in a flash car run at the taxpayers' expense."

"Just came along to see you, Bony," rumbled the huge man. "Friend of yours rang me to ask if I would call on you just to make sure you haven't gone batty. Seems to think the old mind's got off the rails."

"Really!"

Bolt nodded and pushed across the foolscap envelope.

"From Colonel Blythe," he explained. "The Colonel said there's an enclosure from your Chief Commissioner to himself, and that I was to be sure that you read it. Seems to think that too much luxury is affecting your brain, and advises you to take the hint given by your Chief Commissioner and go home."

Bony lifted his gaze from his task of rolling a cigarette. There was no answering smile on his face. He said, slowly:

"There are times when my Chief, and others whom I will not name, causes me intense weariness. It is my Chief's paramount failing to assign me to a case and then impatiently demand instant results. He lent me to Colonel Blythe, and almost immediately demanded my return. I'd not like to think where I would have got in my career if I had ever taken the slightest notice of him. Now then, let us to work—business before pleasure. Have you any developments to announce?"

Superintendent Bolt sighed and shook his head.

"Marcus has slipped us," he admitted. "And none of Grumman's luggage has come to light, nary a single item of it. I'm getting a bit worried at the nix results, and our Commissioner is a bit like yours in the expectation of results. What d'you know?"

"That patience always wins the game," Bony replied. "Have you done anything in re-checking up on those people I named to Mason?"

"Yes." Bolt took a notebook from a pocket and from it abstracted several flimsies.

"The woman, Eleanor Jade, is all correct so far as background goes. She began in a small way, and worked up. There's nothing whatever against her, and when she applied for her drink licence she was supported by the police in her application. Everything is plain and straight-forward. The same can't be said about the drinks steward, George Banks. He told us that he'd been in Miss Jade's employ for over three months, and that prior to being engaged by Miss Jade he had been working at various hotels following discharge from the Air Force. Now he did work at several hotels during the periods stated in the references he showed to us, but when we described him to the licensees who had written the references, not one could recognise him. Banks is dark and pale of face and of medium weight but the man recalled by the reference-writers all agree that the George Banks employed by them was six feet tall, thin, fair-haired and grey-eyed. We think that George Banks is not that steward's name, and that he pinched or borrowed the references. The real George Banks hasn't been traced so far. I haven't had the Chalet steward hauled over the coals, remembering our agreement about spheres of activity."

"Thank you, Super. What about the guests?"

"Well, your artist pal, Raymond Leslie, is clear enough," Bolt went on. "Very well known in his line and the double check failed to shoot holes in his statement. Your other pal, Wilfred Dowries, wasn't staying at Wideview the night of Grumman's murder. I sent a man to make a few enquiries from Miss Jade while you all were having lunch. Miss Jade stated that to the best of her knowledge Downes is just a gentleman of leisure. Away back in 1937 he stayed at her guest house at St. Kilda, stayed with her for about six weeks. He rang her on the 'phone during the evening of that day Grumman was found dead, and then stated he had learned of her new venture up here and asked if he could be given accommodation. That's all we know so far about him. We haven't completed the check on Lee and the Watkins people."

Bony looked steadily at the big man, pinching his nether lip between forefinger and thumb.

"Thanks, Super," he said. "Now, Mason, what did you get from the curators?"

"Chiefly support for your own theory," answered the Sub-Inspector. "The mixture of grass put down in that lawn is quite suitable for the locality. The two experts I interviewed both agree that the marks were caused by abnormal weight when the grass was stiffly brittle with frost. The abnormal weight crushed the grass stems and the surface roots, and then the action of the sunlight during the subsequent sharp thaw burned the bruised grass, which was not able to withstand the effect of frost as the uninjured grass did."

"What's the strength of all these Devil's foot-marks?" interposed Bolt. "Mason told me what you told him, but what's it all about?"

"Well, you see, it turned out like this," Bony began in explanation. "That night Grumman was poisoned, his body was carried from his room down over the lawn to the wicket gate at the bottom and then to the road and into the ditch where it was found. Grumman's weight was eleven stone and some odd pounds. If the weight of the man who transported the body to the ditch was ten stone, there was a combined weight of more than twenty-one stone, or three hundred pounds, or a little more than two and one half hundred-weights, concentrated into the area of a man's shoe sole. When the killer of Grumman walked down that lawn with the body, he left shoe-tracks as plain as though he had walked on sand, the tracks branded upon the grass as though the shoes were red hot."

"Ah!" Bolt breathed. "And you are an expert on tracks, aren't you?"

"I have done a little," Bony modestly admitted.

"Then you know the size of the shoes, eh?"

"Oh, yes! They are size twelve."

"Size twelve! Same boots, or shoes, you saw on the ramp that night Grumman was corpsed."

"I know the man whose shoes most likely made those marks."

"Eh!" exclaimed Bolt. "You know the man who made those foot-marks?"

"Pardon me, but I did not say that. I said that I know the man whose shoes most likely had made those marks."

Two pairs of eyes bored into Bony's eyes. Bony fell silent.

"Well, go on, man!" urged the Superintendent. "Who is he?"

"It would be unfair of me to state the name of the man whose shoes most likely made the marks on Miss Jade's lawn," Bony told them firmly. "When I know the name of the man whose feet were in the shoes belonging to the man who most likely owns the shoes, I shall suggest that you order his apprehension."

"Then you think that the shoes which made the marks had been stolen and used for the occasion?" enquired Bolt.

"That may have been possible. I am not sure of anything. Tomorrow, Mason, I'd be obliged if you called on the Bagshotts and told them that a man alleging himself to be a collector of clothes and foot-wear for the war victims of Europe has been operating in the district. He is known to be a person of ill repute, and the police would like to know if he called on the Bagshotts and if they gave him any old clothes and shoes. Will you do that?"

"Certainly."

"Why put that over on the Bagshotts?" demanded Bolt.

"Because the imprints on Miss Jade's lawn were made by shoes or boots size twelve, and because Bagshott wears shoes of that size."

"O—oh!" breathed the Superintendent.

"My contention is that because a man's shoes have made certain imprints it doesn't follow that that man's feet were inside the shoes when the imprints were made by them."

"And you have reason to think that Bagshott's feet weren't in his shoes when his shoes made the marks on Miss Jade's lawn?"

"That, Super, sums up the situation. Now, let me have a few minutes with the bust of our dear friend Marcus."

Mason went to work unpacking a common butter box.

"Professor Phisgig insists that the result is only a rough approximation," Bolt pointed out. "The face is a remarkable likeness to the photographs; it's the shape of the head which the Professor insists is not accurate."

Mason placed on the table a plaster bust. It was the normal size of a man's head. It might well have been a copy of a piece of Grecian sculpture. The features possessed classical symmetry.

Bony gazed at it for a full minute. For almost that period he looked at it in profile, and then for three minutes he gazed at the back of the head. Eventually he placed it on the floor and looked at it from the back and from a higher level. Bolt stolidly smoked. Mason did nothing but stare at the bust, saying nothing.

"If Lombroso were living today and could study that head, and then was asked to outline the character of the original, he would say that Marcus was the good boy of an upper-middle-class family," Bony observed.

"Instead of which he is the bad boy of an aristocratic family," Bolt contributed. "The Italian criminologist was a bit out—here and there."

"I agree with him, however, that genius is a form of degeneracy," argued Bony. "Further than that I will not accompany him. However, there are exceptions to every rule, and the rule is that evil within the mind is stamped upon the features. Marcus is an exception. By the way, do I remember correctly from your records of Marcus that he was known to be in Victoria in 1937?"

"Yes. He killed a man named Langdon in June of that year."

"And he was not apprehended?"

Bolt shook his head. Bony rose to his feet.

"I'll be getting along," he said. "Thanks, gentlemen and comrades, for your co-operation. I have an intuition that Marcus is not as far away from us as the facts and assumptions indicate."

Chapter Twenty

Shadows Against the Sky

It was fifteen minutes to ten when Bony again entered the lounge at Wideview Chalet, finding it occupied by Sleeman, Downes and Lee. Sleeman was asleep, Lee was reading, and Downes was seated at a table writing letters. The last named said:

"Blowing up for rain, d'you think?"

"Looks much like it," replied Bony. "Wind's in the north and the only stars are those to the east. Won't get that fog-cloud over the valley tomorrow. Worth looking at, wasn't it?"

"Yes, very fine. Care about a drink?"

Sleeman roused sufficiently to mumble something, and Downes regarded him with faint contempt. Bony shook his head, smiled, picked up a magazine and settled into a chair. Downes went on with his writing.

Miss Jade did not appear, and Bony wondered where she was, as the office was in darkness when he passed through the reception hall. Presently Lee rose and came to sit beside him. The big man moved with a minimum of effort.

"How's your place off for rain?" he said, opening the conversation.

Mr. Bonaparte, passing as the squatter whose station was in Western Queensland, was able to answer the question with a fair degree of accuracy, having studied the weather reports over the last six months just in case.

"We had a good rain at the end of July, and another in the third week of August," he said. "The stock are fair-conditioned. I suppose you would like to have more rain on your place."

They discussed pastoral problems and conditions until Downes pocketed his letters and joined them.

"What about a drink—before Sleeman wakes up?" he suggested. "I'd like just one as a night-cap."

"I'll be with you," Lee agreed.

"So will I, but I insist that it's my call, and like you, one will be sufficient," added Bony.

Lee, however, voiced a protest. Downes regarded him with his steady eyes, on his face a cold smile.

"If you really want to indulge in an orgy," he murmured, "I offer the suggestion that after Bonaparte and I have had our little night-cap with you, you might awaken Sleeman. Still, as Bonaparte has insisted that it is his call, and as I broached the subject, we will make it two drinks with my call added."

"Make it three for peace sake," pleaded Lee.

"My dear fellow, I have been magnanimous by declaring the limit at two," countered Downes in such tones that Lee offered no further argument.

Downes crossed to the bell push, summoning the steward, and Alice entered the lounge with her tray.

"What is that place actually like—you know, that place you were telling us about last night where Sleeman wanted to go round on his hands and knees with Bagshott, the author?" asked Downes of Bony.

"Wanaaring!" Bony smiled broadly. "Well, like the majority of outback townships, Wanaaring has fallen sadly from its state of affluence back in the days of old. Why Bagshott should have chosen Wanaaring, I don't know. Many roads converge upon Wanaaring, which is a centre for surrounding pastoral properties. And, of course, station people and station hands all have a thirst to quench when they visit the township."

"How would Bagshott get there—if he did go?" pressed Dowries.

"By car he would go to Mildura, then up the Darling River to Wilcannia and from Wilcannia to the northwest via Momba and several other stations, the names of which I forget."

"Hum!" murmured Downes. "You know, that jaunt is becoming slightly attractive. I've never been up in the real bush. I've got a good mind to buy a car and go and see it. Bagshott writes fairly clearly about it."

The subject held them until Sleeman awoke, when Downes and Bony rose with the intention of retiring to their rooms. They left Lee with Sleeman, and Sleeman was pushing the bell for Alice. They said good night to each other outside their rooms, Downes occupying a room farther along the passage. It was then five minutes to eleven.

At a quarter past eleven, Bony switched off his light and sat in his chair. He waited there for some fifteen minutes, and then soundlessly eased up a window and climbed over the sill into the dark night. He had discarded his evening clothes and instead of the white shirt and collar he wore a blue woollen scarf. Instead of dress shoes, he wore black canvas tennis shoes.

He had no set purpose in leaving the house this early and by his bedroom window, although he did have a purpose which he intended executing much later.

Bisker's rough plan of the house and outbuildings had been most thoroughly done, and by now Bony had memorised all its details. With the main bedrooms and public rooms, of course, he was already familiar, and only a little less so with the staff's sleeping quarters, the store-rooms, and the purpose for which every outbuilding was used.

Having climbed through his bedroom window, he found himself in a left angle of the main building, the angle formed by the bedrooms occupied by the staff—the wine-store, the pantry and the linen room occupying the apex of the angle.

There were no lights in any of the guest rooms on that, the upper side of the building, but there was a light in the cook's room which was at the far end of the staff's quarters. In the darkness he was invisible, for there were low clouds on the mountain. He moved round the end of the staff's quarters and so came to Bisker's wood-stack containing something like a hundred tons. Passing behind this, he then crossed the roadway leading out through that gate by which Constable Rice had come down from the Police Station. After crossing this roadway, he skirted the rear of the several garages until he came to the rear of Bisker's hut.

There was no light from within. Softly he opened the door, when Bisker's presence was instantly betrayed by his snoring. As quietly, he closed the door. With the blind down, the interior of the hut was several degrees darker than the dark night without, but without difficulty, he crossed to the bed, found the wooden case upon which were the alarm clock, the two pipes, tobacco and knife and matches, the corkscrew and the hurricane lamp. He reached for and found Bisker's shoulder beneath blankets, and gently and persistently patted it until the man awoke.

"It's me, Bonaparte! Don't speak loudly," he whispered, and Bisker, having begun to demand who it was, obeyed.

"Wot's up! Doings?" he asked.

"No, everything is all right. I want to talk to you for a little while. Won't keep you long. When did George leave?"

"He went on the half-past three bus. Promised he'd come back tomorrow morning."

"Did he tell you why he wanted to go?"

"Yes," replied Bisker. "Said he wanted to meet a cobber off a ship wot's in port only three days."

"Did you see him leave?"

"Yes."

"How was he dressed?"

"Pretty flash. Trilby 'at, navy-blue double-breaster suit and all."

"Were you close to him at any time?"

"Close as I am to you right now. Why?"

"Did his clothes smell of moth repellent?"

"Can't say as 'ow I noticed it," Bisker replied.

"All right! We'll leave that. Have you ever been inside the wine-store?"

"Yes, plenty of times, carrying in cased liquor, and sometimes taking out empties."

Further questioning informed Bony that the wine-store was fairly large, in area about twenty by ten feet. It had once been used as a bar, but the practice of allowing guests to drink there had been stopped twelve months before. The stocks of wines, spirits and beer, according to Bisker, were always maintained at a high level. And the door was fitted with a Yale lock, whilst on the inside of the window there were thick iron bars.

"George has a key, I suppose?" Bony asked.

"Yes, that's so."

"Would he have handed over the key to Miss Jade or the secretary before he went off, do you think?"

"I couldn't say. Expect so—just in case he never come back."

"But he would surely return for his belongings?"

"Of course. I didn't think of that."

"Have you any reason to think he will not return?"

"No. I only spoke general like."

"All right! Now one more question. What kind of lock is fitted to George's bedroom door?"

"Just an ordinary lock. 'Is room's the one next to the wine-store."

"Next to his is an empty room containing lumber, and then two maids' rooms and finally the cook's room. Am I right?"

"All correct, Mr. Bonaparte." Bisker wanted to ask questions, but remembered Bony's admonition and remained silent. As Bony did not speak again, after a silence lasting three minutes, he did put a question:

"Can I lend a 'and at anythink?"

"If you'd like to, I believe I could make use of you."

"Do me. I can dress in the dark."

"Good! Before you do, did you see Mr. Downes come back?"

"Yes, and seen 'im go off."

"Did he return with the same people with whom he went away?"

"The same man. There was only the one man who drove the car. He arrived about half-past two and they came back just before nine. The car was a Studebaker. The bloke driving it was a little man. He sent me in to tell Mr. Downes that Mr. Jackson was come to see 'im."

"And this Mr. Jackson didn't go into the house at all?"

"No. 'E stayed in the car."

"Good. Now for Mr. Leslie. Did you see him go out after dinner tonight?"

"Yes. 'E left shortly after eight. 'E went down the drive to the main road. I never seen 'im come back, though."

"What about Miss Jade?"

"She went to bed early. I was in the kitchen round about nine 'aving a last drink of corfee when the old cat came in to tell Alice she was going to bed with a 'eadache and that Alice was to lock up the wine-store punctually at eleven and go to bed."

"Hum! Well, I think we have got everyone tabbed, Bisker. Get up and dress, and don't talk. I am going to put you on sentry-go at the wood-stack to watch the scullery door. And I don't want any talking after we leave here."

"Goodoh! I won't be more'n a coupler minutes getting rugged up."

"What about your boots? Have you got any rubber-soled shoes?"

"No, but I got a pair of gum-boots, and I know where all the soft places are to walk about on."

"Excellent. Get dressed, and warmly."

Presently Bisker announced that he was ready, and together they left the hut, Bony leading the way round the rear of the garages and so to the rear of the wood-stack. It was twenty minutes to midnight.

At the end of the stack where Bony halted, a watch could be kept on the scullery door, the roadway to the top gate, and the front entrance, which now was locked and unlighted.

"I want you to stop here and not move away no matter what might happen," Bony breathed. "I'll be back later."

Bisker softly grunted that he had heard, and Bony moved off to be engulfed in the night. The night was full of noise, the gusty wind roaring in the drive trees and those lining the upper road. At a distance above and below Wideview Chalet, the wind roared with volume through the tree-tops like angry giants walking the mountain slopes, coming near and nearer, and passing away and farther away.

Although wearing a heavy overcoat, Bisker was becoming cold when he heard light footsteps on the roadway. The person was coming in through the top gate, and bush-wise, Bisker slid down to the floor of wood-chips skirting the wood-stack that he might see the approaching person against the sky, which although black was not as dark as at ground level.

The steps came quickly, and almost at once Bisker recognised that they were the steps of a woman. Then he saw her quite plainly against the sky. She was wearing some material about her head, and whilst in his view, she stopped and stooped and removed her shoes. When again she went on, she moved without sound, and Bisker watched her walk to the scullery door, pause there, then open the door and pass into the house, re-closing and locking the door behind her.

"Wonder where the old cat goes gallivantin' this time of night?" he voicelessly asked the passing wind. "Now lemme think. She was out the night Grumman was done in, and she was out the night following. Then she missed two nights, and went out and come 'ome about this time. She ain't been out since then until tonight. Wonder if Mr. Bonaparte was expectin' 'er to go out tonight, sort of?" Bisker began to sneer silently to the wind: "Go to bed with a 'eadache, me blinkin' aunt's grandmother! The old cat. Strayin' on the tiles at midnight, or a bit after."

Soliloquising thus enabled him to pass the time and to assist in keeping from his mind the growing chill. A strong gust of wind brought a skiff of rain which bit coldly into his face, and then when the wind passed like a giant to stride away down the mountain, in the abrupt comparative quietness he fancied he heard other footsteps on the road beyond the gate. The next wind-giant came before he could be decided about it, roaring through the trees so loudly as to drown out the noise of a farm tractor. That giant passed, and Bisker strained his ears.

"Musta been mistook," he breathed into his moustache. "By cripes, I wasn't!"

He saw the figure on the roadway, a figure that loomed high from his prostrate position at the foot of the wood-stack. He saw it against the almost black sky. It seemed to drift past him, making not the slightest sound, and Bisker shivered. It drifted towards the open space before the front entrance and vanished from him.

"Musta bin Mr. Bonaparte," he said to himself. "Cripes, 'e can move silent, all right. Like them bloomin' aborigines gettin' around. Well, well, we are 'avin' a great time of it."

Half an hour later he almost shouted. He was lying on his back to maintain that sky background when he felt a hand close over an ankle, and then saw a form loom over him like a vampire. A shape blotted out the sky from his eyes, and then he saw two gleams of steel-coloured light. The voice, he was most happy to hear, although it came to him as an echo flung back by his own moustache.

"Did you see that man come in from the top gate?" asked Bony.

Bisker felt Bony's ear touch his mouth, and he breathed: "Yes. Did you? Where did he go?"

"Into the house by the front door. Had his own key, I think. Went in and closed the door. It was locked when I tried it a minute ago. See anyone else?"

"Yes, Miss Jade. She come back a full hour ago. From the top road."

"You were not able to recognise the man?"

"No. All I could make out was a sorta shadder drifting by, I thought I 'eard footsteps on the road beyond the gate but I couldn't be sure 'cos of the wind."

"How do you know the woman who came in was Miss Jade?"

The question was cause for Bisker's silence, and Bony said:

"You don't know that it was Miss Jade, eh?"

"But we know as 'ow Miss Jade 'as been out late at night, don't we?" countered Bisker in defence.

"Very well! We'll leave it at that. It was a woman, but who, we don't know. Will you stay here a little longer?"

"Too right! As long as you like."

"Good! Stay here until I come back to you. I may be away for some time. I am going into the house by the scullery door."

The shadowy form that had been just above him slipped away, and Bisker did not see Bony, or hear him, depart.

Chapter Twenty-one

The Prowler

Stooping before the scullery door, Bony felt for the key beneath the brick, and with it let himself into the house, then pocketed the key and closed the door behind him. With the shutting of the door the orchestra of the wind played with only one violin and one drum muffled.

Within the house the inner silence was profound, and Bony leaned back against the door and gave himself a full minute of meditation. He could be sure that the woman Bisker had seen enter by that door had been Miss Jade, and that by now she would have reached her room and probably was in bed and asleep. The man who had entered by the front door presented a far different problem because even a guess could not be hazarded to establish him. Bony could not know if he were one of the guests, or a burglar. If one of the guests, then he could assume that this guest had gone to his room and by now was in bed, if not actually asleep. If a burglar, then he would be very much awake and somewhere in the house engaged in his unlawful occupation. In consequence, a burglar would be much more a menace to Bony's plans for that night than a guest.

In his left hand, Bony held a swithy-stick, cut from the bush that evening, green and resilient and about four feet in length. Why does a cat grow whiskers from above each eye if not for the purpose of being warned by them that an obstruction was immediately before it, an obstruction not seen in complete darkness? Bony's swithy-stick was intended for similar use to avoid running against any object which might fall with a clatter, and to avoid tripping over an object and producing the same result. With the stick held before him, he gently prodded with it whilst he crossed the scullery to the connecting doorway with the kitchen. He felt that he would not contact any probable burglar until after he had left the kitchen, and therefore, when he gained the passage beyond the kitchen, he leaned against a wall and listened, listened for full sixty seconds which, under such circumstances, take a long time in passing.

He was aware that this passage was approximately twenty-five feet in length, and that at its far end was the serving door to the lounge. The passage was bisected by another. Along the left angle were the reception hall and the office, whilst along the right angle were the wine-store, the steward's room, a lumber room and three bedrooms occupied by the staff.

If the man observed by Bony to enter the house by the front door was a burglar, then he could be expected firstly to be operating in the office, secondly in the wine-store, and thirdly, well, anywhere. He must be first located before Bony could execute the work he had planned to do.

With his "cat's whisker" feeling the way hidden even to his keen eyes, Bony moved soundlessly over the linoleum covering the passage floor. On reaching the cross-passage, he moved along that to the reception-hall door, now walking on carpet. The door was open, and this did not disturb him because he had not once seen that door closed save on that day the police held their enquiry in Miss Jade's office.

The wall clock in the reception hall ticked loudly, but although Bony gave another minute to listening, he could hear no sound other than the ticking clock and the wind in the trees outside the house. Familiar with the furnishing of the hall, he crossed to the door of the office, finding that closed and knowing that it was fitted with a Yale lock. With his ear pressed against the wood, he listened intently, and eventually decided that the unknown man was not working within on Miss Jade's safe.

Now for the second target. Using the swithy-stick like a rapier, he re-crossed the reception hall to find that he had missed the door by about two feet and was warned by the stick that he had come up against the corner of a straight-backed chair. Out through the door and along the passage, across the passage from lounge to kitchen, and without the slightest relaxation of caution, eventually he reached the door of the wine-store, a door also fitted with a Yale lock. Against this door he leaned with his ear pressing the cold woodwork.

No sound came from within. Other than the moan of the wind outside the house and the ticking of the wall clock in the reception hall, the interior of the house presented to him the silence of a bank's vault. He had his ear still pressed to the door of the wine-store when from farther along the passage a door was softly opened. Normal ears, perhaps, would not have registered the sound, and much later, when he recalled this moment, he was undecided if it were sound or change of air pressure which gave him the warning.

The door of the wine-store was, fortunately, only five feet from the cross-passage and with two swift strides he was round the angle and peering back, confident that he had made no sound betraying him. Listening, he heard no further sound from beyond the wine-store—until he detected a minute noise of periodic rasping slowly becoming more distinct.

His mother's blood was tingling his neck and the roots of his hair; his father's blood was flowing strongly through his heart. The aboriginal half of him was widening his nostrils and dilating his eyes and urging him to flee from the unseen terror; the white half of him was holding him to that corner, controlling his limbs and his mind.

Bony knew what it was—that faint rasping sound becoming slowly more distinct. It was being made by the hand of a man who was otherwise silently approaching, the hand sliding along the wall to guide him through the absolute darkness.

Himself making no sound, not even the slightest rasping noise, Bony, with the aid of his "cat's whisker," slipped along to the door of the reception hall, and there turned and again waited—listening. Now he could hear nothing. The moments passed. The ticking of the clock in the hall had become hammer blows in his ears and he wished that he had stopped it.

The light glow appeared at first as brilliant as a searchlight. He thought it could not fail to reveal him to the man at the point where the passages crossed, and then instantly realised that it was not sufficiently strong, that it was the light of an electric torch shining through two or more folds of a silk handkerchief. Thus dimmed, it would not reveal anything beyond two or three feet to the man holding it.

The light went out, but before it was switched off, Bony saw that the man was about to enter that passage leading to the lounge. He walked swiftly to the crossing of the passages—to peer round the corner, holding his breathing the better to hear.

The light was switched on again, and this time Bony made out the figure of the man as he was about to turn down the passage between the dining room and the lounge door, the passage leading to the guests' bedrooms. Again the light was extinguished. Bony counted three and then, with less necessity for caution with his feet as the floor was carpeted he gained the turn-off passage to the bedrooms, where he stood hugging the wall angle as he peered with useless eyes into the blank space of total darkness.

The light did not come again, and Bony was reasonably sure that it had been switched on only to guide the man into passages leading him to his room. So, after all, it was a guest and not a burglar. But that argument was wrong, surely! If a guest, he could have left the house by his bedroom window and could have returned by that way. If a guest intent on nefarious business, then why had he left the house, and later entered it by the front door? If not a guest, why had he entered the passage to the bedrooms?

Only five of the twenty-six rooms were occupied, the occupants being Raymond Leslie, Downes, Lee, Sleeman and himself.

These questions hammered at his brain almost as loudly as the ticking clock had done. Had the man mistaken his way? Was he even then returning? Bony could hear nothing whatsoever. He waited with the "cat's whisker" held before him, his legs tensed to spring backward at the instant the top of his stick contacted a body.

Then once more he felt the infinitesimal alteration of air pressure and knew that the man had opened one of the bedroom doors. The same alteration of pressure did not occur again, and Bony understood why when visualising that the man would close the door with greater precaution and with slower action than he had when he opened it.

He had certainly entered one of the twenty-six rooms, five of which were occupied. Which room? It seemed unreasonable to accept the premise that he had entered an unoccupied room for the purpose of leaving the house by its window. That would pre-suppose that he knew which of the rooms were unoccupied and which were occupied, and that would further pre-suppose that he must be a guest to know the answer. Bony felt safe in assuming that the man was one of the guests. Still, why break into the house by using the front door?

Now sure that the man had entered one of the rooms, Bony proceeded to move along the passage on the side where were the five occupied rooms, his own being the last. Then he remembered that outside the doors of the occupied rooms would be a guest's shoes against which he might kick with a foot. Following that thought, another flashed into his mind. Assuming that the man he had followed was a guest, that man's shoes might not yet be placed outside his door to await Bisker's early-morning attention.

With the "cat's whisker" trembling before him, Bony passed along the passage, his left hand barely touching the wall. He came to a closed door, then a second, a third, and the fourth, behind which slept, or should be sleeping, Raymond Leslie. Yes, there were Leslie's large shoes close to the foot of the door. Bony stepped over them and went on. He passed the fifth door and the sixth, and came to the seventh, and at the foot of the door he felt with the stick the large shoes of Mr. Lee. He could hear Mr. Lee snoring beyond the door.

The next room was occupied by Downes, and a pair of shoes were outside that door. Bony passed three more empty rooms and then came to the door of Sleeman's room. And outside this door there were no shoes.

The next door to be reached was his own, and at his feet were his day shoes as he had placed them before leaving his room by the window. Bony silently and slowly opened the door and passed inside, where he turned about and leant against the frame so that he could keep watch along the passage, and also keep one ear directed to the interior of the room, where the stealthy gentleman with the masked torch might be.

He had been there for perhaps five minutes when for the third time he felt the alteration in air pressure as a door was opened. That was all. There was no sound. No light was switched on. Which of the twenty-six doors in that passage had been opened, he could not distinguish, and whether the door opener had left to steal back along the passage to the front door, or had re-closed the bedroom door, Bony could not decide.

The only sound to register upon his ear-drums was the ticking of the clock in his own room. The overall noise of the wind outside the house appeared to come as from a great distance and failed to master possible sounds within.

Bony waited at his door for many minutes. No light was flashed on to indicate that the intruder had reached the far angle of the passage, and presently he came to believe that the door had been opened to enable a pair of shoes to be placed in the passage for Bisker to clean. That could have been done only by Sleeman, whose shoes had not been outside the door when Bony had passed.

Bony left his doorway and slipped along the passage wall to the door of the next room. At its foot he felt with the stick a pair of shoes. The door was shut. Bony pressed his ear to the panel, and brought his eye to the key-hole. The key prevented his seeing into the room even had the light been on. And as he stooped he heard from within the faint creaking of a wire mattress.

So it was Sleeman whom he had followed, who had left a room in the passage beyond the wine-store. Surely he had not been visiting one of the maids! Their rooms were in that passage where the wine-store, the steward's room, and the lumber room. And why had Sleeman entered the house by the front door?

Had the man who had entered by the front door been Sleeman? Had Sleeman been out of his room on an amorous adventure leaving his room by the door and returning by the door and was the man who had entered by the front door still prowling about the house somewhere?

Because he, Bony, chose to enter the house by the scullery door instead of through his bedroom window through which he had gone out, it would seem most unlikely that Sleeman had had a similar reason for leaving the house through his bedroom window and entering it by the front door. Bony had chosen to enter by the scullery door because he wanted to examine the lumber room and, perhaps, the room occupied by George, and these rooms could be more easily reached by way of the scullery than through his bedroom. He decided to have a word with Bisker.

Locking his bedroom door and slipping the key into a pocket, he climbed out of his window for a second time that night and eventually, for the second time, clamped a hand about one of Bisker's ankles.

"Seen anything?" he breathed into Bisker's ear.

"Not a thing but a star trying to peep out now and then," answered Bisker. "How did you get on?"

"Well enough. You did not see or hear anyone leaving by the front door?"

"No. I seen nothink and 'eard nothink bar the blinkin' wind."

"You know Sleeman's room, don't you?"

"Number seventeen it is."

"When did you clean the windows of that room last?"

"'Bout a fortnight ago."

"Do they open and close all right?" pressed Bony.

"No," replied Bisker. "The bottom one jams so badly that it can't be raised. There's only one set—not two sets like yours. Miss Jade was gonna get it fixed, but the carpenter hasn't been."

Chapter Twenty-two

Early in the Morning

Once again in the scullery with the closed door behind him, Bony spent a minute listening before proceeding into the kitchen and from there to the cross-passages. Here he waited, listening for two minutes, becoming confident that his presence was unknown to anyone within the house. Almost, but not quite, he had dismissed the presence of a second prowler as an improbability.

However, he did press an ear against the door of the wine-store and could detect no sound from within. The next door he came to was that of the steward's room, and although he halted here for a few minutes, he did not enter but went on to the door of the room given over to lumber. Outside this door, he also paused to listen, to be assured that no one was within, before returning to George's bedroom.

He had with him a bunch of skeleton keys provided by Colonel Blythe when first the Grumman case was assigned to him, but he found on trying the door that it was unlocked and that the key was on the inside. Silently closing the door, he stood for a little while listening. Then he switched on his torch, over the bulb of which he had wrapped his handkerchief.

There was no one there—just as he had thought. He turned to the door and withdrew the key and directed the subdued light of the torch to it. He saw that it was covered with oil, and that the oil was old and not applied that night. Inserting the key, he locked the door.

The blind was down. On the single bed, the blankets were folded neatly at its foot, and on them were the folded sheets and the pillows. The mattress was rolled into a cylinder at the head of the bed, and this struck Bony as queer because George was to be away only the one night.

There were no washing facilities in this room. There was a chest of drawers and on that was a stand mirror and the man's shaving and toilet gear. This was all of excellent quality. A pair of ivory-backed hairbrushes lay beside the leather case. There were pots of shaving cream and hair pomade, a couple of combs and several tooth-brushes and a tube of dentifrice. There were, too, three photographs of groups within small and cheap frames.

All these articles displayed in the dimmed beam of the torch indicated that the owner was careless and slovenly in his habits, and George had not revealed this trait at any time to the observant Bony. There on the bed was displayed neatness in the folding of the bed-clothes, when such folding arrangement appeared to be unnecessary. Here on the chest of drawers all was chaotic. He proceeded to examine the contents of the four drawers of the chest. In them were underwear, shirts and collars, socks and a sports suit. The shirts were washed and ironed. There were five of them and the laundress had folded and ironed them as though they were intended for shop sale. Bony took each from the drawer and closely examined them—to find that the creases and the folds were out of the original. The shirts had been "opened" out and then roughly refolded before being put back into the drawer.

Next Bony gave his attention to a leather steamer trunk, old but still in good condition. The lock was evidently out of order, the lid being kept fastened with only one of three buckle straps. Within lay more garments—a dressing gown, several older shirts, a suit of navy-blue serge, several pairs of shoes, and books and unframed photographs of people on ships and of ships. The contents of this trunk smelled heavily of moth repellent.

Bony went carefully over the blue suit, the trousers of which were keenly creased, as were the sleeves of the coat.

The repellent was the same as that which he had noticed on the suit of the man who had held up both Bisker and himself and had taken the empty fountain pens.

Replacing the contents of the trunk, Bony closed down the lid and proceeded to direct his torch into corners and under the bed and the chest of drawers. Beneath the bed was another pair of ordinary shoes and a pair of good-quality tennis shoes. On pegs affixed to the door hung an overcoat and an old felt hat. Questions! Standing and leaning against the wall in the darkness following the switching off of the torch, Bony asked questions and sought their answers.

Was the blue suit in the trunk that worn by the gunman? It was similar. It smelled of the same moth repellent, of which there are many, which had clung to the gunman's clothes. And the old felt hat on the peg looked something like the gunman's hat.

That the gunman was George, Bony was morally certain, although he had not discovered the kerchief used as a mask or the rubber pads inserted into the mouth to disguise the voice. Neither had he discovered the gunman's pistol or his own automatic.

There was something else of great interest found in that room. Bony had had plenty of opportunity to study the steward employed at the Chalet, and he was sure he was not in error in summing him up as precise in his habits. He was sure that George would not have left his toilet gear in disorder upon the chest of drawers. He was sure that George would not unfold all those well-laundered shirts and then refold them in such a careless manner. Apart from the man's training and psychology, what need had he to unfold those shirts?

Then there was the bed. He was to be away for only the one night, and the bedclothes were folded and placed as though the room was expected to be vacant for some time instead of being unoccupied merely for one night. It was most likely that George made his own bed and himself kept the room clean and tidy. Now it was upset, despite the folding of the bedclothes and the rolling of the mattress.

Just as he was convinced that George was the gunman, so he also felt sure that this was the room visited by Sleeman, and that Sleeman had been searching for something. Instead of remaking the bed, he had neatly folded the clothes and rolled the mattress, possibly to give the absent man the idea that during his absence one of the maids had done this—Sleeman had apparently been unable to remake the bed after pulling it to pieces to get at and to search the mattress.

Probably the hairbrushes had been within their leather case, and Sleeman had forgotten to put them back, as he had omitted to replace any article correctly.

What was Sleeman? He used a light to get himself along passages with which a novice in crime would have become familiar after twenty-four hours' stay at the house. He had come here to ransack a room and had made stupid attempts to hide his work.

Yes, what was Sleeman? What was his interest in George's room? And if it had been he who had returned from some place long after midnight, and had entered the house by the front door, where had he been and why had he been out so late?

Not altogether disappointed, Bony left George's room and proceeded along the passage to that used as a lumber room. The door of this room was also unlocked. The key was on the inside of the door, and examination proved that recently it and the lock had been oiled—recently, but not that night.

The interior of this room was three parts filled with old furniture, wooden cases, rolls of linoleum, old-fashioned lattice blinds and ornate gilt-framed pictures. The furniture, although old, was very good and very solid, bespeaking an era long before the modern guest house at a mountain resort.

The dust held Bony's first interest in this room.

He had not questioned Bisker particularly about its contents, neither had he sought to learn how long the contents had been in it, but the impression which he had received from Bisker was that the place had been a lumber room for a long period. Yet the dust on the surface of this furniture was so slight as to indicate its age as less than a month at the longest.

An interesting point. Well, now he was here, he would see what there was to be seen.

The furniture was stacked and not loosely. He set the torch upon a what-not which he placed beside the door and thus gained its direct light. There was no window blind, but now he was disposed to defy the possibility of being observed from outside.

He proceeded to extract chairs and tables and sofas from the stack, determined to make a passage through it to the far wall. He was obliged to work with extreme care, for the room beyond was occupied by one of the maids. Unused to this kind of labour, as he was unused to this kind of investigation, he yet made not the slightest sound. And when he had worked for nearly twenty minutes he began to hum a tune, to hum unconsciously, so swift was his mounting excitement.

In one of the far corners he came upon two large steamer trunks, three large suitcases, a small leather grip and a bag of golf clubs. Every article was stamped with the letters "B. G." The trunks and suitcases were plastered with shipping-company and rail labels.

So that was why the dust was so light upon the furniture. The furniture had been thoroughly dusted before Grumman's luggage had been taken from his room to be stowed away in that corner. The dust on it now had settled after the luggage had been brought there so that there would be presented no finger- and hand-marks and no fingerprints if the remover had not been so stupid as to work without gloves.

Bony began the task of putting all the furniture back. He used his handkerchief to dust each article as he replaced it, and repeatedly shook the handkerchief, hoping to raise as much dust in the air as possible that it might settle and thus mask his work as a duster.

He was warm when he left the house by the scullery door, which he locked, warm, from exertion, not from mental excitement, which had the effect of making his brain cold. To Bisker, he whispered:

"Have you got any tea and sugar over in your hut?"

"No," replied Bisker. "Got a billycan over there, and there's a water tap 'andy."

"Good! You go back to your hut and make a fire and fill that billy. I'll steal tea and sugar and some eats from the kitchen. Where is it kept?"

"The tea and sugar you'll find on the shelf over the electric stove. The

150

tins ain't large and I could take 'em back when I goes in first thing, sort of," directed Bisker. "In the cupboard near the winder is a tin of biscuits. I seen the cook put 'em there late last night."

"All right! I'll get all that. You make that billy boil fast."

For the third time this night, Bony entered the kitchen, was there only for a few minutes, and then for the last time emerged through the scullery door. He left the key beneath the brick and carried his treasure trove to Bisker's hut.

Already flames from the fire were licking determinedly round Bisker's blackened billycan, and Bisker stood and watched Bony unroll a cloth and display a half leg of mutton, a loaf of bread, some butter, a bread knife, and tins of tea, sugar and milk. "You're a blinkin' corker!" he exclaimed.

"I am a hungry man," Bony admitted. "Night work always makes me hungry. What do you think of the weather now?"

"I'm game to bet it won't rain after all," Bisker replied. "Wind's gone round to the southeast and the stars are breaking out. That suit you?"

"It most certainly does. Now no more talking till that billy boils. Make the tea really strong."

Bisker nodded, and began to remove his outer garments of two overcoats, muffler, battered felt hat and gum-boots. Now and then he glanced at Bony, to see him roll a cigarette and lean back against the wall whilst seated on a petrol case beside the table. Bisker felt happy—really happy. He was cold, despite the wearing of the two overcoats, and the growing heat of the fire added to his happiness. The interior of the hut, the "tucker" stolen from the kitchen, all transported him far away back into his own country.

Bony was smoking with his eyes closed, and Bisker thought he was tired out. Tired out! Bony's mind was clear as crystal and as active as a race horse at the barrier.

The water in the billycan broke into violent eruption and Bisker nonchalantly tossed two handfuls of tea into it, permitted it to boil for four seconds and then lifted the can off the flames and dumped it on the floor to assist the leaves to settle. The sound brought Bony from his meditation, and he stood up and proceeded to cut bread, butter it lavishly and then cut meat to make sandwiches. Bisker opened a tin of condensed milk by stabbing its top with his tobacco knife. He poured milk and then the tea into two polished tin pannikins, and Bony said:

"Like old times, eh?"

"Too blinkin' right!" agreed Bisker, and began to sip noisily at the scalding liquid.

"By the way, did you happen to notice the number of the car which took Mr. Downes away and brought him back?"

"Yes. NX 052 B."

"Smart work, Bisker. Thank you. Now tell me, between mouthfuls, were you ever in the room next to George's where the lumber is?"

"Yes."

"When were you in it last?"

Bisker pondered. Then he said:

"Two months back. The old cat give me the job of going over all the furniture and stuff with the vacuum cleaner. A girl named Joan did it the time before that. She was a maid 'ere. She left soon after, I remember."

"Do you know when that furniture was first put in there?"

"No. Before my time. It's always been gone over about every three months since I've been 'ere, though."

They continued to eat for some time in silence, and then Bony asked: "Do you happen to remember near the door-side of the pile a heavy mahogany chest?"

Bisker grinned.

"I do that an' all," he replied. "I've had me eye on that chest ever since I seed 'er. I asked Miss Jade if she would sell it, and the old cat shut me up with a 'no'! She's a great chest, that. I'd like it 'ere to keep me clothes in— and a bottle or two when I should get me 'ands on a win."

"When you were dusting it, I suppose you raised the lid and looked inside?"

"I did so."

"Was there anything in it when you looked?"

"Nothing."

"No old boots?"

Bisker shook his head and stared long at Bony. Bony was cutting another sandwich for each of them.

"It would seem that Miss Jade values all that furniture," Bony remarked, noting Bisker's stare.

"Musta. Has the stuff dusted and polished every so often. Wonder why!"

"So do I."

After another period of silent eating, Bony asked:

"Have you ever been into George's room whilst he's been working here?"

"Oh, yes, often. Me and George 'as a game of poker now and then. George is a good player and I ain't so bad meself. We play for matches, as I never seem to 'ave any money."

"Hum! Well, tell me this." Bony regarded Bisker calmly but steadily. "When you were in George's room, did you notice if he was an untidy man?"

"Untidy!" repeated Bisker, a snort in his voice, "Why, George is the most particular bloke with 'is things I ever come across. Everythink 'as to be just so. We used to sit playing cards on the chest of drawers, and after we finished, 'e'd collect the brushes and things wot 'e'd took off before we started playin' and 'e'd mess about with 'em, arranging 'em just so. Same with 'is bed. I sat on it once, and 'e went crook and made it all over again."

"He has been here a little over three months. How many times has he gone to the city?"

"Yesterday was the first time. 'E told me 'e was savin' up 'is money."

"You don't know if he had any friends, then?"

"Oh, yes! 'E's got one pal wot 'e called Mick," answered Bisker. "Mick's been out to see 'im a coupler times. Irish bloke, about George's age. Lemme think! Yes, Mick came to see 'im about three weeks ago. Came in the afternoon, 'e did. Came out in a car wot stopped down in the road. The driver 'ooted several times and George went down to meet 'is pal, who was coming up the drive. They 'ad a chin-wag for more'n 'alf an hour, and the old cat got rampant 'cos it was time to serve the afternoon tea."

"If George arrives back by the first bus this morning, what train will he leave by from Melbourne?" continued Bony.

"'Arf-past eight she leaves the city."

"Well, thank you, Bisker," Bony said, contentedly, whilst rolling a cigarette. "I've enjoyed that snack very much. By your clock it's twenty minutes to five, and I have work still to do. If you go along keeping one eye open you will oblige me greatly. Take particular notice of Mr. Sleeman's shoes when you clean them, and if anyone calls to see Mr. Downes or Mr. Lee, just make a mental note of them and the car numbers. You know how to do that without making yourself too prominent."

Bisker gave assurance that he would be as close as an oyster and as wide awake as a Derwent Jackass, and at half-past five, in the bleak air of the hour before dawn, Bony pressed the button of the night bell at the Police Station. Mason appeared in pyjamas and dressing gown to let him in and conduct him to the office.

There was no evidence about Mason's visitor that he had been moving furniture and dusting it, or even that he had been up all night. After leaving Bisker, Bony had returned to his room through the window, where he had changed into a good suit and a smart pair of shoes, after having washed and shaved. The hat laid down on the desk was spotless — the raincoat bore not one crease.

"Sorry to call you up so early, Mason," came the quiet and suave voice. "Needs must when criminals drive. Who is on night duty at the local telephone exchange?"

"One of our men," replied Mason, and Bony picked up the instrument and proffered it to the Sub-Inspector.

"Ask him who was on duty there yesterday afternoon."

When Mason replaced the instrument, he said:

"The postmaster."

"All right! Now I am going over your head, Mason, because I have reason to. Can you contact Superintendent Bolt?"

Mason said that he could and was requested to do so. Whilst waiting for the connection, Bony said to him:

"Please contact the Motor Registration Branch and ascertain who owns the Studebaker car bearing the number NX 052 B. And then, as soon as you think it convenient, interview the Bagshotts about the alleged collector of old boots and clothes. I'll be back here again later in the day. There is — — Thank you."

Bony accepted the receiver from Mason and leaned back in his chair. Mason heard him say:

"Ah—top of the morning, Super. Bonaparte here...Er—with reference to the man, George Banks. You will recall the name... . Oh, yes. That's right! You know, I've been thinking that because he forged those references he ought to be taken into custody... . Not serious enough! Well, perhaps not, but still I think it might be as well. Somehow or other I've gained the impression that he removed certain travelling equipment and personal effects from the room occupied by the late Mr. Grumman."

Bony ceased speaking and the watching Mason saw the slow smile spread over his dark face. After a little while, Bony spoke again:

"Mason is not in the position of effecting an early arrest. Banks went down to the city yesterday afternoon, and he promised his employer to be back on the first bus this morning. To do that he must catch the eight-thirty train from the city. I think it most probable that Banks will be in possession of concealed firearms; I stress the plural because I have reason to think he will be in possession of my own pistol. I like that pistol and I want it back, you understand? It fits so perfectly into the palm of my hand.

"What do I know? Very little when totalled... . No. I cannot agree to that. If Banks should slip by your men, or return by car, then I want no arrest made here at the Chalet. He'll be all right for a few days. You see,

Miss Jade has had quite enough upsets in her house. Oh, I know, but then policemen, real policemen, of whom I am not considered to be one by my Chief Commissioner, are quite in keeping with the background of a Police Station, a detective office, and even a court of law. The same cannot be said of them against the background of a mountain guest house of the quality of Wideview Chalet. Their proximity affects the cook, for one thing, and for another I don't want my friend, Miss Jade, disturbed more than is absolutely essential. Therefore, if you can lay George by the heels without any fuss, I would be obliged. But no arresting here, please. My nerves wouldn't stand it."

Chapter Twenty-three

George Does Not Return

Inhabiting the trees in the immediate vicinity of Wideview Chalet was a family of nine kookaburras. These wise birds knew every cranny of the garden, every foot of the lawn, every branch of every tree, and into this, their domain, they permitted no outside kookaburras. They barely tolerated the day-sleeping opossums. Four of the nine birds had occupied positions on Bisker's wood-stack, and the remaining five were perched within sighting distance all waiting for breakfast scraps, when Bony arrived at the gate in the upper fence.

The morning was cloudy. The valley lay clear of fog. The sun had not risen above the mountains and the wind was cold and dry. Just beyond the gate, the gravel of the roadway petered out into the soft sludge bordering the upper road, and on the sludge were the plain imprints of Miss Jade's shoes and Mr. Sleeman's larger shoes. Mr. Bonaparte had no difficulty in reading them.

Both Sleeman and Miss Jade had, on reaching the public road, gone to the right along the macadamised strip. They had stepped off this strip, crossing the sludge area again in order to reach the gravelled roadway and down into the house, but Bony was interested to ascertain where they had been. He walked along the upper road.

He had proceeded only a few yards when he sighted Sleeman's tracks at the border of the strip. Miss Jade had kept upon the road. Sleeman had continued to walk along its flank on the softer ground.

Bony came presently to a crossroads, and because Sleeman had turned left, he also turned left and went on. The road led him upward and not once had Sleeman stepped off the softer ground edging it. Bony did not again see Miss Jade's tracks until, when opposite a house standing well back within the seclusion provided by a barrier of closely growing fir trees, he saw that she had stepped off the road and had entered by the gate the grounds of the house behind the firs.

Sleeman had walked on. Bony continued following Sleeman's tracks. The man had proceeded for fifty yards and then halted, and had returned to sit on a boulder opposite the house gate.

Having continued his walk for a further half mile, Bony returned and briskly passed the house behind the fir trees, and so walked back to the Chalet. He knew the story. Miss Jade had left her house very late at night to visit the house behind the firs. Mr. Sleeman had followed her, had sat on the boulder whilst she was within the house, and then had returned at leisure to enter the guest house by the front door and to "raid" the room occupied by the steward before retiring to his own room.

Bony certainly had to revise his views of Sleeman.

Of the five men at the one table, Sleeman was the last to appear for breakfast.

"Sleeman is apparently finding it difficult to get up this morning," observed Downes, regarding Lee with his steady eyes. The pastoralist grinned broadly and then chuckled.

"He didn't want to go to bed last night," he said. "Alice told us she had been ordered to close down punctually at eleven. That pleased me because our friend was thirsty but I wasn't—not by then."

"Nice fellow," asserted Raymond Leslie, and no one attempted to argue about that.

Sleeman entered the dining room and received cordial greetings. He appeared well groomed and normally cheerful. He greeted everyone individually, and ordered his food without any finicky regard for his digestion.

How old was he? Bony found difficulty in assessing Sleeman's age. He might be anything between forty and fifty.

He was well set up and the "weakness" did not show itself so very clearly on his face. Like Downes, and unlike either Lee or Leslie, he had never been informative about himself.

"What sort of a day is it going to be?" he asked, glancing through the great window at the magnificent view presented.

"Fine, I think," Leslie answered him. "I'm going down what they call The Way of a Thousand Steps. We were speaking of it the other day, remember? There's a place halfway down where the gulley path goes through a small forest of fern-trees. The tree-ferns are at least twelve feet high, some even higher, and so their age must be great. To sit there under them always reminds me of pictures of the Carboniferous Age and of pre-historic monsters standing on their hind legs to get at the young and juicy ferns sprouting outward from the tops of the trees of that time."

Lee offered to accompany the artist. Sleeman said he had to remain indoors to write business letters. Downes expected a visitor. Bony said he was going to lounge about and read.

After breakfast, Bony put on a light overcoat and took a book out to the veranda, where he occupied a chair in his favourite position. He would have liked better to return to his room to sleep.

A little before ten o'clock, the man from the Riverina and the artist came round from the end of the house and went on down the path to the wicket gate. Leslie was carrying a satchel of drawing materials. They moved slowly whilst discussing the Devil's Steps which so disfigured Miss Jade's lawn, and finally disappeared beyond the gate as they walked down the ramp to the highway.

At ten o'clock, Bony saw the top of the bus from Manton as it drew to a stop at the drive. A minute or two later, he watched Bisker carrying up the driveway a load of suitcases. He was followed by an elderly couple. George did not appear. At eleven, the maid, Alice, brought to him a cup of tea and biscuits. At half-past eleven, Downes walked down the drive, wearing his overcoat and hat, and a few minutes after he had vanished from sight Bony heard the sound of a car coming up the highway. It was stopped somewhere out of sight, turned round and departed the way it had come. Then he saw Bisker appear among the trees lining the driveway, and casually he left his chair and sauntered down the steps to the lawn, where he stayed for a moment or two to regard the Devil's Steps, before wandering to that end of the house near the entrance. He found Bisker washing the tiled flooring of the entrance porch.

"Same number. Same driver," Bisker informed him.

Bony nodded his thanks and walked out to the upper road, turned left and followed it down to the highway as far as the fruit stall. Then he continued along its winding course until he left it and entered the Police Station.

"Where is the Sub-Inspector?" he asked a Senior Constable.

"I was ordered to inform you, sir, that Sub-Inspector Mason went down to Manton. The man wanted did not show up to catch the eight-thirty train from the city, and the Sub-Inspector thought it likely that he would return to his place of employment by car. The Manton officers don't know the wanted man, but they have a description of him. I am to suggest, sir, that perhaps you might wish me to interview the Bagshotts regarding the matter you spoke about to the Inspector."

Bony pursed his lips and considered the situation, then:

"Contact Superintendent Bolt. I'll write a message for you to read to him." The S.C. took up the telephone, and Bony wrote rapidly on a pad and pushed the pad across the desk. They had to wait five minutes for the connection. Then the S.C. spoke, giving his name and station.

"A message for you, sir. Begins: 'Suggest every outgoing ship searched for wanted man.' Message ends. Very well, sir."

"I will stay here while you interview the Bagshotts. This will be the line of the enquiry."

Bony outlined what he wanted, and the S.C. departed. He was away for approximately fifteen minutes, and the result of his mission was the information that a man, representing himself to be a collector of footwear and clothes for refugees in European countries, had called a fortnight previously, exhibiting what purported to be an official card of the Clothes for Europe Committee of Victoria. Mrs. Bagshott had interviewed the man and she described him as well built and having a faint Irish brogue. She had given him several garments and several pairs of shoes, including one pair belonging to her husband.

The Senior Constable opened a desk drawer and took out a slip of paper. He said:

"You wanted to know the name of the owner of a certain Studebaker car, sir. Number NX 052 B. The owner is Mr. William Jackson, Number 17 Myall Road, Southeast Camberwell."

"Ah! Yes, thanks." Bony paused, then added: "After I have left here—wait an hour—contact Superintendent Bolt and ask him to let me have all possible information about this William Jackson. Say, too, that I will communicate with him, the Super, about nine o'clock tonight. Also inform Sub-Inspector Mason that I will be here again round about nine this evening, and that meanwhile I am having quite a nice holiday and do not wish to be disturbed."

In a thoughtful frame of mind, Bony left the Police Station and walked down along the highway, calling a cheerful "Good day" to the proprietor of the fruit stall as he passed. He arrived at the Chalet in time to hear the luncheon gong.

Downes had not returned. Lee and Leslie had told Miss Jade that they would be lunching away somewhere. In consequence Bony and Sleeman lunched alone at their table, a neighbouring table being occupied by a Mr. and Mrs. Phelps who had arrived by the early bus. More guests were to arrive during the afternoon.

"Miss Jade's in a bit of a temper, I fancy," Sleeman remarked softly to Bony. "George isn't back yet, and there are tons of new people coming today and tomorrow. He promised her faithfully that he'd be back this morning. You been out for a walk?"

"Yes. I strolled up the highway for a mile or two. Beautiful road and beautiful surroundings, don't you think?"

Sleeman nodded.

"Charming," he agreed. "I may go out this afternoon. Care to come along?"

Bony smilingly expressed regret and said it was his intention to relax and read a novel. The conversation became desultory, Sleeman evidently a little uncomfortable at being alone with Bony, and Bony being a little tired following the all-night work.

Later, wearing an overcoat and with a rug about his legs, Bony reclined in a chair on the veranda and thought about Sleeman. Had it been Sleeman who had examined his possessions during that night he had spent taking the contents of the fountain pens to Colonel Blythe? He was inclined to doubt it because the person who had gone through his things had been an expert, whilst the work done by Sleeman in George's room was that of an amateur. But wait! If Sleeman knew that George was not returning to the Chalet, there would then be no need for him to be meticulously careful in replacing everything.

Well! Well! Why worry? Time would tell. Time would uncover all things for Bony to know. Meanwhile there were two hours until afternoon-tea time. In the cool and pure air of Mount Chalmers Bony slept the sleep of the just.

The chatter of newly arrived guests awoke him. Ten or a dozen strangers were standing at the balustrade of the veranda admiring the view. He felt refreshed and again mentally alert. What was it he had been thinking about Sleeman? Ah yes! Did Sleeman know last night that George would not be returning to the Chalet?

The possibility occupied his mind even whilst he was being presented to the new guests by Miss Jade at afternoon tea. Afterwards he sought out Bisker.

"Seen anything of George?" he asked.

Bisker shook his head, and then said:

"Mr. Downes isn't back, either."

"You didn't receive from George any impression that he might not be returning, did you?"

"No. 'E seemed all set to come back first thing this morning," Bisker replied. "Wonder what's happened to 'im?"

"So do I. Still, we must be patient."

Guests sat at nearly every table in Miss Jade's dining room that evening. Downes had returned about five o'clock and shortly after that the artist and Lee had come in: The Way of a Thousand Steps and the beauties they had seen formed the major part of the conversation that night, both Downes and Bony being entertained by the artist, who had also the gift of word painting. Sleeman evinced more interest in Wanaaring.

A little after eight, Bony slipped away and walked up to the Police Station, where he found Bolt waiting for him with Sub-Inspector Mason.

"What's all this about?" the huge Superintendent demanded without any preamble.

"Ah—good evening, Super," countered Bony, smiling naively into the hard eyes. "Good evening, Mason. Nice and warm in here. Well, now, have you located our friend?"

"No," snapped Bolt. "Not back at the Chalet?"

"No, he hasn't returned."

Bolt stared at the little half-caste who, with irritating calm, was rolling one of his fearful cigarettes. Then he burst out:

"What d'you know of this George Banks? Come on, Bony, out with it!"

"Can you recall a man answering to the name of Mick? About eleven stone in weight, medium height and having dark eyes and speaking with a faint Irish brogue?" inquired Bony.

Bolt shook his great head. Then he exclaimed:

"Wait! That might fit Mick the Tickler. But then he left the country about the time the war broke out and was reported to us as being in London in, I think, 'forty-three."

"What was his speciality?" Bony asked.

"Tickling military secrets from the wives of Service officers comes first. A close second was blackmail. What of him?"

"Merely that your Mick the Tickler might be the man who is friendly with our George Banks. If you get in touch with Colonel Blythe he might be able to tell us more concerning this Mick the Tickler."

"Oh all right!" snapped Bolt. "But start at the beginning and let's have it. What about Grumman's luggage? Where is it? What d'you know about this George Banks?"

"You become more like Colonel Spendor every time I see you, Super," Bony complained. "One doesn't get anywhere by being impatient. Bad for the blood pressure, too. Now listen, calmly. This Mick—he may be your Mick the Tickler—called on Mrs. Bagshott, alleging that he was a representative of a clothes-and-boots-gathering organisation, and she gave him several pairs of shoes, including a pair of her husband's shoes.

"I've been much interested in the tracks made about Wideview Chalet. The size of the shoes that made them is twelve. Those shoes made what are known as the Devil's Steps on Miss Jade's lawn. I was telling you of them the last time you were here. You will remember that I was doubtful if Bagshott's feet were in his shoes when those tracks were made. The shoes which were given away by Mrs. Bagshott, and which made the tracks about the Chalet and on the lawn, are now in a chest in a lumber room at the Chalet. In that same lumber room is Grumman's luggage. In George's trunk in his bedroom is a blue suit which might have been worn by the man wearing a mask and carrying a pistol, and who stuck up Bisker and myself in Bisker's hut and robbed me of two fountain pens."

"Robbed you of two fountain pens!" barked Superintendent Bolt.

"Yes. Good pens, too. I want them back. They are mine. I promised one to my wife and the other to my eldest son, Charles."

Bolt regarded Mason with desperation in his eyes.

"Give us a fag, Mason," he grunted. Then to Bony, he said:

"Go on. Me and Mason can easily sort it all out—I don't think."

"Excellent! I thought you could," murmured the smiling Bony. "However, I find it all a little vague at present. The evidence is strong against Banks, and it is by no means complete. It is sufficient for his arrest, but I am not yet quite ready to make you a report. That is why I suggested that you charge him with being in possession of another man's references, anything to hold him quietly for a day or two. There are many matters still outstanding, your friend Marcus being one of them."

"Marcus!" Bolt regarded Bony steadily. Then he said, almost shouting: "What d'you know?"

"I must confess, Super, not very much, not enough to feel warm. Let's get back to this Mick the Tickler. Have you a photo of him in Records?"

"Don't know. Ought to have." Bolt's exasperation changed to a period of calm grimness. "Now look here, Bony, I'm talking to you as one pal to another. Marcus is dynamite. If you are playing around with him, you're playing with dynamite. He's just a ferocious wild tiger. If he gets the slightest suspicion that you're onto him, he'll blast out your life—as quick as he did poor Rice."

Bony rose to his feet. He stood regarding the top of the great domed cranium before permitting his gaze to sink to meet small and unwinking brown eyes.

"Thanks, Super," he said levelly. "I'm not quite ready to complete this investigation, but the end is not far off. Now be a sport and leave me to it for a few more days. Meanwhile, get onto Banks's pal, whom we will assume is Mick the Tickler. Get hold of Banks too. He must have removed Grumman's luggage to the lumber room, and he or his pal must have carried the body down to the ditch when wearing a pair of Bagshott's shoes. Why, we may learn when the fish are netted.

Those two men were responsible for Grumman's death. If you do have a picture of Mick the Tickler, see if Mrs. Bagshott can identify it. Leave it here for me to pick up tomorrow night. I want to show it to a man who has seen this Mick. But no policemen at the Chalet, yet."

Bolt relaxed and sighed tremendously.

"I've a damned good mind to arrest you, Bony, and put you away into safety," he growled. "I know all about you, your record, and I know that this slick, grease-quick gangster type of criminal is outside your experience."

"That's what makes the work all the more interesting," Bony countered. "Did you get anything on that William Jackson, the owner of the Studebaker?"

Bolt glared at Mason, and the Sub-Inspector produced a flimsy.

"Nothing known against Jackson," he read. "Paint manufacturer. Office in Flinders Lane. Works at East Richmond."

"Does the report not state if he owns a house here?" enquired Bony.

"No. But—I've got a list of every house owner on the Mount."

"Have a look for William Jackson."

Mason became busy with a file, running his finger-tip down the columns of names. Then:

"Ah! Yes! William Jackson owns a place named Ridge House. I know it. It's about two miles down the highway."

"Strikes the bell, looks like," growled Bolt on observing the mirthless grin which flashed into Bony's blue eyes. "By crikey! I've an even better mind to put you away for safety sake."

"Super—if you make a move off the wrong foot you'll lose your dear friend, Marcus," Bony told him. To Mason, he said:

"On a road leading from Wideview Chalet, which then turns left, there is a house standing behind a line of fir trees. Who lives there?"

Mason's mind raced.

"A woman named Mrs. Eldridge and her daughter. The daughter is a confirmed invalid."

"Thank you, Mason. And you, too, Super." Bony put on his hat. "I'll be getting along. I'll call again tomorrow evening at this time. Cheerio!"

"One minute," snapped Bolt. He also stood up. "Will you let us plant one of our fellers in that Chalet, just to keep an eye on you when your back is turned to prevent a bullet? Got a man who can do the play-boy act very well."

Bony shook his head. He smiled into Bolt's worried eyes.

"I'll be all right, Super. Tomorrow night, perhaps I will be able to give you the hammer to strike the gong."

Chapter Twenty-four

Mick the Tickler's Story

The following evening, when towards eleven o'clock Superintendent Bolt and Sub-Inspector Mason had decided that Bony would not be calling at the Mount Chalmers Police Station, they heard his voice assuring the wife of the Senior Constable that he could find his way to the office.

"Must have come in by the back door," observed Mason.

"He can come down the chimney so long as he does come," growled Bolt. He gave vent to one of his tremendous sighs and then added: "I was becoming fed up. Now you keep quiet and listen. He might make a remark indicating who he thinks is Marcus."

The door was opened and Bony came in, glanced at the cheap clock over the fireplace and beamed at the seated men who had been impatiently waiting for him for more than two hours. Mason regarded him with an impassive face; the big man glared. Bony said:

"Sorry I'm late, but I was persuaded to play a game of draughts with one of the guests. He proved to be a very good player and I wasn't able to bring the game to an end until half-past ten."

"Interesting game, eh?"

"Very," Bony assented, seating himself opposite the Superintendent at the desk. "My opponent was clever with his kings. You would like to know him, I am sure. I'll introduce him to you one day. He would be certain to enjoy a game or two with you."

"I'm not much interested in draughts—just now," Bolt said, rudely.

"You ought to be interested in draughts at any time, day or night," Bony said, as he rolled a cigarette. "Great brain exerciser and also it sharpens one's interest in one's fellow men. Well well! What have you got for me tonight?"

"One of your friends in the bag, and another of your pals in the mortuary."

"H'm! A little progress, eh? I hope you don't think you've got friend Marcus in the mortuary."

"A milkman, when on his rounds this morning, found the body of a man lying just inside the front gate of a house in Coburg. The occupants of the house state that they heard a car stop in the street at something to three o'clock this morning, and as they state that they don't know the dead man, it is assumed that he was carried from the car to the place where the body was found. The gate, by the way, is midway between two street lights. The body is that of your friend George Banks."

Whilst Bolt had been speaking, Bony regarded him with brows slightly raised, and if the Superintendent expected to see astonishment lower those fine brows he must have been disappointed. When Bony made no comment, he went on:

"In the pockets were employment references in favour of George Banks. There were two letters from Mick making appointments for past dates. There was a pair of thin rubber gloves and a wallet containing Treasury notes to the value of fifty-three pounds. Besides a few silver coins, there was a heavy solid-gold cigarette case with the initials 'B. G.' engraved on it."

"No pistols, of course?" Bony commented.

"No pistols."

"And death was due to ... ?"

"A bullet in the brain—following a bashing."

"Dear me!"

The small brown eyes of the Superintendent bored into the wide blue eyes of Inspector Bonaparte. He said:

"The obvious assumption for the bashing was the need for information."

Bony nodded his head in agreement.

"Either desperate need or iron determination to get it," he said. "The gold cigarette case bearing Grumman's initials is an interesting item. The rubber gloves are still another. Who of my friends have you arrested?"

"Mick the Tickler. We located him on a Black Funnel liner now in port. Ship was due to sail tomorrow. We took him to view the body. After that, he broke down and gave us a statement. Here is a copy of it."

Bony accepted the sheets without speaking, lit another cigarette and leaned back in his chair to read:

My full name is Michael Francis O'Leary and I was born in Sydney in the year 1907. My father was Irish and my mother English. I had one brother, Daniel, who was born in London in 1911.

Early in 1945 I was in Germany on an especial assignment, being then in the employment of the British Government. I was thus employed because, having completed my education in Germany and subsequently got around a good deal in that and other European countries, I was able to speak the language without accent and was familiar with the German psychology. And also because I have always been able to manage women.

While on that particular assignment, I met the mistress of a high Army officer by the name of Lode and through the woman I learned that he was a member of the German General Staff. Lode was infatuated with the woman, and as the woman became infatuated with me, I found myself in a strong position.

In March of that year, the collapse of Germany was seen to be inevitable by the German General Staff and Major General Lode was commissioned to take out of the country certain highly secret formulas of both drugs and explosives, and much other information of great importance to the General Staff, the members of which knew that it would be forced to dissolve for several years after the defeat and occupation by the Allies. At some future date, it could be reorganised and set about the job of preparing for the next attempt to conquer the world.

The possibility of defeat, it seems, had been recognised before the war, when it was recognised also that Hitler would start a war before the country was ready for it.

In the United States there was a man named Grumman, a German who had been naturalised shortly after the first World War. He visited Germany in 1937 or 1938, when it was discovered that he was remarkably like Lode, and the following plan was then arranged.

It being decided by the General Staff that their secrets must be sent out of the country for safe-keeping until such time as it could be reorganised, photographs of the formulas and plans, etc., were made and reduced to the size of pin heads on micro-film. The film was to be wound on spools and inserted into two fountain pens. Two other similar copies were to be made, a set of each to be taken charge of by two other officers, who also were to get out of the country before the crash took place. I know nothing about them.

Lode left Germany by submarine and landed somewhere on the coast of Florida. He was met by Grumman, who handed over all his identification papers, his personal effects and details of his business. Grumman went aboard the submarine and returned to Germany. Lode became Grumman, an American citizen.

I left Germany early in April 1945, having accomplished the work for the British Government. Certain officials objected to my severance with their department, but I gave them no chance to kick.

Early this year I arrived in Australia on the same ship with Grumman. On the ship I chummed up with Grumman, who was Lode, and I recommended to him Wideview Chalet on Mount Chalmers as a good place to stay at nice and quiet and away from the city. I did that because I knew my young brother had a job there as drinks steward, and thought that he and I between us could rat Grumman of his secrets, which would sell for enough hard cash to put my brother and me on velvet for the rest of our lives.

Grumman landed in Sydney. So did I. Unknown to him, I kept him under observation during the whole week he was in Sydney. No German contacted him. He came to Melbourne by rail, and I came here on the same train. For a week he stayed at the Australia, so did I. Still no one contacted him. Then he took my advice and went to stay at Wideview Chalet and I went up there and stayed at another guest house.

My brother kept me informed of Grumman's actions and habits. Grumman felt himself to be perfectly safe, for he adopted no extraordinary means against molestation and /or theft. During his absences at night, when he went out for a short walk before going to bed, my brother Daniel went through his gear, and Daniel was a master at that sort of thing. He didn't find the pens, and I did not expect that he would, although there was the distinct possibility that they were buried in the leather of his steamer trunks or in the soles of a pair of used shoes he would not actually wear.

I was sure that he still had the pens, that he had not passed them to anyone else, and that he would never do that until he was instructed to do so by a member of the German "Order of the Swords," a secret Prussian military organisation which is said to be higher still than the German General Staff.

Daniel told me that shortly after Grumman arrived at Wideview Chalet there arrived also a man named Sleeman. Daniel got wise to Sleeman when he saw him sneaking out of Grumman's bedroom window when Grumman was out for his usual short walk. We could not make up our minds what Sleeman was—whether he was just an ordinary crook after what he could pick up or was a member of some organisation after Grumman's secrets. Daniel said he drank pretty freely during the evenings, but Sleeman was the type of man who is on top when there's whisky inside him, and he made the most of this by pretending he was semi-drunk when the reverse was the case.

I felt confident that Grumman still had the pens in his possession. His higher-ups chose pens in which to conceal the micro-film, because in addition to fountain pens being very ordinary objects they have to be kept in a top pocket of a civilian waist-coat and therefore draw attention to themselves every time their owner changes his clothes, like an ordinary watch and chain which crosses a man's stomach and has to be handled every time he undresses. I was positive that when Grumman took off his day clothes he would pin the pens in their holder to the pocket of his pyjamas coat.

When Grumman was visited by two men and two women, I began to be anxious. It was the first time since he had arrived in Australia that any friends came out of the blue to contact him, and so I decided we could not delay any longer.

The night that Grumman was murdered, Daniel added a stiff bromide to his last drink before going to bed. He doped Sleeman's drink, too. That was before eleven o'clock, when the veranda light was switched off.

When the veranda light was put out at eleven o'clock, I went up from the road to the veranda and waited outside Grumman's windows. After about an hour the windows were opened from the inside by Daniel. I went in, drew the curtains and the blinds and switched on the light. Instead of Grumman being held by the bromide, we found that he was dead. He did not die from the bromide because Sleeman got the same measure.

We did not know what killed Grumman, but I got the idea then, and still have it, that Sleeman poisoned the water in the carafe, because Grumman had poured some into a glass and drunk it— Sleeman intending to overhaul Grumman as we had planned to do after giving him the bromide. Anyway, believing that Sleeman had poisoned Grumman, and knowing that Sleeman would be asleep for at least four hours, we went over the body and found the pens pinned into the pockets of the pyjamas coat. Daniel actually took the pens, and both of us being upset at finding Grumman dead, I did not think to take them with me when I left, walking down the main lawn to the main road.

The next morning, a man whom I don't know called on Grumman and shot a policeman. Daniel got the wind up, and when he went to bolt the front door to keep out the guests until the police arrived, he pushed the pens in their holder into the earth of a tub where a shrub was growing, thinking that he might be searched by the police.

After the first fuss and examination was over, Daniel saw towards evening that the yardman was most interested in that shrub tub. And so, when after dark he went to the tub to get the pens and found that they had been taken, he naturally assumed that the yardman had seen him push them into the tub and had taken them.

He reached the hut in time to see a guest named Bonaparte going in, and he thought that this guest wanted the yardman to run an errand or do something for him the next day. After Bonaparte left the hut, Daniel stuck up the yardman, but the yardman swore that Bonaparte had taken the pens. Daniel put the yardman to sleep, but he found that he had spoken the truth because the pens were not on him. He went after Bonaparte, and then he saw him coming back to the hut. After Bonaparte had been inside for a few minutes, Daniel got him to open the door by playing a ruse. He stuck up Bonaparte and got the pens from him.

I forgot to state that before sticking up the yardman, Daniel changed into an old suit of clothes and made a mask for his face out of a neckerchief.

Bonaparte went away from Wideview Chalet late that night and did not return till the following afternoon.

Eventually, after waiting for the police to calm down, I telephoned to Daniel and he arranged to come to the city. We met in a cafe and Daniel produced the pens. I found in the end of each a screw which, I knew, was attached to a spool round which was wound the microfilm inside either pen.

The guest named Bonaparte must have removed the micro-film while he was away from the yardman's hut, and he must have taken it to the city to hand it over to someone there.

I have viewed the body of my brother, Daniel. The foul work done on him before he was killed is the kind of work that the German "Order of the Swords" would do to get from him the whereabouts of the contents of the pens. Who Sleeman and Bonaparte are working for, I don't know, but I am sure neither of them belong to the "Order," as they would not be eligible.

Bony set down the statement on the desk and, without commenting, manufactured a cigarette. Bolt remained silent until after Bony had struck a match, and then said:

"Well, what d'you think of that?"

"Have you seen Colonel Blythe and shown this statement to him?" enquired Bony.

"Yes. He says that O'Leary was an espionage agent employed by the British Government, and that the first part of the statement might be substantially correct."

"That's my view, Super. With regard to several matters in the latter part, I think that the statement is far from being correct. O'Leary denies complicity in the actual poisoning of Grumman, saying that his brother added a sleeping potion to Grumman's last drink, and yet when he walked down the lawn in Bagshott's shoes he was carrying a very heavy object, that object being the body of Grumman. However, those details can wait for the time being. Of more immediate interest is the brother's fate."

"Too right!" agreed Bolt. "You have no idea even who they might be? What about this Sleeman?"

"Sleeman may be in that, but Sleeman has not been away from the Chalet excepting for a few hours yesterday afternoon when he went for a walk. Let us imagine a tale of fiction with the bare facts in our possession. A party suspected that George—we'll refer to Daniel O'Leary as George—killed Grumman and stole the pens. They kidnapped George in the city after he had left his brother—who, by the way, does not state what happened to the pens after they discovered the micro-film had been extracted from them. They find the pens on George, and they find that the secrets they contained have vanished. What had George done with the micro-films? George won't talk. They apply pressure, and perhaps under pressure, George relates the adventure he had with Bisker and me. They say that is a tall one to put over. Who was the man he met that day in the city? George won't tell. They apply more pressure. Still George won't speak, won't say anything which might lead his torturers to his brother. And so in the end they shoot him. I am inclined to believe that George died a hero.

"Well, then, having killed the stubborn George, they will recall the story about his adventure with Bisker and me, and doubtless they will endeavour to check up on it. H'm! That might prove interesting."

"You'll find it so if they apply to you their methods of—persuasion," Bolt said slowly, with emphasis.

For the first time Mason offered an observation.

"Might not the people who collared George be friends of our pal Marcus?" he said. "Marcus did call at the Chalet to see Grumman. He knew Grumman."

Bolt waited for Bony to counter Mason's suggestion.

"It is quite likely, though we have no evidence. O'Leary in his statement makes no such suggestion, although he must have known that the man who killed Rice had called to see Grumman. However, neither of the brothers would know what we know about Marcus. Although without evidence, I am much inclined to the thought that Marcus is at the back of killing George."

"And that being so, you and Bisker might be for it," Bolt said.

"Let me think," pleaded Bony.

"Don't think," urged Bolt. "Tell us where Marcus is, if you know."

Bony smiled and Bolt felt like leaning over the desk and clouting him.

"Tell me, how did you come to get O'Leary to make that statement?" Bony asked.

"Well, after we picked him up on the gag of taking him to Headquarters for questioning, the body of George was put into the mortuary, and I took O'Leary to the mortuary to identify it—if he would. When he saw the body, O'Leary broke down, and I don't blame him for that. After a bit, he calmed down, and then he said that the dead man was his brother, and that he would make a statement in order that he would himself gain safety in gaol. Subsequently, it came out that he firmly believes that the people who dealt it out to George are members of that secret German 'Order' who have been covering Grumman ever since he landed in America."

"And he might well be right, Super," Bony added. "No, we won't pounce on Marcus yet. Neither will we raise an argument with our Mr. Sleeman. Not yet awhile. We'll give this torturing crowd a chance to make a move."

The huge Superintendent slouched over the desk and glared into Bony's eyes. When he spoke, his voice was like the sound of tearing corrugated iron.

"Assuming that they take you for a ride and bump you off good and proper, how do we get to nabbing Marcus? If you know him and where he is, tell us before you get nabbed and tortured and bumped off."

Slowly, and returning Bolt's baleful glare with steady eyes, Bony said:

"If I am bumped off I shall be astonished, as I've never been bumped off before. Now, good night. And you watch that blood pressure of yours."

Chapter Twenty-five

Revellers Three

Bisker was not the only member of Miss Jade's staff who was supplied with an alarm clock, the other member being Mrs. Parkes, the cook. Unlike Bisker, she was unable to voice hatred of clocks and Miss Jade and the world in general, for the reason that she never slept with her teeth in her mouth and was in any case speechless until she had moistened her throat with hot tea.

On opening the kitchen door this particular morning, she was astounded to find the place in total darkness. Not only were the lights not on—there were no fires lit in the range—there was no pot of tea made by the waiting Bisker—and there was no Bisker.

Following this decided shock Mrs. Parkes thought that her clock had called her much too early. Then she saw by the kitchen clock that her alarm had not played a trick on her. It was, indeed, five minutes past six.

Five minutes past six! And no fires lit—no pot of tea made—and the boots to be cleaned for forty-odd guests! No tea made! That fool of a Bisker must have forgotten to set his clock and even then was sleeping away what little brain he had left.

Toothless and now in a towering rage Mrs. Parkes swept across the kitchen, switched on the hot-point of the electric stove placed thereon the kettle and sallied forth to arouse Bisker. She shivered as she advanced through the darkest hour before the dawn, and her arm-muscles tensed and relaxed in preparation for the real work ahead.

To her astonishment and chagrin, she found Bisker's bed empty, and because Bisker made his bed once every month, she was unable to decide if he had or had not slept in it that night.

Back again in her kitchen, Mrs. Parkes noted that the kettle on the electric stove was "singing," but that encouraging sound failed to have any impression on the weight of fury pressing on her mind. From the kitchen she thudded along the passages to the staff's quarters and aroused the two maids, who were not due to rise until seven. When they entered the kitchen, Mrs. Parkes had lit the range fires and was drinking tea and smoking her first cigarette.

"One of you go and tell Miss Jade that the guts 'as fallen out of the works," she said with unnecessary vigour, to add: "George still away, and now Bisker's gone orf, too. The guests will have to clean their own shoes for once."

To make the beginning of this day still more tragic for Mrs. Parkes, one of the maids giggled and fled. The vast proportions of the cook, the state of her ensemble, the square white face with the tiddly-winks marker of a nose in the centre of it, and in addition, the cavernous, toothless mouth, and the cup of tea held high in one hand and a cigarette in the other, were far too much for Alice.

Five minutes later, Miss Jade entered the kitchen. She was wearing a scarlet silk dressing gown and wearing slippers of rabbit fur edged with white satin.

"What is the trouble, Mrs. Parkes?"

It took Mrs. Parkes a little more than two minutes to relate her woes. Miss Jade listened without attempting to interrupt the cook, and, when the mechanism ran down, all she did say was:

"When Bisker does appear, send him to me."

From such small events do Empires totter and crash into ruins.

When the maid with the early-morning tea knocked on Bony's room door, he slipped out of bed and removed the arrangement of empty tobacco tins forming a booby-trap to announce any unauthorized entry by the doorway during the night, and from her he learned that Bisker had failed to report for duty. Miss Jade sent her compliments, and regret, and would Mr. Bonaparte, under these unfortunate circumstances, clean his own shoes this morning?

Bony switched on the electric heater, and sat down before it to sip his tea and smoke a cigarette.

He had not seen Bisker since the previous afternoon.

In his dressing gown and with a bath towel over a shoulder, Bony left his bedroom before his cigarette was smoked. He strolled along the main passage towards the bathrooms, meeting none of the guests, and eventually passed through the reception hall and out through the main door which had only just then been opened for the day.

It was a beautiful morning. The risen sun was flooding the trees and the garden with colour. Over the floor of the valley sailed small patches of fog looking like wool scattered upon the floor of a shearing shed. No cloud sailed in the clear and vividly blue sky. No breeze disturbed a tree leaf.

On arriving at the cinder path leading to Bisker's hut, Bony read the latest edition printed upon it. He saw the wide imprint of the cook's slippers. He saw the tracks of Bisker's boots, the most recent impressions indicating that the last time Bisker had passed that way he had been leaving his hut. There were no other tracks of recent date.

Bony entered the hut. The blind was not drawn, but there was little significance in that, as Bisker seldom drew down the blind. The bed was unmade, as has been stated, but Bony felt with his hands among the blankets and decided that Bisker had not slept in his bed the previous night. Upon the case beside the bed was Bisker's alarm clock, but nothing else excepting the pipe which was habitually loaded with "dottles" in preparation for the first smoke of the day.

The pipe told Bony a little story. The bowl was empty. It would have been filled by Bisker just before going to bed. It had not been filled, so Bisker had not returned to the hut the previous night to sleep.

Bony circled the hut before returning to the open space before the garages. He had seen no fresh tracks, and here on the path were those left only by Bisker and the cook. As he dressed his mind was not on clothes.

Had those people who had tortured and killed George now got hold of Bisker? If so, then the outlook for the yardman was, indeed, bleak. There was, of course, the possibility that Bisker had gone to the local hotel and there had stayed overnight. His pal, Fred, who mowed the lawn, might know something of him.

Bony was far from being easy in his mind concerning Bisker when he went to breakfast to join the artist, Downes, Lee and Sleeman, and another man who had arrived the night before. The newcomer to their table was big and solid and weather-beaten, and Bony wondered if he was one of Bolt's men sent along in defiance of the arrangement between the Superintendent and himself.

"Didn't inconvenience me," the squatter was saying. "I'm used to cleaning my own shoes."

"Must make life a little difficult for Miss Jade, what with George staying away too," supplemented Sleeman. "Perhaps he went along to the pub for a bender, and found it too good to leave."

Lee recounted stories of bushmen he had employed who, if they merely smelled liquor, simply had to demand their money and rush away to the nearest hotel. Downes listened but said little, offering once the remark that there must be plenty more yardmen to engage.

After breakfast Bony sought Miss Jade in the office. "What's this about Bisker being absent?" he asked.

"He's just cleared out, Mr. Bonaparte, and just when he knew we were short-handed with George being still away and the house full of guests." Miss Jade was angry, really angry, and he thought she looked more beautiful this morning than he had ever seen her.

"Perhaps he's up at the hotel," he suggested.

"No. I've just been talking with the manager. They haven't seen Bisker for two weeks."

"Has he ever been away before without permission?" Bony pressed.

"Never. I'll say this in his favour, that he has never been away in the morning, and he has never overslept." Miss Jade smiled with her lips only. "The man has a good many virtues, I must say in justice, but all his virtues are now nullified when my house is full and the steward also is absent."

"It's very unfortunate," Bony murmured.

"Mrs. Parkes, my cook, you know, is furious," said Miss Jade. She was in perfect control of herself, but the anger was written plainly in her dark eyes. "Good cooks are hard to get and hard to keep," she went on. "Men, too, are hard to get these days. I must ring up all over the Mount and try to get a man."

"What about Fred?"

"He might come—if I could locate him. But he goes here and there on day-work."

"If you could tell me where he lives, I would go there for him. He might be at his home. If not, then I'll try and find him for you."

"Oh, Mr. Bonaparte, would you?" Miss Jade was genuinely relieved. "You go up to the top gate and turn down the road to the highway. Then you go up the highway to the fruit stall and take the left road towards the gulley. Fred's little house is on the right-hand side near the gulley."

"Excellent. I'll take a walk down to the place right away," the now-smiling Bony assured her, and Miss Jade went so far as to press his forearm.

Bony bowed, saying:

"Might I use the telephone here before I hunt for Fred?"

"Of course. Use it as much as you wish. I'll leave you alone, and go to breakfast."

Miss Jade again smiled at him, and again he bowed to her. She closed the office door after her. He rang the exchange and asked for the Mount Chalmers Police Station. The Senior Constable spoke.

"I want the Sub-Inspector, please."

"Sub-Inspector Mason? Who is it speaking?"

"Never mind the name," replied Bony. "I'm speaking from the Chalet."

The S.C. metaphorically jumped.

"Oh! Yes, sir, I'll get the Sub-Inspector at once."

The line remained dead for thirty seconds. Then Mason spoke. Bony said softly:

"Can you hear me?" On being told that he could be heard, he went on:

"I want you to communicate with the Super, and tell him he can collect both his friend Marcus and a guest here named Sleeman. Marcus's latest alias is Downes. Get that? I'm leaving it all to the Super."

"Right! I'll be along with a couple of men."

"Wait, Mason," pleaded Bony. "You will do nothing until you have communicated with Bolt. Remember, the place is full of guests. Remember also that if you lost Marcus, your career would be ruined. None of you know Downes. You'll have to leave it to me to point him out."

"H'm! Suppose I would. All right! I'll contact the Super. Where can we get you in a hurry?"

"I can't make any arrangement," Bony said. "You remind the Super of Marcus's pal, what's his name, who lives at Ridge House, down the highway. I suggest that that place is raided efficiently and with speed. Have you seen anything of Bisker? Wait!"

The door of the office was opening.

"Well, thank you," Bony went on, his voice raised a fraction. Over the telephone he saw Downes standing beyond the opened door. "Yes, I will inform Miss Jade. Yes, thank you so much!"

Bony set down the receiver on the instrument and with his free hand reached for the call handle to contact Exchange.

"Miss Jade has gone to breakfast," he told Downes.

"Oh!" murmured Downes. "I came in to use the 'phone. Didn't know you were here. Finished yet?"

"No. But I won't be long."

The eyes of Marcus were slightly narrow. He drew back and the door closed. Bony turned the call handle. He was certain that just beyond the door Marcus, alias Downes, was standing, and that the door was such that Downes could hear what he would say into the telephone in a normal voice. When Exchange answered, he requested to be put through to the Bus Service proprietor, and of him enquired if it was known where the man Fred was working, purposely lowering his voice.

The information was not available. From the reception hall came the voices of several guests, and Bony became sure that Downes would not remain just beyond the door, if he had done so after leaving the office. Still, he waited whilst rolling a cigarette, and then passed out of the office and, seeing nothing of Downes, strolled out through the main entrance and so up to the top gate.

On the soft sludge between the Chalet roadway and the macadamised public road he saw the imprints of Bisker's boots, showing that he was headed down the road to the highway.

Bony continued at a leisurely pace down the road to its junction with the highway. There he paused to admire the view, now and then turning to glance up that side road he had just come down. He saw nothing of Downes.

Standing there, he saw no human being either up or down the highway, and continuing to stroll, he walked up along the highway. He was midway between the side road's junction with the highway and the wayside fruit stall when he heard a car coming along behind him. The car was travelling fast, and before it reached him, he stepped casually off the road and leaned against the trunk of a magnificent mountain ash. As the car approached he stepped farther back, ready to leap behind the great trunk at the first sign of attack. There was only the driver, however, and he failed to see Bony.

Bony stepped out to the centre of the road, and there with his hands clasped behind him, he stood staring upward at the mighty tree. The dwindling roar of the car was the only sound in the stillness of the sylvan scene. After a little period spent in admiration of the tree, he proceeded on along the highway, now and then turning casually to look back.

On coming to the fruit stall, not yet opened for business, Bony took the side road falling in a fairly steep gradient and rule-straight. This road was surfaced with gravel, and along its right side there was a path for pedestrians. And there on that path were the tracks made by Bisker's boots.

Those marks brought Bony profound relief, for it was evident that when he made those marks with his boots, Bisker was on his way to visit his friend, Fred. Bony began to hum a little tune. He walked a little faster, and had proceeded about halfway down the road when he observed two figures emerge from the bordering trees at its bottom and stand in the centre of the road.

"Now that would be about where Fred's house is situated," he said aloud. "By the manner those two men are standing it would——"

Again he began to hum, and presently he ceased to hum and began to chuckle. The two men were walking up the road towards him. Now they drew close to each other, and now they moved apart. One was tall; the other short. One was thin; the other rotund. The tall man carried a hurricane lamp.

The lamp was alight and smoking. Bony stopped beside a tree and waited.

Onward came the inebriates. The warm sunshine mocked the tiny flame of the lamp but could not mask the film of smoke issuing from its top. Bisker stumbled, and Fred said, complainingly:

"Why don't you look where you're going? Wot in 'ell's the use of me bringing a light if you can't see to step over a bit of a log?"

"You want to shine the blasted lamp properly," countered Bisker. "'Ow d'you think I can see the ruddy logs and things if you keep on waving the lamp about like you're signalling a young tart in a winder."

Along the perfectly made gravelled road the pair staggered past Bony, who then left his tree and walked on to the road behind them.

"Flamin' good mind not to go 'ome till morning," growled Bisker, finding great difficulty with his speech. "'Ow many bottles of Scotch left in the kip, Fred?"

"Four of Scotch and about a coupler dozen of beer," replied Fred. "They'll keep, and you can come down tomorrer evening for another bender. Gripes! Wot a night we've 'ad, Bisker. Wot a night!"

Bisker hiccoughed and then laughed uproariously.

"The best flamin' night me and you ever 'ad, Fred," he said, and both were unconscious that Bony walked only two paces at their rear. "Y'know, Fred, when I whistled to you on Sat'day afternoon that Black Prince had won, and when I seen you wave your arms, I says to meself, I says, 'Wot a bender me and old Fred gonna 'ave with the doings. A 'undred and ten quid ain't a bad win,' I says. 'That'll buy a lot of the real poison,' I says."

"Too—hic—right, Bisker, it will," Fred agreed. Bisker abruptly stopped.

"I'm not goin' 'ome," he announced. "The old cat can go and take a running jump at 'erself. I'm goin' back for some more of that grog. Why, we ain't properly drunk yet."

"Yes, we are," argued Fred. "Look! Look where you're going! Can't you see that log a'ead of you?"

They halted to regard with great solemnity a stick of about half an inch in thickness which had been parted from the parent branch and had fallen upon the road. Fred held the lamp close to it, and then stepped high over it, turned and held out his hand to assist his companion. Bisker absurdly took his hand and high-stepped over the stick. Bony stood close to them, and neither saw him.

"'Bout time the ruddy Reserves Committee give you a few days' work cleaning up this track, Fred," Bisker said, and Fred pointed out that he was engaged to work for a "'undred people" for the next two years.

Slowly, the party moved up the road towards the highway. Then Bisker straightened his body, stared about and saw Bony.

"Hey, Fred, the ruddy sun's ris. Blow the flamin' lamp out."

"'Ow d'you mean, the sun's ris?" demanded Fred.

"Yes, gentlemen, the sun has risen and we are far from home," Bony said gravely.

Bisker shaded his eyes with a grimy hand.

"Cripes!" he said, and added nothing.

"They will be wanting wood cut for the fires," Bony went on. "Miss Jade is most anxious about you Bisker."

"She would be," Bisker agreed, with biting scorn.

"The old — —"

"Fred, please. Miss Jade is not old."

"Course she ain't old," swiftly asserted Bisker. "Friend of yours, Mr. Bonaparte?"

"A great friend, Bisker."

"Then she's a friend of mine. All your fren's are my fren's. Come on, Fred. What you dawdling for? Come on up and give us a 'and to split some flamin' wood for Mrs. Parkes."

"Thank you, gentlemen," Bony said. "I knew that you would not let a lady down over a stick or two of wood. Take my arms and let us homeward bound."

With Bisker clinging to his right arm and Fred holding onto his left arm, with the hurricane lamp in Fred's free hand, still burning and still smoking, they came to the highway. And down the highway they rolled and tripped, singing at the top of their voices.

They met a car and the driver pulled up. He was the Senior Constable stationed at Mount Chalmers. His eyes were as big as small pumpkins. Bony stopped singing long enough to say:

"Bolt must mind his step."

The S.C. stared after them, Bony in the centre—leading a chorus about an old grey mare a-restin' down on the farm.

Chapter Twenty-six

The Mistake That Marcus Made

Bony took lunch with his customary table companions in excellent spirits.

Having accomplished his Boy Scout act for the day, he had been amply rewarded by Miss Jade with her sweetest smile, the memory of which was to remain long in the mind of the impressionable Bonaparte.

On nearing the top gate into the Chalet grounds, Bony had put the brake on the singing, and then having arrived at the wood-stack, with fine diplomacy he put his walking companions to work introducing the competitive element by suggesting to Bisker that perhaps he would like to sit down and allow Fred to do the splitting for Mrs. Parkes. The result, of course, was that Bisker refused to remain inactive and Fred declined to do any sitting about so when the luncheon gong was struck there was enough wood split for all the fires to last for several days.

The work accomplished, Bony conducted his new friends to Bisker's hut, returned to Miss Jade from whom he obtained a refresher in a bottle, administered the tonic and saw the two men safely into the one bed for the afternoon. Meanwhile, Miss Jade had secured the services of a local man to take the place of George, and once more the organisation of Wideview Chalet was running efficiently.

After lunch, a goodly proportion of the guests departed for walking exercise. Others, chiefly the elderly people, retired to their rooms for a nap. A hire car arrived and took yet others for a drive round the mountain, and when that had left there remained on the veranda less than a dozen people.

Of these Bony was one, occupying his favourite chair placed at the far end. In a group sat Sleeman and Lee and the new guest at their table, whose name was Tully. Downes occupied a chair beyond them, whilst beyond him were grouped several men and their wives.

The day had continued fine and gently warm. The kookaburras were silent, but the whip-birds in a distant gulley now and then gave forth their peculiar notes. Over the valley floor the scattered "wool" had been swept up and away by the heat of the sun, and now this early afternoon the distant mountains were receiving their Joseph's coat of many colours. The only blot on all of Nature's vast and beautiful scene were the Devil's Steps on Miss Jade's lawn.

To doze, of course, was impossible for Bonaparte. His mind was charged with the electricity of expectancy for at any moment now Bolt and his men would appear and go into action against Marcus. He wondered if by now the house belonging to Marcus's friend had been raided, and just how the preparations for arresting Marcus were shaping. Bolt would take no chances. He would have half the Police Force of Victoria on the move, moving grimly and with machinelike precision towards the focal point of Wideview Chalet.

A kookaburra laughed lazily. It was high up among the foliage of a mountain ash growing near the main entrance, and Bony wondered if the bird had sighted anything unusual. Other than that laughter, faintly mocking, faintly satanic, there was no sound. The quiet air appeared held within the grasp of a giant, careful that nothing should vanquish the spell exerted by the valley and the distant mountains.

Bony had decided not to take any action in the arrest of Marcus unless compelled to do so by circumstances. For one thing, he was not a member of the Victorian Police and was not even on loan for duty to that Department. For another, he had agreed to co-operate with Bolt, and he had done so by establishing to him the man responsible for a Victorian policeman's death, and, moreover, a man having an international reputation for ruthlessness, a man whose capture would give great credit.

For Bony, the minutes passed laggardly, and then the first move of interest since he had reclined in that wickedly luxurious chair was made by Downes. He left his chair and, passing behind Sleeman and his companions, he approached Bony with an easy motion like that of a cat.

"Care for a game of draughts?" he asked. "Not the right time for a game, but I don't feel like sleeping—or reading."

Bony swung his feet over to the floor and sat up. "Yes, I'll play," he consented. "Where? Here?"

"Might as well. I'll get the board, it's in the lounge."

Downes went away, again passing behind Sleeman, Lee and the hefty Tully. Bony noticed that both Tully and Sleeman watched Downes until he had disappeared through the french windows into the lounge, and both appeared to be careful not to be looking that way when Downes reappeared, carrying the board and the box of draughtsmen. He picked up a card table en route, and placed it near the balustrade, and before Bony could assist him he had arranged two chairs, one on either side of the table, and had occupied the seat facing the lawn, Bony thus having to be content to sit with his back to the lawn. It was all done with casual politeness.

"It's your choice of colour," Downes said, evenly, placing the draughtsmen.

"Then I'll choose black. I am not taking any chances this afternoon—not with an opponent like you."

"I never take chances with an opponent," Downes declared with a faint smile. "Draughts, like any other game, and like life too, isn't to be taken lightly. A mistake can rarely be retrieved, especially an initial mistake."

"I agree. Well, you make the first move."

Dowries played without any affectations and, when playing with Bony, never with defensive tactics. He went swiftly into action, and then leaned back in his chair whilst waiting for Bony to make his move. Bony took time to consider, and then moved with greater deliberation. Under which arm-pit did Marcus carry his gun? He wore single-breasted coats, slightly full in front and with padded shoulders. Neither side pocket was out of place.

It was Marcus's turn to study the board. His pale face was expressionless. His hands resting on the table on either side of the board showed no signs of nerves. Never once did he raise a hand to stroke his chin, or to stroke his moustache which was so perfect that even in that light Bony could not detect its falsity.

Bony's next move followed after several minutes of studying the board and attempting to elucidate the reason for Marcus's last move. That last move had not been the one he expected. Pity he could not detect which arm-pit concealed the nesting gun, so that he could anticipate which hand Marcus would use when he went into action.

Following Bony's move, Marcus took only three seconds to make up his mind how to counter. He forced Bony to take two of his men, and then he removed three of Bony's men and brought his "jumper" to Bony's rear line of defence. That wouldn't do! Bony would have to remove his mind from armpits and guns and hands, and concentrate on this game. It was about time that Bolt turned up and earned his salary for the day. But then Bolt mightn't arrive until after dinner. Oh, forget it and play, Bony!

Ah—Marcus had left himself wide open! But wait! That might be a trap. If he, Bony, moved thuswise, that would make Marcus move sowise, and then he could follow up with a thencewise. No, that would leave his centre too vulnerable. Better try and dig into Marcus's left flank. Seems to be more interested in the view than in the game, but he wasn't playing as though his mind was occupied with anything else.

Bony made his move and sat back in his chair. Tobacco smoke drifted before his face, and its aroma he did not like. It came from Tully's pipe, and Tully was half reclining on his wicker chair, his hands placed at the back of his head. The quiet of the afternoon continued. There had been only one car past the Chalet since the game of draughts began, and that had gone down the highway.

Then Marcus made a silly move. Why had Marcus made that move? It had been unlike his play. The minutes passed, and still Bony studied the board—until he became reasonably sure that his opponent had, indeed, made a move without intent. What did this mean? Was his mind wandering? What was he thinking?

What was he seeing?

Bony's hand hovered over the board, was withdrawn whilst he fell to studying the board again. Marcus was sitting back, apparently relaxed, his gaze directed past Bony to something beyond the balustrade. The temptation to turn became strong in Bony, but to do so might be to make a physical movement as silly as the move Marcus had made with a draughtsman. If he did turn to ascertain what Marcus was seeing, Marcus would know that he was on edge about something, and it was essential that the man's suspicions be kept to a minimum until Bolt arrived. What *was* he looking at? Bony made his move, taking advantage of the stupid move by Marcus.

"H'm! I seem to have made that initial mistake after all," Downes said, seeing that he was compelled to remove two of Bony's men and to suffer more severe loss himself. "Sorry, Bonaparte, I'm not feeling very well. Indigestion, I think."

Downes stood up, slowly and with both hands resting on the table.

"Perhaps if you walked about for a little while," suggested Bony, easing himself on his chair and so turning a quarter-circle. That brought him round to face along the veranda towards Sleeman, Lee and the big man known as Tully. Downes moved back and away from the table. Bony saw him "opening" his chest, and the action increased the distance between the lapels of his coat. Then he saw Bolt and Mason, with a third man, on the lawn.

The three policemen were halfway up from the wicket gate. The Superintendent was pointing to the Devil's Steps as they walked slowly and with a hint of deliberation towards the veranda steps.

Nonchalantly, Bony cleared his throat and took up from the table his tobacco pouch and papers. Downes was moving slowly back from the table. Sleeman was watching the advancing police officers. Tully was sitting on the edge of his chair and staring intently at Bony, and Bony felt more sure than ever that Tully was a policeman whose job it was to protect him.

"I'll go and get a tablet," Downes said coolly to Bony. "I'll not be long. Remember, it's your move next."

Bony nodded. Whilst Downes had been speaking his eyes were directed towards Bolt and his companions. Then, for an instant which seemed to be a minute long, he stared into Bony's eyes, and Bony saw a tinge of scarlet behind the black pupils.

Bolt and the two with him were now within twenty feet of the veranda steps when Downes made a half turn and began to walk between Tully and the line of french windows. Then Mason pointed to something beyond the far end of the house, and Bolt slowed in his walk. Mason said something, and Bolt stopped to gaze at what Mason was pointing to. Bony could not see what was interesting Mason, but actually the three were delaying in order to permit Inspector Snook and his troop to reach the main entrance. Other plain-clothes men were coming down from the top entrance to enter the house by the scullery door. Beyond the boundaries of Wideview Chalet, a hundred policemen entirely surrounded the property.

Still staring at Bony, Tully rose to his feet. With the merest motion of his head, he indicated Downes, and Bony nodded. Then, casually, the big man turned to his right and to Downes said:

"Better stay put—for a minute or two. It seems that the place is surrounded."

Tully's right hand was thrust into the pocket of his tweed coat. He was now standing squarely on his feet, facing Downes, and Downes halted to stand slightly raised on his toes with his arms hanging loosely. The fingers of both hands were splayed outward, as Bony had observed them that evening when they had rushed to the kitchen on hearing the screams of Alice.

Bony, whose gaze was now directed towards the tableau, heard heavy boots on the veranda steps almost behind him. He was gripping the table with his hands, his body leaning forward and resting partly on his toes. It was then that Downes moved with incredible speed.

His body appeared to lift and move two or three feet to the left all in a fraction of a second. A pistol shot crashed into the silence of the afternoon when Tully fired from his pocket. With such swiftness—that Bony barely followed the movement, Downes had altered position so that the bullet from Tully's weapon smacked into the wall behind him. His right hand flashed upward and then flashed halfway down. It was empty when it rose, when it came down there was an automatic pistol in it.

The man's face had fallen into a devilish grin. His eyes were wide and big—and red. To Bony they grew even larger in the small fraction of time. In that face was the exultation of the killer, and Downes paused before firing to savour the thrill. That pause saved Tully's life.

He fired, intending to kill Tully with a bullet between and above the eyes, as he had killed Constable Rice and others, but even as his finger pressed the trigger, the table on which he had played draughts crashed against his legs. It was not a heavy table, but the impact was enough to spoil his aim. The bullet took Tully in the right shoulder.

Having thrown the table and cascaded the draughtsmen over Mason and Bolt, who were leaping up the veranda steps, Bony dived for Tully's chair, and even before Tully fell the chair was on its way towards Downes. Downes dodged it and fired at Bony, who was crouched behind another chair. A woman screamed. Bolt's great voice came like one of the wind-giants. Downes fired again at Bony the instant he disappeared into the lounge through the open windows.

Racing through the lounge, Downes arrived at the cross-passages, there to see policemen at the kitchen door. He turned right and rushed to the reception hall and the front entrance—to see Snook and others coming in. He turned left—into Miss Jade's office.

It had been a bad day for Mrs. Parkes. It had begun badly for her when she entered a dark and cold kitchen with no Bisker and no tea waiting for her. The giggling Alice had not improved the cook's temper, and when, later in the morning Mrs. Parkes witnessed Bisker and Fred at work under a guest's supervision, the day was wholly ruined.

The day had not been easy for the maids, both having to do work normally done by George, and so during lunch tempers rasped and struggled for outlet until, when the staff sat down to lunch, open warfare broke out.

Mrs. Parkes had all day felt the need for exercise—violent exercise, the exercise giving both mental and physical relief from a condition of pent-up imprisonment, and when the second maid told Mrs. Parkes that she was a "nasty old gummy," the climax was reached.

Mrs. Parkes removed her apron whilst she struggled for articulation. She threw the garment on the floor and stood on it. Then, with the index finger of her right hand stabbing to death the two girls, she managed to say:

"I'm finished, d'you hear? I'm finished, I tell you. You can do the blasted cookin' between you. I wouldn't stay in this lousy, rat-infested joint for all the tea in China. You can have it—all the—all the—the—ruddy lot of it. You can kiss my back—so there—you couple of—of——"

Turning her enormous bulk upon her comparatively small and slippered feet Mrs. Parkes stamped from the kitchen along the passage, turned left and arrived at the reception hall. Without knocking, she entered the office where Miss Jade sat at her desk writing a letter.

"Mrs. Parkes!" exclaimed Miss Jade, outraged by the cook's appearance in her working clothes in that part of the house where guests frequently moved. "What do you want here?"

"I'm finished," Mrs. Parkes dramatically announced. "I won't be called a nasty old gummy by anyone. I'm leavin'. I'm finished. You can make up my money to last night. I'm going by the half-past four bus."

Miss Jade was petrified. She sat and stared at the infuriated cook. She was obliged to fight the fright produced by the prospect of no cook, a calamity far greater than the loss of a steward and of Bisker. She rose to her feet and stood in all her regal slimness. Mrs. Parkes broke out again, and Miss Jade vainly tried to stop her, to obtain a real explanation. And then the door was opened and slammed, and both women turned to be confronted by an automatic pistol menacing them below a pair of dark eyes gleaming red fire.

"Back!" Downes snapped. "Into that corner or I'll snuff you out like candles."

The threat backed by a pistol was less frightening than the man's eyes and affected the two women in different ways. Miss Jade's growing feeling of despair was replaced by a feeling of mounting anger, a feeling even inexplicable to herself. In contrast, Mrs. Parkes's anger swiftly subsided as the heat of her brain was replaced by a coldness she often had experienced when her husband required correction.

"Back into that corner," shouted Downes. "I'm giving no chances."

Someone was banging on the door. Beyond it they could hear the voices of many men. By some freak of acoustics, or by reason of their mental excitement, neither woman had heard the firing on the veranda, and this sudden dreadful threat of death came upon them with terrific force. Miss Jade found herself wanting to scream, and yet realised she was incapable of screaming. She remembered seeing a pair of flame-lit eyes, and the crumpling body of Constable Rice. The hardness of the wall at her back was like a giant hand holding her steady whilst she was about to be killed. She did not see Mrs. Parkes, but she felt the woman at her side.

The door withstood a fearful shock. Again came the shock against it. Downes fired through the door—once. Yet again the door was shaken by some object without. This time there was the sound of splintering wood. And now Downes waited, a pistol in both hands, and it was now that he made his fatal mistake.

No great man can avoid making a mistake now and then. The greater the man, the sillier the mistakes he makes. Marcus was a great man in his sphere of activity, and yet he made a mistake of such enormity that his career ended on a note of farce. The mistake he made would never have been committed even by Bisker, and for him there was no excuse, for he had seen with both eyes wide open Mrs. Parkes kill a running rat with a flat-iron.

He actually turned his back on Mrs. Parkes.

There was only one missile handy to that woman's great hands, and that was the secretary's portable typewriter. This machine was a little too large for the normal hand to grasp and the normal arm to throw, but the hand that did grasp it was not ordinary, and the arm attached to the hand was as large below the elbow as is the leg of the average man above the knee, and much harder with muscle.

The machine struck Marcus on the back of his head and he went to the carpet with the terrible abruptness with which Constable Rice had fallen. With astonishing agility, Mrs. Parkes picked up the typewriter, held it up at arm's length as she stood over one of the world's most dangerous men, and over her wide face there hovered a tiny smile as though she were willing poor Marcus to sit up and beg for another jolt.

Miss Jade began to laugh hysterically. The door was burst inward. Policemen appeared at the window. Bolt and Snook and Mason almost fell in through the splintered door. Bony came in after them. They saw Mrs. Parkes calmly and contemptuously drop the typewriter onto the small of Marcus's back, and then turn and take the over-wrought Miss Jade into her arms and press the dark head against her enormous bosom. They heard her say:

"There, there, dearie! Now don't you take on so. It's all right! When I throws things I throws 'em."

Chapter Twenty-seven

The Rebel Goes Fishing

"You will be interested to know, Colonel, that Superintendent Bolt's friend, known locally by the name of Marcus, is now recovering nicely from the impact of a typewriter. It was not a large machine. You will remember the story of Mrs. Parkes."

"Wonderful woman," breathed Colonel Blythe. It was the fourth day after Mrs. Parkes had thrown the typewriter, and Bony was making a farewell visit. He went on:

"It appears that Marcus was very friendly with the American Grumman, and having read the first statement made by Mick the Tickler, you will recall that the American Grumman changed places with General Lode, and was taken back, it is assumed, to Germany.

"Marcus was unaware of all this, and when he heard that an American named Grumman was staying at Wideview Chalet, he naturally desired to call on him. Firstly, however, as he was staying with his friend Jackson on Mount Chalmers, he contacted ex-General Lode at the Chalet by telephone. And when Lode could not remember Grumman's friend Marcus he endeavoured to put Marcus off but Marcus isn't the kind of man to be put off.

"Ridge House, where he was staying with his friend, Jackson, is only two miles down the highway from the Chalet, and being reasonably able to assume that he wouldn't meet a policeman, he didn't trouble to disguise himself in addition to the removal of a genuine moustache—removed several weeks previously.

"Under the circumstances which, although rare, are not fantastic, no one noted the number of his friend's car when Marcus was driven to the Chalet. That there was no one outside the house during Marcus's visit is not extraordinary, considering the time of the visit and that Bisker the yardman was inside the office with Miss Jade waiting for the local policeman. After leaving the Chalet, Marcus crouched down on the floor of the car until Jackson stopped it outside his house. There Marcus left the car and Jackson drove on down to the city and his office. He must have just got through before the road-block was set up.

"Marcus then built himself into the personality of Downes. He went by bus to the city, where he telephoned to Miss Jade for accommodation, returning to the Chalet per bus. He believed that nowhere would he be safer, and also he would work to learn what had happened to his pal, Grumman, and why."

"Pretty cool customer," interjected the Colonel.

"Oh, yes, he's all that," Bony agreed. "Get Bolt to let you read his record. Coming to believe that George Banks knew what had happened to Grumman's luggage, and, therefore, to Grumman himself, Marcus determined to ascertain from the steward what he did know. He assigned that task to his friend, Jackson.

"Jackson and two accomplices picked up George shortly after he had parted from his brother, Mick the Tickler, and they took the steward to Jackson's factory, where they proceeded to extract from their victim not only what had become of Grumman's luggage but also why and how Grumman was killed. Having then shot him, they disposed of his body, as you know.

"A point of interest is that Banks said nothing to them about his hiding of the fountain pens in the shrub tub, and what they contained. The pens were found on Jackson when they arrested him, and are now in my possession. I think a lot of them.

"Bolt and his crowd worked fast and well, following their raid on Jackson's house on Mount Chalmers. What I have related to you is what the Victorian Police have built up with evidence and statements obtained from Jackson and his accomplices. Those statements fill in the blanks in that made by Mick the Tickler and Bolt now has the story clear-cut.

"The brothers planned to put cyanide in the water carafe in Grumman's room, and then to remove the body and the luggage to make it appear that Grumman had 'flitted' to avoid paying his bill. Mick was to steal a truck which habitually was left outside the gate of a house tenanted by a wood carter. This place was two miles up the highway, and the truck was so parked that all Mick had to do was to release the hand-brake and steer the vehicle down the road, without the engine running, all the way to the Chalet. Then, having placed on the truck the body and the luggage, the vehicle could be steered for three more miles down the mountain road without having to use the engine. Here they would arrive at a place where luggage and body could be safely hidden perhaps for months in a natural hole several hundred yards down the slope from the highway.

"Having entered Grumman's room and having found the pens, Mick set off for the truck, and George, wearing a pair of Bagshott's boots, carried the body down to the highway and waited for the truck to arrive. It did not arrive, for the simple reason that the wood carter had accidently damaged a wheel the day before. The truck had been towed to his house, and he had removed the wheel and sent it away for repairs.

"They then decided to hide Grumman's body in the ditch, and take it away the following night, but they had to work in the dark and their efforts to conceal the body were not successful. The luggage they carried through the house and 'buried it' in the corner of a lumber room behind a stack of Miss Jade's unwanted furniture.

"That, Colonel, was a very neat piece of work," Bony said. "Just think. Amid a houseful of sleeping guests and others, they carried heavy steamer trunks along passages and shifted stacked furniture without awakening anyone. Their planning was good, we must admit. They went to the length of wearing a pair of Bagshott's shoes because of their abnormal size, just in case the police should be interested in the departure of Grumman, but they had not taken into consideration the accident to the wheel of that truck.

"I think that covers everything, bar the bone I have to pick with you. I stipulated with Bolt that I was to be left free to investigate in and about Wideview Chalet, but Bolt went so far in breaking the agreement as to place a policeman named Tully inside the Chalet on the excuse that he was to protect me from the persons who had killed George Banks and who, it was thought, would find out that I had taken the films from the fountain pens. The result was that Tully had been severely wounded. And then you did not tell me that you had already sent a man to the Chalet before I came down from Brisbane, so that not only was he severely wounded by Marcus during the uproar on the front veranda, but I have been put to a lot of inconvenience and have had my time wasted unnecessarily."

"My dear man, what the devil are you talking about?" Blythe asked.

"I am referring to Major Sleeman of Military Intelligence, assigned by Military Intelligence to investigate Grumman. Major Sleeman was a guest at Wideview Chalet when I arrived there."

Colonel Blythe waved his hand in mock despair. Then he pressed a bell button, summoning Captain Kirby.

"Kirby, do you know anything of a Major Sleeman staying up at Wideview Chalet?" he asked the ex-Scotland Yard man who entered.

"No, sir."

"I thought not." Blythe rose to his feet, a very angry man. To Bony, he said, witheringly: "If you were to gather into one place all the country's village idiots, and then compare them with these alleged Intelligence Officers, you would find the village idiots a thousand per cent more intelligent."

"I am so sorry that your stay here has been disturbed by the extraordinary things that have happened," Miss Jade said earnestly to Bony. "I hope you will come again sometime."

"Thank you, Miss Jade. I hope to come again, and to bring my wife with me. My stay here has been delightful and it is with genuine regret that I have to return to Brisbane. I am going to let you into a little secret. Actually, I am a Detective-Inspector on a busman's holiday."

Miss Jade's brows rose high and she exclaimed:

"Mr. Bonaparte—are you, indeed!"

"Yes, that is so, and unbeknown to you, I have used a little influence to keep your name out of what is bound to follow, what with inquests and trials. Mr. Sleeman is an officer of the Military Intelligence, who were interested in Mr. Grumman, and he found out that very late at night you visit at a house up along the higher road. It has devolved upon me to ascertain from you just why you visit that house so late at night."

"But—but that hasn't anything to do with Mr. Grumman," expostulated Miss Jade, a flash of fear entering and leaving her eyes.

"Possibly not. Personally, I don't think your visits to that house do have anything to do with the Grumman case, but Mr. Sleeman does, and I have so engineered it that my word for it will be sufficient to stop any future enquiry. You see, the Grumman case goes very much deeper than his murder."

Miss Jade sank back farther into her chair in the lounge of the Chalet and regarded the dark face and the dark sympathetic eyes. Like all women who came to know this gentle, almost wistful man, she discovered that she could trust him. She wanted, quite naturally, to put the events of the past few days far behind her, and to get along with her peaceful business of running a guest house high up on this peaceful mountain. She asked Bony a strange question:

"How old do you think I am?"

"Thirty-four, or perhaps -five," he ventured.

"I am forty-one," she said. "I have never been married, but when I was twenty-five, I had a baby girl." Miss Jade spoke softly and no longer was looking at him. "Her father didn't refuse to marry me, or desert me, or anything like that. Everything was arranged for the wedding. But, you see, the day before we were to be married, he was killed in a motor accident.

"When the child was five she had infantile paralysis and she has never recovered despite all that has been done for her. That was before I started a guest house in St. Kilda, and I rented a house and furnished it with the things my husband-to-be and I had saved for and bought. I got a woman to live there and look after the child, who is also not quite normal. When I came up here and built this place, and was warned even then about the scandal-mongers, I still wanted my daughter near, and so I obtained that house on the upper road, and brought up the furniture. Some of it I had to store here. I'll always keep it just because it was bought by the man I loved and the father of my unfortunate daughter. That's all, Mr. Bonaparte. There's nothing else in it but that. I have had to be so careful about going there to prevent people finding out."

For a while there was silence between them. Then Bony said, and he placed his hand on her wrist:

"Your secret shall be kept. And with regard to your motive for keeping the matter secret, I fancy that Clarence B. Bagshott would fully concur."

"Thank you, Bony."

He beamed. She realised her error and bit her nether lip.

"Oh, I'm so sorry, Mr. Bonaparte!" she exclaimed. "I didn't——"

"But why not? Everyone calls me Bony—from my Chief down to my youngest son. There comes a time in all our lives, you know, when we need a friend, and you can regard me as such. I understand that you are not intending to accept any guests till after the summer. In fact, I have to thank you for not turning me out. You ought to consider a holiday. Take a trip up to Brisbane and come and stay with my wife. The spring up there is very lovely. I'll get her to drop you a little note. We live very quietly; nothing so grand as this, but our hearts, I am glad to say, are in the right places. Ah—that will be Clarence B. Bagshott."

They rose at the sound of a motor horn being worked like the Morse Code. He held out his hand and she took it, regarding him with eyes that were misty. He smiled at her, and she did her best to smile back at him. Then he bowed to her, walked to the french window and bowed to her again, and she said:

"Au revoir, Bony! And thank you—oh, so much."

He left the veranda and walked down the path skirting the Devil's Steps. Cloud fog swirled about him. Halfway down he turned to wave back to Miss Jade and to see her answering wave. At the wicket gate he could no longer see her.

Bisker stood beside a car at the foot of the drive.

"All your things are stowed away, Mr. Bonaparte," Bisker told him.

"Thank you, Bisker, and good-bye. When you really want to leave

Miss Jade, and I think you would be foolish ever to do so, you have only to write to Windee Station and the owner will send you down your fares."

He gripped Bisker's grimy hand and got into the car beside Clarence B. Bagshott, who said:

"Settle down, settle down. Friend of yours in the back." Bony turned and looked behind—to see Colonel Blythe.

Blythe was dressed in very old clothes and on his head was a disgracefully shabby cloth cap.

"Well, I never!" Bony exclaimed, rare astonishment plain in his eyes.

Blythe chuckled.

"Secret Service, me!" he said. "Detective-Inspector Napoleon Bonaparte declined to return to Brisbane by air because, so he said, air travel makes him sick. Despite Colonel Spendor's ramping and roaring, little Bony planned with Bagshott to travel back to Brisbane by car, and the car was to break down at Bermagui for three or four days, while little Bony and Bagshott went off tuna fishing, as the swordies are not about at this time of the year. And so, as Colonel Blythe was instrumental, in the company of the said Napoleon Bonaparte, in obtaining for the British Government plans and formulas of priceless worth, the said Colonel Blythe decided to have a few days' tuna fishing. Drive on, Clarence B."

Bagshott broke into delighted laughter. The car rushed into unlawful speed down the fog-masked highway.

"This is going to be a real bucks' party," he shouted. "Do we stop at the first pub?"

More from
Arthur W. Upfield

Other Titles by Arthur W. Upfield and published by ETT Imprint:

1 The House of Cain

2 The Beach of Atonement

3 A Royal Abduction

4 Gripped by Drought

5 Breakaway House

6 The Murchison Murders

7 The Gifts of Frank Cobbold

8 The Great Melbourne Cup Mystery

9 Follow My Dust

10 The Devil's Steps

11 Up & Down Australia

12 Up & Down the Real Australia

13 Up & Down Australia Again

14 Beyond the Mirage;
An Autobiography

forthcoming
Walkabout

Upfield's own drawing of Bony

First time Published

BEYOND THE MIRAGE

An Autobiography

Originally written in 1937, Upfield's own story of
life in England, and travelling around Australia
with his camels, working the Rabbit Proof Fence,
and his encounters with Snowy Rowles. A big
book, heavily illustrated with photographs from
the Upfield family archives. First published
by ETT Imprint, Exile Bay, world-wide in 2020.

Lightning Source UK Ltd.
Milton Keynes UK
UKHW010247180221
378934UK00005B/529